THE SPIRE
CHRONICLE

Anonymous

ISBN   978-1-4475-4062-5

Cover Art: **SJH**

The Wretched Life Of A Scoundrel

September 8th 1910

To Whomever It May Concern

Dear Reader,

As a cover note to the attached manuscript I wish to simply convey how it came into my possession before passing it to another generation. Beyond assigning this extraordinary tale to the confines of a safety deposit box to be read once more in the future I feel no duty to share this script at the present time but rather send it on to another time in the same spirit that I received it.

Now I trust that you will find this story as intriguing as I. It is dated as June 16th 1861; nearly 50 years ago to the day that I have chosen to re-secrete the now delicate and yellow tinged pages.

And so to how the script came into my possession. If you will excuse my own literary prose, it was one dark December evening last year that I was struggling to enjoy a book by my fireside as the rain battered hard on my Drawing Room window. I was then surprised by a very loud knock at the door. My visitor turned out to be a very nervous and sheepish young stranger of few words, but I was able to glean that he was a builder's apprentice who had been working on a house in The Close in this fair city of Salisbury. Whilst assisting in the renovation of this property the young lad came across a dusty leather bound book of pages which I now present before you. He was candid enough to admit that he hid the script from his employer assuming it was of value. For this reason he would not reveal his name or precisely where the script was found. To be honest I was ready and willing to tell him to leave immediately but I was quickly drawn to the book as I examined it closely. It left me spellbound and as I have wealth I paid the rogue ten pounds to be on his way, which he readily accepted before fleeing. He had come to me due to my reputation and standing in Salisbury as a celebrated writer of this age and as a lecturer on English Literature of some repute. I gather he was directed my way by another as the awkward youth appeared poorly educated, in many ways.

That evening I sat down to do as you are about to do now. Dismissing the ghastly and boisterous din generated by the inclement weather I opened a bottle of Cognac and took my place once more by a roaring fire and set about reading this engaging tale. I read through until dawn so enthralling was the yarn.

Is this truth or fiction? I would not like to say but the romantic spirit in me revelled in the experience and prompted me to send it another 100 years into the future for another to enjoy. I have left instruction with a local legal firm that the box be opened on September 8th 2010 and the script made available by advertisement to whoever may choose to read it.

Yours, Anon.

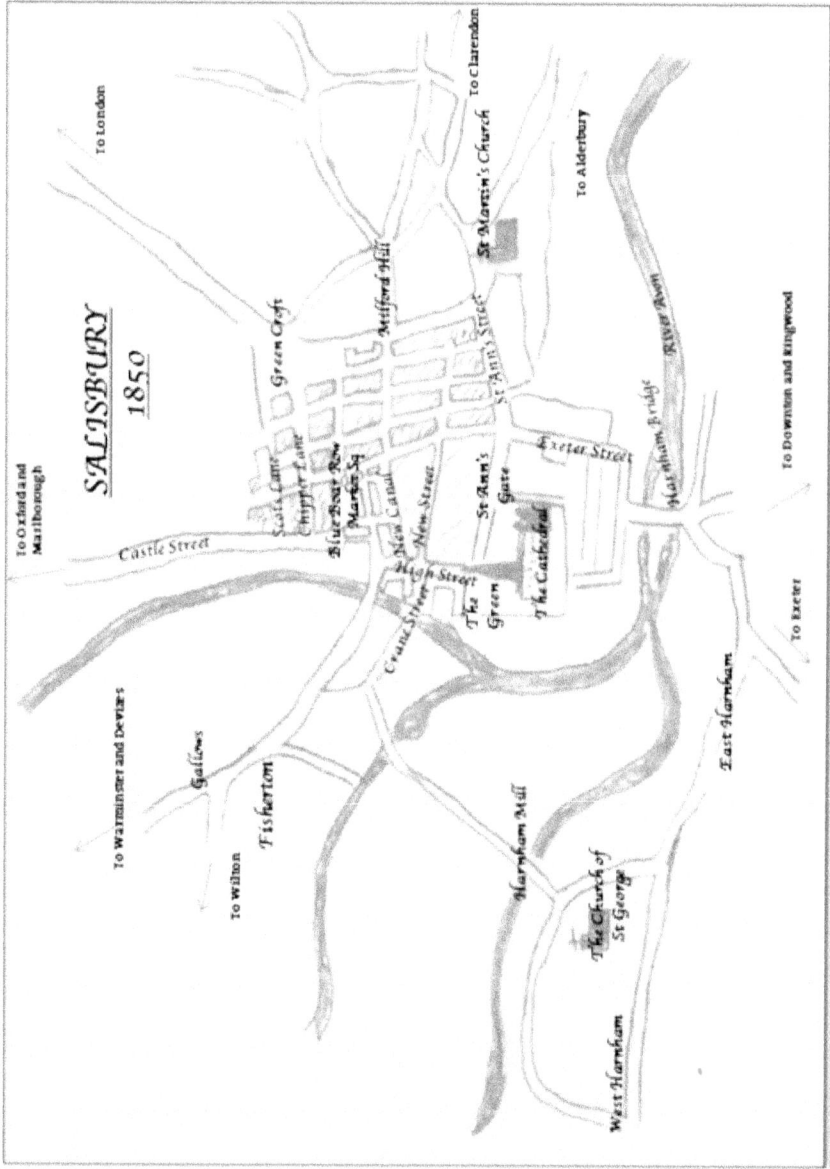

SALISBURY
1850

To Oxford and Marlborough

To London

Castle Street

Green Croft

Mitford Hill

St Martin's Church

To Clarendon

To Alderbury

Scots Lane

Chipper Lane

Blue Boar Row

Martin's Sq.

St Ann's Street

New Canal

New Street

Exeter Street

St Ann's Gate

Crane Street

High Street

The Green

The Cathedral

River Avon

Harnham Bridge

To Downton and Kingwood

To Warminster and Devizes

Gallows

To Wilton

Fisherton

Harnham Mill

East Harnham

To Exeter

West Harnham

The Church of St George

- 7 -

CONTENTS

On this Sixteenth day of June in the year of our Lord Eighteen Sixty-One.

Story-reader it is desirable that we establish an understanding from the very beginning. I am conscious that my tale would be the cause of alarm and great commotion if it were made public at the time of writing. It would not be agreeable to my wretched conspirators in this matter that I should commit our wrong doing to words but in order to somehow repent I do present to you story-reader a true record of my deeds. To begin with I humbly and emphatically acknowledge the main part in the devious events herewith described. My actions remain unaltered and history is what history is. The innocent pawns in this game remain heedless to my thoughtless conduct. And so it must remain. Forgive me if you believe I am unjustified in what has been decided but I am quite alone in the world and presently of a haunted disposition. Haunted by what I must now reveal.

I once considered myself a worthy gentleman of chivalrous spirit, coming from a family of good birth. For that reason I choose to assign myself a fictitious name so that I am not disposed to blacken or inconvenience my innocent relatives in the telling of this tale. Henceforth I will be known as Ralph Chatterforth, whilst feeling obliged to remain truthful in all other detail.

Chapter I - *The Circumstances of my childhood in Salisbury and setting forth the pedigree of the Chatterforth family. Certain characters are introduced that will remain integral to this tale, notably my dear sister Lilly and both Thomas and Dorothea Endstreet.*

I was born the son of a doctor in the year Eighteen Thirty within the district of Harnham that is encompassed in the boundaries of the market town of Salisbury. Being of sound reputation in medical circles, my father delivered me to the world himself. As indeed did he also deliver my beautiful young sister, Lilly, just over a year later. Let it be clearly established that the Chatterforth family were of good standing and acquaintance in Harnham and of fashionable notoriety in the coffee houses of Blue Boar Row in the town. My dear mother Charlotte was herself a caring and diligent schoolmistress at an establishment for a limited number of young gentlemen that was kept in The Close by the sisters Mary and Nancy Twizzle.

It is a fact that my father was a man of strict conduct and notwithstanding both Lilly and I were taught the value of respect, always speaking with the utmost politeness to the man we called Sir. I remember him as a stout gentleman, proud of his appearance that included a beard of such prominence that it took the eye away from his unfortunate and constant ruddy faced complexion. Like many notable physicians of the day my father maintained a room in our house for the purpose of a surgery. As a child I was never allowed to enter this room nor the study to which my father would retire daily for peace and solitude.

My dear mother was a plump lady of jovial and frivolous nature with many friends in Salisbury and beyond. Always the beaming hostess at numerous and frequent suppers, my mother would also enjoy weekly excursions to the cathedral and be enthralled by the orchestral concerts therein. The places of amusement in Salisbury have never been very numerous but my mother was not diminished in her search for pleasure. Often she was drawn to the bookshops on the High Street, returning with volumes on many different subjects that would be thoroughly enjoyed by the fire on quiet evenings.

And now to sweet Lilly, who always held the most girlish countenance and daintiest of dispositions. Her delicate and extremely pretty face was often described as perfection when she was in the full bloom of adulthood as I know for a fact that Lilly was declared as strikingly beautiful by so many admiring callers. Coupled with her beauty was an advancement in thought for her years from as tender an age as I can remember. To this day my sister has been above all comparison in my heart to all those acquaintances I have had the fortune, and sometimes misfortune, to make.

So there you have it first of all, the Chatterforth clan. We lived in a charming house under a hospitable roof in a town of character and distinction that was a good distance from London. There are no doubt many notable stories to be told of events in Salisbury, surrounded as it is by wonderful green fields and overseen by the magnificent dominant spire. And it is with close proximity to the cathedral that I will now introduce my fellow protagonists in this tale.

Although now retired, my mother was able to secure a place for me at the Twizzle School in The Close at the age of eleven and under the tutorship of Nancy Twizzle herself. When it fell upon the day that I was to start on my scholastic journey it was understandable that I was full of nervous apprehension. I still shudder even now as I remember the day when our honest and caring Governess, Violet Straybody, took me by the hand and led me to the quaint establishment that stood innocuously in the corner of The Close.

Whilst Mary Twizzle was renowned to be of amiable temper, her elder sister is best described as having a fierce reputation that had no reservation to humiliate or openly chastise. Nancy Twizzle's uncertain temper was evident from our very first meeting when I was instantly scolded for wearing uneven socks in such severe terms that it was as if I had committed a major crime. All this was very unpleasant and I tearfully took a seat at the front desk in the classroom. However it soon became apparent that I had not been singled out as my other classmates filed in to join the lesson. Nancy Twizzle stood tall by the door to dish out a spiteful rebuff to every new pupil that entered. In no time she had four students who knew their place.

Sitting before the domineering schoolmistress of high principle were the following:

The tall and lanky figure of Edwin Gurden, who always stooped as he sat to bashfully refrain from showing his features in full view, placed as they were under a crop of unkempt hair. Always short on confidence and with a shameful stammer, Edwin was never the cleverest of pupils but was nevertheless pushed to the limit by his determined father, Randolph Gurden. The Gurden family resided in Fisherton near the mills from which they had made their name and fortune as Clothiers. By-and-by the overbearing and authoritarian Randolph Gurden was earnestly forced towards a new way of living as the success of Lancashire cotton forced his hand. Becoming a member of the Guild of Tailors he established a shop that always dresses to the height of fashion and in so doing his family's standing was preserved.

Behind Edwin sat Thomas Endstreet, a suave and dapper character dressed to immaculate perfection. The Endstreet family, known for the making of cutlery, had been part of Salisbury society for generations. The family home was located in Wilton but Thomas was given weekly board by a wealthy relation who resided in St Ann's Street. Often absorbed within his own thoughts, Thomas rarely had time to contemplate the well-being of others unless there was profitable outcome to himself.

Finally to the back of the class where sat the son of a Banker, Daniel Drumdale. A slimy natured individual whose pitted face spoilt an otherwise handsome profile. My experience of Daniel, and indeed of his entire family, is that he would stoop so low as to connive, cheat and lie at any opportunity to gain an upper hand.

Rather curiously considering our disparate characters, we four became a strong band of friends. I perceived from an early stage that all our labours where intent on succeeding. The days, weeks and years of my time at school never once dragged slowly. It has habitually and often been said that children's prospects are decided by their schooling and status in the early years. I have never doubted this to be true from those past days and up to the present time.

As well as her temper and strict application, Nancy Twizzle's other memorable attribute was her constant unwavering soprano voice as she lectured on the fundamentals of arithmetic or read chapter and verse from literary masterpieces. In her own words Miss Twizzle had nothing but admiration for the exquisite novels of Jane Austen, or The Lady as she was then referred to in the words of our schoolmistress. In many respects Nancy Twizzle was ahead of her time as only now at the time of writing is it true that Jane Austen has found acceptance and general popularity. Whilst four keen boys hoped for a Walter Scott recital I still recall the time that Nancy Twizzle gazed through the small schoolroom window towards the cathedral as she narrated, without reference to the book, a passage from Sense and Sensibility. For the only time I can remember, her voice quivered slightly at the romantic inclinations of Marianne Dashwood. At this very moment, behind her back, Thomas Endstreet did place his thumbs in his ears and stuck out his tongue in Nancy Twizzle's direction. Although this was the cause of inward hilarity to us all, it was Daniel Drumdale who could not suppress a snigger. Nancy Twizzle instantly stopped her recital and spun on her heels in a moment. Red faced with anger she demanded to know which one of us had guffawed. Daniel remained silent, as did we all, and for so doing we were individually beaten across the bottom with our schoolmistress's prime birch rod, which she kept constantly resting in a jar of water on her desk to ensure it was supple for its purpose. I am sure that Nancy Twizzle took enjoyment from these beatings and as if to make a point she gave Daniel two extra strokes. She had known the culprit all along but our bond could not be broken from that day forth.

Nancy Twizzle was never one to spare the rod in my years at school and I clearly recall that her punishments were not always physical. Next to the birch in the jar, taking equal pride of place upon her desk was a tall red dunce's cap. We all wore it in humiliation at some point for not trying hard enough, but if ownership was based on usage then Edwin Gurden was a street ahead in this regard. The more nervous he became the more he stammered and the more Miss Twizzle shouted. In the end a spell in the corner stood with the red cap on his head became a daily occurrence for poor Edwin.

It was outside of the classroom that my classmates and I truly united. Free to explore The Close, it was the only time during the day that we escaped the unwavering gaze of Nancy Twizzle. In contrast the five pupils under Mary Twizzle's tutelage would stay near to the school and on the whole seemed a very dull lot. Thomas Endstreet did entice them to play football after he was able to secure a suitable pig's bladder from Butcher Row. However Mary complained to her sister that her class were too hot and bothered when returning to lessons and so Nancy confiscated our ball. It was not long before Thomas secured another and the game was saved, although with the other class now excluded.

My early school years persisted in providing a hearty intent to find enjoyment in life. In truth there really should not have been much to amuse as four schoolboys were driven to earnestly cultivate knowledge of the world. But in spite of it all our youthful hopes were bred as a team and so it would be that our fortunes were to remain ever entwined. And our leader as such was the ever suave and enigmatic Thomas Endstreet. Whilst Edwin, Daniel and I were often driven to cry like a newborn by the severe attitude of Nancy Twizzle, Thomas defiantly remained unaffected. Only once did Miss Twizzle break his spirit after he had missed several lessons on account of his mother being very ill. Thomas's inability to recite clearly from the bible brought vicious admonishment from a furious schoolmistress who sensed her chance. Finally Thomas's tears flowed as Nancy Twizzle cruelly sneered in victory. Thomas was instantly set on revenge and confessed to us all that he would find Miss Twizzle's weakness and ensure ridicule won the day. We did not have to wait long. It was on a fine autumn day in Eighteen Forty-Two that Nancy Twizzle entered a silent classroom as normal, totally unaware as to the mischief that would follow. As she walked along the row of desks to inspect us all, I believe I was the first to spy the two small rodents scurrying behind the tall rotund Miss Twizzle. Momentarily I heard Daniel gasp in shock, instantly causing Miss Twizzle to turn severely with a finger pressed to her lip to demand silence. Her eyes then followed Daniel's gaze and the frightening powerful lady quickly began to quiver upon the awareness of the two brown mice at her feet. Whilst grabbing the hem of her long black skirt, Miss Twizzle scurried from the room screaming at such a pitch that I swear my ears did nearly burst. Once she was gone, Thomas announced to us all that he felt he had acquitted himself to his own satisfaction and that he hoped that it was true too of his audience. Indeed it was.

That Christmas saw the coming together of the Chatterforth family with the Gurdens, Endstreets and Drumdales. My mother truly loved the festivity of Christmas and did put all her heart into it. At this time of the year our house was always filled with guests and so it was that my dear mother decided to host a festive dinner party on the night before Christmas Eve with the guest list to be confined to the families of my classmates. In truth my father loathed industrialists of any kind but he always remained submissive to the wishes of my mother. And so the event took place, even though the weather was very severe as to bring snow so deep that it was almost impossible to navigate a path to our front door, let alone the hill up to Harnham. However our Christmas guests did all arrive safely and the adults were instantly presented with a glass of hot punch by the fire. I do recall that the drink did seem to make everyone extremely merry and very quickly too.

Edwin and Daniel had between them a tribe of younger brothers and sisters, who quickly filled our drawing room with their presence as they sat quietly on the floor. In contrast Dorothea Endstreet, the elder sister of Thomas and his only sibling sat with the prominence of an adult by her mother's side. I recall that mother and daughter were dressed almost identically in long heavy thick brown gowns and both maintained the same aloof stare for the entire evening. In comparison my sister Lilly held a gentle countenance throughout, dressed as she was in a light pink silk gown. Dorothea was by far the eldest child in the room with her sixteen years, some four years older than I. As our fathers discussed how Salisbury, and Wessex in general, was behind the game when it came to signing up to the advantages that the railways would bring, our mothers all spoke softly about their preparations for Christmas. Both conversations came to an abrupt end as Kitty Endstreet, Thomas's mother, announced that Salisbury had no desire to sign up to the railways as it wished to remain hidden and without promotion. She then made the indignant remark that it would be best if ladies took a hand to business for the benefit of all and leave housekeeping to the servants. As nervous coughs ensued the moment was saved by the clock in the hall loudly chiming, causing my delicate sister to start with nerves. Our housemaid then appeared to lead the children to the table put aside in the kitchen. It was now time for Dorothea to take centre stage.

"I wonder," Dorothea announced as the meat was being carved, "that I may take pity on your school friend Thomas and be allowed to marry him one day."

It was I that Dorothea positioned her gaze upon, causing me to flinch and then blush with embarrassment. My eyes focussed away and I stared upon the roaring fire, watching the glow of the red-hot coals and hoping the moment would soon pass.

"Come do not be shy young Master Chatterforth for I am a good judge of character and have already seen the affection you have for me in your young innocent eyes." Dorothea announced with great confidence and several of the children giggled.

"Please Miss Endstreet I ask you not to put such a disposition upon my brother and embarrass him so," Lilly spoke with a restrained but sharp tone.

"Oh do let the man speak for himself young girl for there is no insinuation in my statement purely fact. Is it not so Master Chatterforth? If you just confirm your intentions I believe we can move on and enjoy this fine feast and then join our doubtless merry parents in some dancing and singing," returned Dorothea

"You are incorrigible Miss Endstreet, totally without scruples," Lilly was now angry.

"Let your brother speak Miss Chatterforth and I am sure my reputation will remain in good standing." Dorothea's big brown eyes once again set upon me and were joined by the attention of everyone else present.

Lifting my chin from my chest I somehow found an albeit quivering voice to speak. "I beg your pardon Miss Endstreet if I have made you feel uncomfortable in any way by paying you undue attention but I am still young and did not have any motive but greeting you as the sister of my friend Thomas." I bowed my head once more.

"Oh my gosh so you do not find me pretty to look upon at all."

Dorothea fanned her face with a quick hand and appeared to be on the verge of tears.

"No you misunderstand, I indeed think you have a real beauty and would challenge any man or boy who said otherwise." My intention was just to be polite but I knew instantly that I had really gone too far by way of correction.

"Then it is settled." Dorothea instantly refrained from weeping, "I will arrange for you to accompany me on a walk along by the river from the mill down the road. The view of the cathedral is the most stunning from there and the stroll will allow me to assess your true credentials. If you impress then I may decide to make you my husband one day. I will impress upon my mother to organise for a chaperone for the first Sunday after Christmas." Dorothea turned toward Lilly in triumph, "there Miss Chatterforth we are done."

My only recollection of that meal as I narrate was an exquisite plum pudding ornamented with a real sprig of holly. A typical festive touch from my mother. Just as Dorothea predicted after dinner we were all summoned to the main drawing room, where the adults were indeed extremely merry. My mother played on the piano and sang beautifully to entertain us all. The gentlemen then retired to my father's study for a smoke and a glass of brandy before returning to joyfully clap as the children all attempted an erratic but well-intentioned polka.

To be honest I thought no more of Dorothea over that Christmas, save for the fact that she had so overpowered us all during the dinner party that even her confident and normally self assured brother Thomas had been reduced to the role of dumb spectator. I still recall Thomas's parting words to me as the Ensdtreet family left to take the carriage that night. "I'm afraid my sister is completely impenetrable and beyond any form of rejection," Thomas semi whispered. I now fully understand this as a warning that I did not heed.

The main reason I had no time for idle thinking was that the Christmas of Eighteen Forty-Two was the most wonderful and festive occasion that I can remember. On the twenty-fourth day of December Lilly and I were taken by our parents to a wonderful toyshop in the High Street and were allowed to select our Christmas presents unaided. I believe we must have spent nearly an hour in the small shop before our choice was made. The shopkeeper was a very pleasant old man who showed no impatience at all in our pondering. Indeed, and rather oddly, neither did my father. Maybe it was because this was to be my last such trip as a child to the toyshop as from that day forward, and for two more years, such presents were confined to being presented to Lilly as the only remaining child in the family. My father did not believe in sending gifts beyond our family home, although I know my mother would buy many splendid gifts for her social circle. On Christmas day the Chatterforth family attended the service at the parish church of Harnham, dedicated to St George. The snow had fallen heavily that evening and my father suggested we make our way on foot to the very old building that had been standing longer than the cathedral itself, which stood tall in view from its place on the other side of the river. I distinctly recall the bells pealing to herald our arrival at the church with an almost poetic charm. On the way home, father decided that we should visit the nearby meadow up the top of Harnham Hill, to take in the wonderful view of Salisbury in the snow. By the time we returned home dinner was prepared and that afternoon we all slept soundly by the fire.

The following Sunday my appointment with Dorothea Endstreet was fulfilled upon a reminder from my mother. The Endstreet Governess, a surprisingly timid woman called Martha Cornfield, was presented as chaperone for our stroll. At first I felt rather restless and ill at ease as Dorothea walked briskly and silently across the frost hardened grass, which was now devoid of the deep snow that had marked Christmas so magnificently. Dorothea daintily held a flimsy white parasol that protected her sufficiently from the bright morning sunshine as it beamed strongly from beyond the glistening spire.

"I believe that this cathedral is the most beautiful work of art I have had the fortune to see. Wherever I might be in any part of Salisbury I know I can just look up and find comfort from the spire looking down on me like a proud parent or guardian angel. Do you not feel the same Master Chatterforth?" Dorothea stopped walking and looked straight at me.

"I had not really thought of it in that way Miss Endstreet," I replied after a considerable pause and whilst taking time to peruse the spire from our location. "I must confess that I am not well travelled at present and so the cathedral is something I am conscious of but do not hold in such significance."

"Oh dear I am clearly going to have to educate you in many things Master Chatterforth for I fear you may grow older to be a wretched individual with no passion or time to appreciate what is around you." Dorothea looked back towards the Old Mill from where we started our walk, "a question; tell me what beauty is clearly visible in the scene yonder?"

"The Mill," I answered quickly after staring back at the grand old building.

Dorothea giggled, "and is that all?"

"Yes," I blushed without further ideas on the subject.

"I fear you have a blindness when looking for the delights of the world. My first lesson for you today is take time to observe before committing so readily to what your head tells you. In truth there is a beauty in the flint and stone that form the mill but stand it alone and it is just a building. Set by the waters edge and alongside the soft meadows, it is nature that gives the real definition. The cathedral spire simply has the sky to frame it and could stand proud in any location," Dorothea announced.

I had leisure to ponder as we continued our stroll by the waters edge as Dorothea maintained an admirable calm manner. And so we continued until reaching the bridge at East Harnham, stopping only to greet a small band of travellers departing from the Rose and Crown Inn. The old hostelry has served purpose for visitors going back many hundreds of years and I do confess that I have always walked briskly by on my way to school through concern over the ghost stories often told in respect of the building's history. Many I am sure are fables but others have been sworn on oath as truth.

A small carriage awaited our arrival. "I shall be happy to continue your education Master Chatterforth and begin to coax out a man who can truly understand what life has to offer. In so doing I will create a gentleman whom it will be fully worthy to marry. If it should suit your convenience, I will be happy to see you on the first Sunday morning of each month after church.

"I believe that will be agreeable," I intimated without commitment, suggesting that the decision would need to be made by my parents.

"Then it is confirmed and for our next occasion I will arrange a meeting at the Old Castle." Dorothea beckoned for the carriage man to proceed, as Governess Cornfield remained mute.

For every month of the new year the arrangements were made and always fulfilled. As Nancy Twizzle continued down a strict academic path, Dorothea would impart upon me her own unique view of the world. To begin with I often dismissed her musings as popular fancy but by the end of that year I proclaimed a great deal of enjoyment in our meetings. It was pretty clear that Dorothea viewed me as a challenge like a lump of battered clay ready to be moulded into a fine sculpture. Her often haughty and pompous exterior would eventually melt to reveal a companion with a most engaging manner. The subject of our continued acquaintance was never discussed when I was in the company of Thomas Endstreet and in fact it was as if his sister did not exist, so infrequent was she mentioned. Although I do recall the time that Daniel Drumdale expressed a personal liking for Dorothea only to be punched by Thomas on the nose without warning. It was Daniel who then apologised stating that on reflection that he was in the wrong. From such an early age Thomas had a complete hold over the unyielding loyalty of both Daniel Drumdale and Edwin Gurden. They both found security in the strong and confident position he held and would never have an appetite to challenge Thomas from our schooldays and into adulthood.

At the end of that year my meetings with Dorothea were promptly ended before the advent of another Christmas as my companion was dispatched by her mother to assume a position in one of the finest hotels in Paris. On our parting I could sense a loneliness in Dorothea although she wanted to convey that it was her desire to go to France and learn a language of beauty and that she had in fact grown weary of her efforts in turning me into a gentleman of standing and substance. I could sense an emotional struggle within but Dorothea departed with a rather cold disposition, uncommon to our recent meetings.

Chapter II - *Containing particulars on my time at the Varndell Academy and the unpleasant situation with the urchin Nick Strapless.*

And so the years fell by briskly as I continued a worthwhile education that assured I would become an admirable member of the Salisbury community. In progressing from the Twizzle classroom in 1845 I moved on to the other side of The Close and the sophistication of the Varndell private school. My erstwhile classmates made the move too and we now came under the tutorship of the dapper Mr Carrywater. He never failed to cut a dashing figure in the finest tailored suits and waistcoats that I have ever seen. Even in the foulest of weather Mr Carrywater would arrive wearing shiny spotless shoes, although it was said that he hired an urchin to walk with him daily from St Ann's Gate and attend to any blemishes about his person before making a grand entrance. He would enter the classroom with an extremely light step save for an instant sharp click of his heels. Stroking a highly groomed and extensive moustache that even curled symmetrically at each end, Mr Carrywater's morning greeting never varied.

"Gentleman there has been given to me this fine day an important obligation and that is?" Mr Carrywater would recite with an overstated pronunciation of the first syllable in every word.

"To strenuously ensure that we demonstrate intelligence through charm, grace and dignity," we all chanted in reply, mimicking our tutor's diction and tone.

Mr Carrywater was an exceedingly tall man who towered over

most adults and could be easily spotted in any crowd. He never stooped to speak to his small charges and treated us all like peers, clearly extolling the desire that we all become virtuous and exemplary characters through a love of the finer things in life. Every lesson was delivered in a theatrical manner and for each regard or notice given to the fundamentals of literature or arithmetic came an aside on how all learning was a base for etiquette. The written word to expand vocabulary for the occupation of both leisure and business whilst the science of numbers assured an alert mind. On frequent occasions Mr Carrywater would have us all stand and then proceed to march his class over to the cathedral. He would then proceed to lead us through the nave and into the cloisters, whereupon numerous laps were completed at considerable pace around the cedars planted some eight years previously in honour of our Queen's accession. To the rhythm of Mr Carrywater's clicking heels we would receive a varied recital that could one day be an epic poem or on another day be basic Latin verbs. Mr Carrywater would recite on the first lap and each pupil would then in turn repeat the subject matter upon designation until at least five clear laps had been completed. It was more if a boy dared to make an error and would then have to take his turn again. To this end Edwin Gurden's stammer proved an early obstacle but he somehow overcame his infliction within the Cloisters without being able to remain as assured elsewhere. In truth it was Daniel Drumdale who found least favour with Mr Carrywater through his inability to retain a smart countenance throughout the mobile lesson and for having the misfortune to perspire profusely. "Perspiration betrays anxiety, apprehension and uncertainty Mr Drumdale and will disturb any other gentleman with whom you may wish to converse with in both social and business circles. Only ever work within a pace that has a necessity for cold reason and consideration and you shall go far." As with all his carefully delivered statements, Mr Carrywater would stand upright on his heels for several minutes whilst he solemnly glared above our heads, enveloping his upper lip with the lower lip. Once he was assured that the point had been made and understood, he would continue.

Away from the Varndell School, Daniel Drumdale was truly

displaying a shameful character that would develop further into adulthood and by all accounts was a collection of irksome traits that were accustomed to the main Drumdale household. Daniel had no aversion to use his position to manipulate those less fortunate for his own gain. The first example I present is the sad tale of a young urchin called Nicholas Strapless. Young Nick was no more than ten years of age and without a mother since the age of five. His father had re-married and allowed his heart to fall captive to an impatient and unkind lady who demanded luxury despite the widower holding a simple clerk's job at an accountant's office in New Street. The family lived in a slum courtyard off Castle Street but the stepmother, a rather regal looking Mary Bigglemore, insisted on dressing in the finest cloth and eating to such extent that the amount of material required to cover her ample body increased by the month. Nick's elder sister Molly was quickly put to work as a chambermaid at the White Hart Inn. At a very early hour each morning the short slight wisp of a girl would set a quick pace across the town wearing the same frayed bonnet and uniform but with no sign of despondency and always prepared to offer a smile to all those she met. But when it became apparent that her husband and Molly's pay could no longer sustain Mary Bigglemore's lifestyle, it was time to put Nick to good use. Mary's roguish brother Charles secured an opportunity for Nick to sell matches along the line of the filthy rivulets that ran through Minster Street. Often mingling with merchants selling fruit and vegetables out of baskets and pots, Nick would either sit pitifully near the market cross on the corner of Butcher Row or try his fortune with more affluent traders near the Cheesemarket.

Daniel Drumdale's father was also an early starter in opening the Bank in Blue Boar row, so meticulous in ensuring it was ready for business several hours before opening. In fact it was to be proven many years later that his intentions were of a criminal nature. Mr Drumdale was carefully adjusting the books to use assets and money that did not belong to him for his own personal gain. In short he lied and cheated to make profit from other people's investments that initially reaped reward before a mistake was made and Mr Drumdale was exposed and sadly many people lost their money. He was to spend his last days in the County Gaol north of

Fisherton, somehow surviving the public clamour for his stout body to hang from the nearby gallows. But at this time Mr Drumdale seemed simply intent on excelling in his profession, and as he went through the books of customer accounts his son Daniel was left alone to find amusement or useful service before the school was opened. Daniel would wander outside and look for mischief and in so doing he became aware of the daily routine of Molly Strapless, and of his very smitten attraction to her beauty. Every morning Daniel would take a position on the corner of Chipper Lane with only the company of two very old women in rags selling boiled water by the pot. He would offer a hopeful and respectful bow as Molly would purchase and collect the water to make up her stepmother's bath in her last domestic duty before setting course for the White Hart. Molly was evidently uneasy and embarrassed by Daniels attention and offered no warm riposte. Daniel was undeterred and expressed to us all that he would soon be delighted to make Miss Strapless's acquaintance. The next day he proposed a romantic arrangement only to see a horrified Molly steadfastly decline the offer before scurrying home. The two old hags cackled loudly at the situation by all accounts but Daniel made no allusion that he was defeated in love. If he could not obtain her heart with honour he would have to steal it through cunning and deception. Step forward the hapless urchin brother, Nick Strapless.

I still recall the gaunt tearful face of Young Nick as I watched Daniel stooping down to confront the shivering boy as he sat cross-legged on the cold pavement with his meagre pile of matches.

"Dear me, I just don't know how this can be," Daniel spoke in the manner of a posh gentleman. "One would suppose that you did not come by this through honest means," Daniel held up an exquisite pocket watch.

"That aint mine mister," Nick replied in bewilderment, "never seen it before until now."

"Well I do not wish to insinuate at all but I would say that this watch has an uncanny resemblance to a piece stolen from a customer of my father's bank this very morning." Daniel announced with loud smugness before shouting "Jerry Sneak" in the direction of a nearby constable.

The stern Peeler instantly marched over as a small crowd of sellers gathered round. Resplendent in his bright blue frock coat and top hat, the Peeler lifted Nick with one hand until the boy's smudged and tearful face fell level with the arms of Salisbury on the Crusher's collar.

"You're a bold boy indeed," the Peeler sneered as Nick started to weep. "I dare say we can have you before the Mayor this very afternoon and believe me he will have you on the next ship to Australia before the sun sets over the spire. Sent two boys that way just last week for stealing a fowl from Mr Jacey's farm."

 Nick was terrified and looked pleadingly towards his snide accuser, Daniel, who was delicately inspecting the timepiece. "Oh my word what a bad disposition this has turned out to be. I did believe with the best intention that this was the very watch that was stolen this morning but I do declare it is not so, and now I do recall that in fact the watch was in the gutter and that furthermore the child was probably not aware of its presence."

The Peeler now released his grip on Nick and placed him back on the pavement. "I am inclined to let you go but I shall keep watching as I have no time or patience for beggars. To my mind, beggars are nothing more than thieves that should only inhabit a prison or workhouse"

As the Peeler turned to go, and make a hasty retreat to the police station in nearby Butcher Row, the small crowd turned on him by shouting abuse.

"What have the poor innocents from the cradle ever done to harm you? Go and pick on someone your own size." One old cackling fruit seller shouted from her stall to the accompanying chorus of jeering.

The undeterred mob followed the red-faced policeman all the way down Minster Street, as he struggled to breathe colour into his own cheeks through a combination of indignation and the tight thick leather tie that was almost choking him. The irony being that the very part of the uniform that was there to protect from garrotting just about did the job by itself.

With the crowd occupied by the shamed policeman, Daniel calmly moved over to ease Nick to one side. "Now then Nick I am very sure that you already appreciate my act of kindness towards you and that any further insinuation on my part would lead to a situation from which you sha'n't escape."

Nick's innocent face was full of fear and worry as his blinking eyes were met by Daniel's sinister expression. "How do you do sir, I beg your pardon sir and I am very sorry I am sure to have offended you in some way. Please sir do not send me to the ship or to the jail."

I felt extremely uncomfortable as the quivering urchin stood with the misfortune to be in such a weak position with his devious foe.

"Now my friend I am sure we shall not fall out with one another and create a positive partnership to a very mutual benefit. For your part you shall be left to enjoy the freedom of the town without fear of being taken from your family." Daniel now stood tall as he pushed out his paunch of a stomach in displaying an arrogant prowess.

"That is very kind sir," Nick smiled at last. "Is there anything I can do for you?"

"In short, yes there is," the victorious tormentor was ready to strike. "I have observed your sister Molly on several occasions and I am drawn by her sullen disposition. This is not a character that I like to see in such a pretty creature and I have endeavoured to make every effort for an improvement. I will not be shunned in my bearing towards your sister and will therefore impeach you to ensure that we are both bound by frequent association." Daniel lent forwards to confront the shocked urchin, "now Nick I wish to meet Molly at six o'clock sharp in the morning by the front of the Cheesemarket yonder, from where I will provide a noble escort to her place of work. Do you understand me and do you know what the consequence will be if you fail to obey me?"

Nick simply nodded, defeated and clearly weighed down by the obligation he had to bear and with no possibility of refusing the task. Daniel ushered him away without further remark, as I for my part felt somewhat ashamed, not sharing in the laughter and congratulations provided by Edwin and Thomas.

"I had a great mind to say that I would not entertain your trickery to get me here," the normally shy Molly spoke with an angry tone on her first arranged meeting with Daniel. For the love and concern of her brother, however, Molly was present to greet her enforced acquaintance.

"Dear me," blustered Daniel, "I do declare that you have a strong spirit about you. I have no doubt we will pull together to forge a strong relationship and my devious way will soon be forgotten."

Molly gave Daniel a reproachful look that spoke louder than words.

"Shall we," Daniel smugly offered Molly his arm, which she reluctantly accepted. He would then proceed to parade his fancy on an early morning stroll through to The Close, ensuring the envy and respect of all the boys boarding at the various schools as they milled around before breakfast. Molly maintained a silence throughout on that and every day that followed, despite Daniel's attempts to ensure her of a very prosperous union. Molly would simply bury her face in her thick shawl and coat from beneath an oversized bonnet, protecting her from the cruel sharp October wind as well as the odious stare of her companion. Once delivered to the White Hart Inn, Molly would simply scurry inside.

By chance of the season Daniel's plot to secure Molly as a prize was as soon undone as from when it had started. Since the time from when the cathedral was built a charter had been granted to hold a fair in Salisbury on the third Monday in October. Involuntarily, Molly escorted Daniel in attendance at the fair, along with both Thomas and I. Indeed we were both forced into a reluctant admission that we were in the presence of an agreeable coupling, despite Molly's pitiful position. It was with relief that I found distraction within the fair itself, which seemed to be more extensive than it had been for the last two or three years, with numerous colourful stalls and shows. Most of the establishments charged only "one halfpenny", as bellowed by the stallholders as they offered everything from a performing pony to a magic mirror. Daniel took Molly upon an exquisite carousel, whilst Daniel and I took our chance on break-neck-looking swings. That year even saw the introduction of several new wooden machines upon which a gang of fairground urchins propelled you on a ride. These were becoming ever more popular attractions and offered an escape to many unfortunate boys left to the mercy of the streets. Step forward Nick Strapless.

At the end of the Fair's time that year the square once more stood empty as the travellers made their onward journey to the next town. The wheels rumbled, dogs barked, children whooped and the crowd waved as the procession was heralded away. If Daniel Drumdale had taken care to look he may have spotted the grubby face of young Nick that day, seated amongst a handful of young boys of similar age and appearance in the back of the final cart in line. It was with a wry smile that I spied the lad, grinning like never before, and it was an observation that I kept to myself.

"Do you mean that he has deserted his family?" Daniel exclaimed with some indignation as the normally timid Molly confronted him pointedly with the news that Nick was now beyond his reach. "The boy is nothing but a runaway rogue. He is a vagabond and no mistake and I now regret the very day I chose to apprentice him in surviving the streets of Salisbury."

"Shame on you sir," Molly yelled in reply, "you had no interest in the welfare of my brother and indeed your only intention was to secure my forced companionship by the threat and hold you had over Nick."

"I have no misgiving to explain for it was always in your best interest to remain by my side, and you cannot deny that I was always courteous and the perfect gentleman in your company. Indeed I stress that you are one lucky female now at a pinnacle of satisfaction and with your brother out of the way we can continue to grow our relationship." Daniel was full of smarmy utter arrogance as he stood before Molly at the entrance to the old Charter Coffee House in the Market Square. I stood idly in the doorway with Edwin and Thomas as we simply observed the meeting as bystanders.

"I'll give you to know sir that I have no feelings for you in any regard. My family is humble and my father is unfortunately affectionate towards a woman who is not fit to take my mother's place. But now my brother has a new life and I am now contented to support my father until he befits that I am able to go out into the world and live to know better." Molly stood tall and confident as she spoke with indignant satisfaction in putting Daniel firmly in his place "Be in no doubt that my future has no place for the sad wretched individual that is Daniel Drumdale."

Molly looked as if she would strike Daniel but instead she moved away at such a quick pace that left Daniel to loiter and gather the amused attention of passers by. Dear Reader it was in fact the last time that any of us set eyes upon the small frail figure of Molly Strapless. I can indeed inform you that a matter of days later came the news that Molly's intolerable Stepmother, Mary Bigglemore, had met a very sudden death, choking on the bone of a fish being devoured for supper. Molly's father did not mourn long past the bells that heralded the funeral in the grounds of St Edmund's. Mary's brother Charles felt that the circumstances of Mary's death were of remiss and would voice his opinion in all the Ale Houses he frequented. However being such a man of disreputable character, Charles was caught in the possession of another man's wallet and dispatched to jail in a short period of time. Edwin swore that he saw him hung at the gallows and although it was true that young Master Gurden had an unnatural fascination for these unseemly spectacles, I cannot confirm that was really the truth of the matter. As for Molly, she departed Salisbury in haste the following year, eloping with a young Stockbroker from London who had made a fortune in the year of the railway. His work brought him to Salisbury to assess the investment potential in a proposed rail link and in so doing he would board at the White Hart Inn. In short he made a considerable impression on Molly and it was said that the pretty chambermaid distracted his attention constantly. It did not take much musing to affect a decision to elope as both were blinded by love and I trust found happiness away from the gaze of the spire.

Chapter III - *Wherein I find employment with the Salisbury Journal. Containing a full account of the pursuance of Katherine and Agnes and the occasion of the Assembly Room Dance.*

The railways did finally arrive in Salisbury in 1847, seemingly bringing London to our doorstep as you could now journey to the capital and back in a single day. I was now seventeen and had developed an affinity with writing that brought me an apprenticeship on the Journal as a penny-a-liner. My father frowned upon my chosen profession, as he felt no connexion whatsoever with any position outside of politics and medicine. It was distinctly due to the influence of my mother that forced my father's hand, and he in turn was able to secure influence upon a political acquaintance with further connexion with the Journal's owner. Edwin, Thomas and Daniel were all apprenticed in their respective family businesses.

Thomas would secure the opportunity to travel from Wilton to Salisbury at least twice a week and on the occasion of every Wednesday I would meet him alone at the High Street entrance to The Close. After a hard morning's labour we both now found recreation in watching the punctual daily exercise routine of the girls attending the Diocesan Training College. The College supplied female teachers for the surrounding church schools and seemed to have a remarkable habit of selecting those of a certain beautiful disposition. At first as we both crouched out of view by a small stone wall and I felt a very uncomfortable sensation that we would be spotted by a passer-by and exposed as a nuisance loiterer and thus marked as being of questionable character. My fear was soon overcome as I relished the weekly show and for one significant reason; the rousing of my heart in setting eyes upon Katherine.

The Diocesan Training College had only opened some six years previously and quickly established a good reputation far and wide in the townships beyond the spire as to be a superior institution. By chance Thomas and I spotted the delightful students going through their ritual exercise regime. It was during a simple lunchtime stroll and from that day it would have taken the strength of many wild horses to pull us both away from our often prolonged viewing. Notwithstanding, we were lured to be hangers-on and quickly identified our favourites. Thomas without hesitation or timidity selected a very thin, pale looking girl, whose name was later to be revealed as Agnes. Acute shyness ensured a gallant effort to reveal the girl soon to be named Katherine as the object of my own affection. I truly remember that I could have crouched peering at that pretty face for as much as an hour and been content in my work for the remainder of the day.

It so happened that one fateful summer's day our spot by the wall was taken by a number of pupils from the Twizzle School enjoying a picnic. Undeterred, Thomas prevailed upon me that we could climb a nearby tree from where our view would be clear whilst our position undetected. I hesitated through fear of spoiling my favourite waistcoat and shirt, selected with the motive that Katherine may spot me by chance at any moment. Thomas was already assuredly making his way to the first branch and giving me a look that goaded a reaction. Accordingly I followed, cursing an inability to climb with the same dexterity as my friend. Thomas coaxed me to his position on a thick branch surrounded by substantial foliage that offered sufficient protection in hiding from view. Almost immediately the College students moved on to the garden lawn and were quickly into their exercises, led by a tall lady of considerable girth. Unfortunately Katherine was obscured from view, standing at the end of the back line. I crouched lower on the branch for a better sight whilst ensuring our situation remained clandestine. I soon had a wonderful glimpse of Katherine as her shiny brown hair glinted in the sun cascading away from a perfect white-as-porcelain face, save for two rosy red cheeks. I was truly engaged and giddy with joy. In fact so giddy that I did not conceive that the branch upon which I sat with Thomas had buckled considerably in light of my changed position. Irresolutely and with carefree abandon I lowered even further until the branch was distressed upon repair and gave way with an instant, and very loud, crack. The suddenness with which Thomas and I fell to the ground and appeared at the feet of the girls that we had been observing still entices a twinge in the shoulder upon which I landed every time the memory is stoked. A chorused scream echoed around The Close as the girls all reeled in shock, bringing a look of astonishment from any passing observer. With apprehension I slowly climbed to my feet but the pain in my right shoulder and arm was severe and even worse my frilly white shirt and blue striped waistcoat were stained green in patches by the grass as the shocked face of Katherine gazed upon me for the first time.

"I humbly apologise," I said trembling, "for interrupting your class."

"Oh dear I do declare that you both look rather foolish," the Class Instructor interposed without anger, "but I fear your friend is of a more concerning disposition."

Thomas lay motionless on the floor having landed heavily on his head. All the students gathered around Thomas's stricken body with a common look of gravity before they all flinched and took a step back as Thomas coughed loudly and stirred from his position.

"What is this? Where are you mother?" Thomas was very weary and seemingly delirious.

"Ah," the Instructor knelt beside Thomas, "do not distress yourself sir. We shall attend to you." She then signalled for me to assist her in helping Thomas from the floor.

Slowly and gingerly we supported a very unsteady Thomas into the main college building where he was placed on a chair.

"Katherine there is some chloroform in Principle Castermore's office, please go and collect it. Agnes, please go and collect some

hot water and towels from the kitchen". The Instructor clapped her hands as the two girls who had been the individual objects of our desire responded in time. Was this fate? I considered, momentarily forgetting the plight of my friend Thomas. "The rest of you please go and prepare for afternoon classes," the Instructor clapped her hands again and the other girls quickly dispersed.
I moved over to see how Thomas was coping as he continued to murmur and moan. "Oh dear I am very fearful for my friend."

"Why, do you think he will soon be dead?" The Instructor stated rather sharply. "Believe me when I say that I know the pair of you are not innocent and blameless in your actions. Would you like to explain why you were up in that tree in the first place?"

"There is good sense as to why we were up the tree," I replied nervously as if I was once more a child of eleven and stood before Nancy Twizzle herself. "I will explain all when my friend has been tended to," I crouched down to tend to Thomas, praying that a stay of execution had been won.

"I look forward to you explaining the situation sir," the Instructor huffed as Katherine and Agnes returned with the requested items. "The girls will repair your friend to a more sober position and I will then be ready to hear you qualify the reason for falling from the sky and ruining my lesson." The Instructor left the room with a quick nod to the girls to proceed with assisting Thomas, who was now inanely and drowsily chuckling to himself.

"Good gracious sir, what a state you are in," Katherine sighed as she patted Thomas's head with a warm sodden towel, "although the good news is that no bruise has appeared."

"Thank you kind lady, I confess I am feeling more like my true self already," Thomas spoke very clearly.

"Would you care for some chloroform sir?" Agnes held up the bottle along with a swab for application.

"No that will not be necessary at all," Thomas now sat upright and seemingly cured.

Katherine and Agnes exchanged glances as I shot Thomas a puzzled look. I received a very exaggerated wink in reply that confirmed his feigning of disposition from the outset.

"My dear ladies, Thomas Endstreet at you service and in your debt," Thomas stood up and casually bowed. "And may I present my good friend, and respected journalist on the Salisbury Journal no less, Ralph Chatterforth."

"I am rather considering Mister Endstreet that you were not injured at all or truly delirious when you were brought in here," Agnes spoke dubiously.

"Please spare us kind Agnes and Katherine, for my friend and I acted only in the interest of love," Thomas gushed as I immediately turned as red as a rose with embarrassment.

"I beg your pardon sir," Agnes fanned her own rosy complexion, " I mean I can make some allowance in such circumstances but in truth your boldness leaves me both vexed and awkward."

"Please sweet Agnes I beseech your assistance on two fronts," Thomas moved over to hold Agnes's hand. "On the first please do Ralph and I a favour and allow us to leave this establishment before your Instructor returns."

"And on the second?" said Katherine.

"The second is your agreement to accompany my friend and I on a leisurely stroll in The Close tomorrow evening," Thomas glanced my way in total confidence of securing the engagement.

An intolerable hush followed as both Agnes and Katherine retreated into a shell. The pause seemed relentless until I recall noticing a change in Katherine's expression as her face became less fixed and instead beamed a warm smile. "Will you allow us a few moments?" Katherine spoke softly in my direction.

"Of course," I replied instinctively, and watched Katherine lead Agnes from the room.

"The fact they both willingly quit the room so quickly is a very good indication," the cunning Thomas pounced to his feet.

"I will be obliged to admit that your acting performance was worthwhile if we do secure a friendship," I stood shaking with nerves in anticipation.

"What are you afraid of?" Thomas goaded, "are you not charmed by Katherine? I am sure that you will now become more than good friends as will I with the prized beauty of Agnes. Never has a fall from such a height brought such good and immediate fortune."

At that moment Katherine and Agnes returned and another uncomfortable silence ensued as they stood before us.

"Do we have an answer?" Thomas announced with impatience.

"Your confidence is priceless sir," returned Agnes, "and indeed it made Katherine and I initially shrink within ourselves with such a brash proposition. I am glad to say that in consultation we have softened our consideration and that we will accept your invitation. We will meet you tomorrow evening at five o'clock near the large horse chestnut tree by Chorister's Green. Do you know it?"

"Truly I do," was my own highly enthusiastic response.

"Now please sirs will you have the goodness to leave here quickly as our Instructor has a keen eye and inquisitive mind. I fear she already suspects your intentions and is not cordial in her present opinion of you," Agnes ushered for Katherine to check outside the door.

Katherine held out a hand and waved for Thomas and I to make our move. As fugitives we were rendered a service by the College Cook, who had engaged the Instructor in conversation at the far end of the hall. She was an extremely large lady who I swear could have veiled the cathedral itself and made it easy to creep from the room before bolting beyond the open main door, across the lawn and to the shelter of the tall tree from which we had earlier fallen.

And so it was, with arrangements so hastily made, that on the following evening Thomas and I went across to Chorister's Green at five o'clock. It was a wonderful evening in the summertime and I recall the calm tranquillity bestowed upon the numerous couples enjoying a stroll, whilst in comparison I was struck with excessive nerves. I could not discern the same traits in the familiar stance of the confident Thomas, as he stood with a turned up nose, resplendent in a purple waistcoat and shining white buttons. I felt even more uncomfortable stood next to him in a poorly tailored and unseasonal black suit. We were thankfully not kept waiting for more than five minutes after the appointed hour, when the gentle delicate Katherine appeared out of the early evening low haze accompanied by the charming but quite indignant Agnes. I swear at that moment the birds sang out loudly and the butterflies fluttered away from the roses on which they had rested.

"Your humble servants ladies," Thomas bowed theatrically causing Katherine to blush and Agnes to roll her eyes.

"Good evening," I spoke with a wide mouth, red cheeks and true humility.

"Whilst we are both flattered by your admiration, please do not be mistaken that our acquaintance will be of a great fancy." Agnes spoke with a quite disconcerting air. "We are both agreeable to enjoy a leisurely engagement and consequently we shall take a stroll with you this evening before contemplating further meetings."

"It is understood sweet Agnes and may I add what good fortune we have with the weather this fine evening," Thomas held out his right elbow, which after a pause, Agnes joined with her own dainty arm and the couple moved at a steady pace along North Walk.

I felt obliged to follow suit and offered the pretty Katherine my own arm as we nervously, and blushing, followed our more overly confident friends. I can make no claim that I knew at the time how much Katherine would enter my heart but suffice to say that this first meeting went very well indeed, despite the very few words spoken between us. I also watched and closely observed how Thomas entertained Agnes sufficiently, and with a very false humility won her acceptance for future meetings. Secured through a respectful prompt from myself, Katherine and Agnes agreed to accompany us once more. Thomas secured the engagement with an invitation to a dance at the Assembly Rooms the following week. Katherine's sweet and placid expression and Agnes's disagreeable but pretty demeanour now tied together in open-mouthed disbelief. In fact my own face painted the same picture, I mean how on earth would we secure a place in the Assembly Rooms?

 The elegant and notorious Assembly Dance was held every second Wednesday and it was to be of fashionable notoriety to be in attendance. In the first instance you could only be granted permission to be admitted by personal declaration from the ladies of distinction who oversaw and conducted the events. At this time Miss Fanny Mudpath and her cousin Miss Jane Handora ruled over the dances. Fanny Mudpath had a gift for making even the most regal gentry or the highest class of lady feel somehow inferior when they stood in her presence. She always looked older than her actual years, insisting on applying so much powder that her complexion could be mistaken for the whitest of spirits sent to haunt for eternity and shown with even more prominence because of the tightly held black hair that sat like a bun on top of her head. She would continually wear a musty brown shawl, often covering a bright satin frock, which confirmed an old-maidish position. In contrast Jane Handora would over adorn her complexion with bright red and smudged blusher under a shock of red hair that was held just above the neck. Often she would stand behind her elder cousin in a fragile gauze dress covered in flowers and always with her shoulders bare to the world, desperate to catch the eye of a would-be suitor. All of Salisbury's society knew of the reputation held by Fanny Mudpath and Jane Handora and how admission to the Assembly Dance was through an arduous application of the utmost difficulty. And yet Thomas had boldly offered and captivated our new delightful female acquaintances with a place in the finest of rooms on the High Street.

It quickly transpired that Thomas's mother had influence over the two highly superior ladies who would decide our fate in gaining entrance to the dance. She secured what is best described as an audition and we were to present ourselves at five o'clock sharp on a Friday. I arrived before Thomas some ten minutes before time, hurrying from the Journal's office down New Canal before loitering nearby in front of the George Inn with a hope that my friend would show particular briskness or that I may otherwise allow my nervousness to grow and compromise our chance of success. I whiled the few minutes away observing the striking medieval and famous Inn as a carriage passed under the throughway, bringing new guests. A young couple climbed out and set foot on the very courtyard where Shakespeare and his players had once performed. I held a passion for Shakespeare and Romeo and Juliet was my favourite of all his works. Suddenly in my mind it was as if I stood upon the famous cobbles looking up at the black leaded windows at the rear of the Inn holding a rose as Katherine appeared, "Ralph, Ralph, where for art…"

"Ralph, come now, where do you find yourself? Thomas was chuckling as he stood directly in front of me with his hands in his waistcoat pockets.

"Where am I?" I was quickly aroused from my contemplation, "I suppose I was considering my steps and demeanour in preparation for our task."

"With such a smile upon your face," Thomas winked, "come let us face the music."

After Thomas had knocked firmly on the thick oak door, we were directed upstairs for an immediate audience with Fanny Mudpath. She was found sitting in a very large carved chair, the back of which rose some distance above Fanny's pale and haunting face. Her sour look alone ensured we knew our place in the presence of a superior. The mood was extremely sullen as Thomas and I stood nervously in the dark dusty room, lit only by the few rays of sunshine creeping through the small gap left by the mostly drawn curtains.

"Miss Handora, the lamp if you please," Fanny finally barked to her companion.

In an instant a flickering flame illuminated the room behind us as the previously obscured Jane appeared from a dark alcove, causing an impulsive nervous twitch on my part. Jane looked her two young male visitors up and down as if inspecting a prize Ox from the cattle sale in the Market Square. Coming before us and out of the shadows, Jane gave the most peculiar of smiles as she somehow puckered her lips and revealed a truly rotten black set of teeth. "Charmed, I am sure," Jane spoke in an exaggerated posh and very squeaky voice.

"If you please," Fanny returned our attention. "I am told Mister Endstreet that you wish me to receive you and your friend with an intention of being accepted to the next Assembly Dance."

"Yes indeed," Thomas replied after a short cough to clear his throat, "Mister Chatterforth and I are great admirers of the Waltz and it is our ambition to be able to perform its majestic steps in the hall yonder, which my dear mother often describes in the most colourful of terms."

Fanny shook her head discouragingly, "spare me the performance Mister Endstreet, the only reason I have granted you this opportunity is because your rather disagreeable mother insisted. If I should avail you of my permission it will be a sound judgement through yours and Mister Chatterforth's appreciation for etiquette and an ability to Waltz correctly. Heaven forbid that you should prove worthy in both matters being of such a young age."

"We could hardly have hoped for a more favourable opportunity," Thomas semi-bowed once more, "is that not so Mister Chatterforth?"

"Quite," I replied rather simply.

"So let us begin," Fanny clapped her hands to signal the ascendancy in assessing our prospects. "Question Mister

Chatterforth, how should one dress for the Assembly Waltz?"

I stood uneasily before stuttering in response, "Not..not in a conspicuous way but with good taste."

"Adequate," Fanny said through gritted teeth. "Mister Endstreet, I understand that you have two ladies that you wish to bring as guests. Who shall act as escort?"

"The Endstreet Governess, Martha Cornfield," Thomas said swiftly as I recalled the timid creature who had chaperoned Dorothea and I all those years ago.

"I hope that I am not left finding fault with her or the Endstreet name will be tainted here," Fanny leant her extremely white face towards us. "Tell me, how would your ladies be expected to behave?"

"They should not indulge in excessive chatter or whispering, and they should always be pleased to dance and clearly show this in their demeanour," Thomas raised his eyebrows respectfully.

"Anything else Mister Chatterforth?" Nancy turned her head my way.

"They should never cross a ballroom unattended and should wear white gloves at all times except when eating," I now fed off the confidence shown by Thomas.

"Adequate," Fanny stated again, "but no more so. Now I must judge if your ability to Waltz is sufficient for the Assembly. Miss Handora, please open up the Ballroom and show these gentlemen in."

Jane led Thomas and I through to the grand Assembly Room which was illuminated by the sunlight pouring through the numerous bay windows and ensuring the magnificent chandelier glistened perpetually. It was instantly observable that this was indeed a fine establishment. Fanny took her place with a stiff recline on a very elaborate window seat that was adorned with numerous colourful and intricately stitched cushions.

"Very well," Fanny clapped her hands loudly, "Mister Endstreet by my side and Mister Chatterforth please lead your partner on the floor and take up a position in order to lead. I shall clap you a beat in order to keep your steps in time."

I led Jane to the centre of the floor and turned to face my erstwhile partner. In truth there was more advantage in viewing her face in the darkness of the side room as I was left to contend with the simpering fat cheeked girl with wild red hair, who continually sniffed with nerves. I feigned a smile of amenable acknowledgement before placing my right hand on Jane's rather generous waist and extending my left hand to hold her limp cold palm. With a loud snort she nudged her other hand on to my shoulder. What a fright this truly was.

"And so begin," Fanny announced with a sudden clap of her hands, to which I reacted and ensured my step timed with the next beat and each subsequent resounding blow, humming silently to myself to keep focus on the waltz and avoid the distraction of my unfortunate ragdoll partner. I seized upon the memory of dancing with my sister Lilly as our mother expertly tutored us both. After a couple of dances around the shiny floor, Fanny bellowed "enough" with a haughty refrain.

"Adequate," Fanny presented no change in her face to betray any further opinion on my performance. "Mister Endstreet, take you position please and follow the same routine."

"My dear Miss Mudpath you may depend upon me to deliver a fine performance faced with a partner of such delectable grace and beauty," Thomas bowed towards Jane with a sly wink and a smug grin.

Jane snorted once more in reply as her cheeks glowed so red as to overcome her thickly applied blusher. Before taking his position Thomas whispered in Jane's ear causing the unfortunate girl to almost fail in her breath

"My goodness this should not be a bashful arrangement but rather an opportunity to express your ability to waltz." Fanny scowled with a countenance of striking impatience.

As Fanny signalled the beat with a series of loud claps once more, Thomas led Jane at a fast pace in a gliding motion, twirling round and round as if floating on summer air. I had to admire his skill and self-confidence as Thomas swept his partner away with perfect timing and rhythm.

"Enough," Fanny finally brought the delightful performance to an end. "I have to say you entertained me Mister Endstreet and I truly had no intention in wanting to convey such a confession."

"Very good Miss Mudpath," Thomas bowed once again with a cheerful expression that caused no stir or reaction upon Fanny's stony face. In comparison he cast Jane a calculated affectionate look that quite and rather easily disarmed her.

There was a long silent pause as Fanny considered her decision. "It is apparent that you both have the required ability to dance at the ball but at the same time you are both so young and overly full of youthful spirit that you may frighten our many older members. If I should choose to commend you it will mean reposing a great trust and it is this knowledge that gives me caution in placing such reliance."

"To remain quite confidential Miss Mudpath, your opinion of a gentleman's prospects holds the highest sway for as far and wide as the Avon flows" Thomas raised his eyes to mine with cunning, "if my friend Mister Chatterforth will allow me, we feel that your decision here today will mark the fate of both of our affairs from this day forth. I hope you do not object to me mentioning this as I truly did not believe it would be possible to have such an infamous audience. I am also obliged to admit, and I know this to be true of Mister Chatterforth as well, that I felt daunted in your presence at such a confident manner and powerful beauty, which of course is complemented by Miss Handora's tender, cheerful disposition and endearing prettiness."

Jane Handora laughed and blushed at the same time as I was at a loss to express any comment on Thomas's fabricated and convenient statement delivered with such zeal. Instead I hoped my uneasy manner would not be transparent to the hard-hearted and astute Fanny Mudpath.

With a reproachful glance, Fanny rose from the window. "Oh spare me the piteous plea Mister Endstreet as it has no influence on my duty here today. I see a conflict currently with your youthful outlook being a general disadvantage but the joy of your dancing gaining more compatible regard. By-the-by, Miss Handora please render us with your opinion."

Jane's eyes flickered wildly before she remarked with an uncommon clear tone, "I am glad to hope that there is a place at our Dance for these fine gentlemen as I believe they will make good acquaintances and gain us all fine repute from their accomplishments in dancing so well." Jane thrust her chin towards her chest as she took deep anxious breaths like a child who had spoken out of turn. For an instant she lifted up her head again and looked affectionately at Thomas before laying it back again.

Fanny had in the meanwhile clasped her hands tightly before her, whilst her face showed no sign of being softened by her cousin's engaging opinion. "I believe that you are both of good nature, although undoubtedly frivolous, but I truly hope that I am not making this decision through a light head. Your attendance at the Dance next Wednesday is granted. Be warned that this chance is given against my initial inclination. Our regular assembled circle behold a refinement in manner and standing for which I venture that you will prevail through gentlemanly approach and worthy behaviour."

"We owe you both a complete debt of gratitude and will surely repay your faith," returned Thomas as continuing spokesman.

"Very well, now go as I have quite a headache," Fanny ushered us both away with a swish of her hand and a deep frown as if we were tiresome servants.

Jane was clearly engrossed in observing Thomas and offered a feeble wave to send us on our way. Thomas waited to the last moment before nodding a farewell, "thank you for expressing such a favourable opinion Miss Handora, I look forward to our next meeting."

I simply nodded too and followed my charismatic friend down the stairwell as more blushing and giggling ensued.

"What a situation," I commented as we came out on to the High Street. "Whatever did you say to win such favour with Miss Handora and make her such a simpering wreck?"

Thomas laughed loudly and slapped me hard on the back, "my dear Ralph you have so much to learn if you want to succeed in this life. It has always been a trait of the Endstreet family to be able to influence any situation by preying on a quickly observed weakness. With Miss Handora there was no need for extraordinary powers of persuasion but rather by simply inferring that there was an attraction to her on my part I gave the poor creature the hope that she would not become the spinster she so dreads. She is therefore happy and so are we because we shall go to the Ball."

I replied with firmness that I did not hold with Thomas's methods but what was done was indeed done and we would be going to the Assembly Dance with Katherine and Agnes after all.

The following Wednesday came around quickly and both Katherine and Agnes were both elated and nervous to be attending such an auspicious event in the Salisbury social calendar. Thomas secured the assistance of Edwin Gurden in getting his father's best seamstresses to alter two grand Parisian dresses owned by Thomas's mother. I can with almost the upmost certainty state that Kitty Endstreet was oblivious to this act. Within the year an Endstreet maid was to be fired from service and sent to ruin after being accused of stealing garments from the household. It takes no great detective to find the true connection.

A carriage was arranged to transport Katherine and Agnes to the ball, with Martha Cornfield in attendance. A directive was given to take a longer route out of The Close and round to New Canal by way of Catherine Street. The ladies could at least enjoy their arrival rather than being transported in an instant by way of the Norman gate on the High Street. In contrast, Thomas and I arrived on foot from St Ann's Street after dressing at the home of Thomas's eccentric uncle, General Basil Bumbledere, a rather stout retired military man with the bushiest and longest moustache I have ever seen. My remembrance of that fine summer evening was that we both strolled together in almost identical black tailcoats, white shirts with collars turned up and fine black silk bow ties. I am sure we greeted every passer by on New Street with such hearty acknowledgement that it was as if we had been declared as joint Mayors of the city.

After a brief pause and deep breath, I accompanied Thomas up the Assembly Room staircase to mingle with the height of Salisbury's society. I felt slightly awkward and hesitant as we were greeted by our stern hostess, Fanny Mudpath. As we approached Fanny seemed irritated to be distracted even for a moment from her exclusive audience and simply said, "do not disappoint me" . She then started to smilingly nod her head to enter into familiar discourse with a Lord and Lady from Clarendon. In contrast Jane Handora was of happy temperament and taking obvious personal interest in Thomas.

Katherine and Agnes did not look out of place in their fabulous gowns as they flicked their fans with delicate lace gloves in perfect time to the sweet music played by a virtuoso string quartet. Katherine's hair was arranged in simple sweet ringlets whilst Agnes looked older and less pretty with her hair held in a formal bun.

"Good evening to you fine gentlemen," Katherine spoke with the utmost politeness.

"What gentlemen are you referring to?" Agnes interposed, "oh my I do behold it is the two young men who would try to fly like birds. Someone has indeed dressed them as gentlemen." Agnes hid a mischievous smile behind her fan.

"You have a free and unique humour," Thomas replied with a degree of irritation.

"You are quite right!" exclaimed Katherine as she exchanged glances with me.

I was able to pleasantly converse with Katherine for the short interlude that preceded the first waltz and found her to be of good nature and kind heart. Thomas did not prosper so well in his conversation with Agnes and was to usher her on to the floor with a sneer and distinct air of unease for the opening dance. Katherine accepted my own more thoughtful and softer invitation to join me for a waltz. I found it to be a truly enchanting experience as I guided Katherine with grace, poise and elegance around the floor, moving with faultless ease. In contrast the stance of Thomas and Agnes was decidedly frosty as he took a rough lead in being excessively far from genteel. It was abundantly clear on our return to the waiting Martha Cornfied that Thomas was both incredibly impatient with Agnes and prepared for a quarrel. Those around stood aghast with consternation at the rather embarrassing spectacle as Thomas and Agnes began to exchange barbed comments with each other, both loudly and without intermission. Among the general hubbub of disapproving voices, the Governess Cornfield was oblivious on account of enjoying several drams of whiskey offered by another Governess. The performance, as it was referred to by one overbearing lady of some stature, drew to an end with the next dance.

"I have no further inclination to dance with a woman so bankrupt of charm and respect for any gentleman such as I." Thomas announced with coarse anger audible above the sweet music.

"At last fortune grants me a favour," Agnes responded with equal admonishment.

Thomas simply trudged away and headed for Jane Handora, whom he promptly led onto the dancefloor. Agnes grimaced towards Katherine whilst tapping her foot impatiently on the floor. A gentleman by the name of Charles Dasher, who I knew to be an apprentice attorney, stepped forward with the utmost civility to request a waltz with Agnes. She duly accepted the invitation. It also gave me the encouragement to lead Katherine to the floor once more.

As the evening progressed it became strikingly obvious that there would be no reconciliation between Thomas and Agnes, and therefore any chance of romance between the pair had withered. However, Thomas now seemed aggravated with indignation at the attention bestowed by Charles Dasher upon Agnes. In order to remonstrate, Thomas seemed set on dancing in earnest with every young female in the room, including Katherine.

Despite the unfortunate turn of events I was determined to prosper in my relationship with Katherine. I found her to be very pleasant company with an agreeable nature and a beauty that absorbed my attention. By the end of the evening I was totally without embarrassment in requesting another meeting, reflecting our easygoing conversation on a manner of subjects that was on the whole unaffected by the misgivings of the behaviour of our friends. Unfortunately as we left the ballroom as the dance came to an end, Thomas witnessed an event that finally pushed and affected his temper to the limit. Charles Dasher now had an irresistible inclination towards Agnes, who in turn seemed suitably charmed by her suitor, or as charmed as far as her rather melancholy expressions would reveal. With an unexpected motion, the dapper Mister Dasher planted a kiss on Agnes's limp but willing hand and a further meeting was agreed. To make matters worse, Martha Cornfield let out a loud yelp of delight, magnified to full effect by the copious drams of spirit that the hapless Governess had by now imbibed. Thomas observed the scene along with all those in attendance but simply and quietly made his way from the room, seeming to be of amenable spirit. I embarked to follow, bidding our hosts farewell, before Fanny Mupdath could impart any harsh observation.

As I hurried out on to the High Street, Thomas was to be found stood stiff and tall with a look of darned embarrassment. The Assembly guests now began to walk out onto the street, where a line of fine carriages waited to to take the refined company home. I walked over to check on Thomas but he was inspecting those behind me and then, in a moment of blind madness, he marched past and with deliberate intentions headed for Charles Dasher. Interrupting a conversation between Charles and an eminent Magistrate, Thomas offered a handshake. After a slightly startled moment of consideration, Charles put out his right hand only to find himself struck hard upon the nose by a cunning but despicable blow from Thomas. Charles fell to the floor and Thomas marched away as a mortified audience looked on. I followed my fiery friend, admonishing his action as we made our way towards The Close, stating that there was no profit in punching a man of such harmless nature.

"On the contrary Ralph there is a principle involved," Thomas stopped marching to confront my reflection on the matter, "I found that gentleman to be distasteful and as a matter of principle, and to be honest duty, I expressed my opinion and put the wretched stranger in his place. He now is in no doubt as to his lower state compared to my own. That is how you prosper in life Ralph, by being of independent and single-minded spirit. Otherwise you will be marked as a grovelling weak character who will never establish a winning role. My dear mother has never let me forget that I am always to be a man of standing, never to blacken or humiliate the Endstreet name."

"I still feel obliged to offer my opinion in that your action was rash and did not assist any circumstance or gain you any credit," I commented firmly.

Thomas shook his head and I feared for a moment he would strike me too. Instead he returned no answer but just pursued his way towards the spire. I took the same course at the rear without further conversation and we both refrained from discussing the event for the rest of the evening.

Chapter IV - *Whereby the Reader will become acquainted with Emma Toopey and will determine if I was foolish in my sentiment towards her. Catastrophe and despair are to follow.*

As my relationship with Katherine grew, Thomas remained earnest in his desire to ensure it was understood that any woman fortunate to accompany him should be both subservient and outwardly grateful. Under the circumstances though he continued to be attracted to a strong minded type of female, contradictory to his intentions and yet there seemed to be an appeal in that a change of character could be won. I can testify that due to Thomas being a man of considerable impatience he never found victory in this game.

On one occasion in the winter of 1848, Thomas met by chance a lovely lady by the name of Emma Toopey, a member of the highly respected timber merchant family. Thomas had begun frequenting the Kings Head and Brewery on the Avon along with Edwin Gurden. I was now a year into my courtship of Katherine and becoming established as a renowned writer on the Salisbury Journal. In truth this had removed me from being a close acquaintance of Thomas as I enjoyed a life far removed from his social circle. How fateful that our paths were to cross again. I understood that Thomas had sunk several jars of ale when he simply sat himself down by Emma Toopey as she was in dialogue with a friend by the Kings Head fire. Far from being affronted by the intrusive interruption it was told to me that Emma was highly amused by the attention. Her friend was a well known actress from London called Florence Thistlewood, who was due to perform in a new production at the New Street Theatre. Thomas secured the chance to accompany Emma to the opening night under the premise that they would be joined by a fine young upstanding couple of his acquaintance. And so I was contacted by Thomas in regard of the situation and he was back in my life again.

Katherine was agreeable to the invitation as she was strongly interested in the Theatre, although there was a sense of recoil upon the realisation that the evening would be spent with the capricious Thomas. However she overlooked her unease and graciously consented to attend in that I gave a personal declaration of confidence that there would be no sufferance or aggravation.

In truth it was I that behaved most out of character that evening as I was rendered both foolish and weak in the presence of the beautiful Emma Toopey. At regular intervals I found myself looking round at the girl of such beauty with her long brown hair cascading over delicate shoulders and with such deep hypnotic eyes that truly left me in a trance. I struggled to retain composure but did bear well in her company without being noticed by Thomas or Katherine.

The play was called Lady Bumbley's Secret and Florence Thistlewood played the lead as a trembling weak maiden living in fear of the overbearing local Squire and desperate to have her honour upheld by the heroic politician. It was my first time in the New Street Theatre, and I could not help but to be overwhelmed by the lavish auditorium decorated so precisely in gold and red, although the hot and dry air created by the gas lighting grew in intensity in line with the developing drama on the stage. As the wonderful orchestra played a rousing finale, the smell of the lamps overpowered a number of ladies in the audience and it was with some relief that we once again tasted the fresh air outside. Although the play had quelled my artistic thirst, I could now relate to why my father despised the theatre experience.

The relationship between Thomas and Emma truly began to flourish and I noticed a change in his character, even to the point of taking walks by the River Avon for pleasant amusement. Emma had a big heart, was sprightly in every regard and always showed concern and interest in the welfare of others. This was in contrast to her father, who held considerable wealth despite coming from poor agricultural stock. It was well known that he had married to his advantage but of sad consequence when his wife died giving birth to Emma's brother, James. It was a long time after the evening at the theatre that Thomas was introduced to Mr William Toopey. Thomas endeavoured to find favour with the man through a sincere desire to win Emma's hand one day.

"Well sir it is not for me to say if you are a nice person," the stout ruddy-faced gentleman huffed as he paced around his drawing room, failing to even glance at Thomas as he stood still by the fire. William Toopey was certainly not going to be praiseworthy of the young suitor brought to the house by his precious daughter. Now a young woman, she so much resembled her mother and the wife that William had tragically lost. "Even though you boast of the family to which you belong and that is certainly known throughout Salisbury, it does not find instant popularity with me. Indeed I know your own reputation to be a man of mischief who is not disposed from making coarse threats and finding remonstrance through physical assault. I observed the attack on the unfortunate Charles Dasher outside the Old George that was not precipitated and in my view of a cowardly nature."

"I am deserving of your opinion," Thomas bit his lower lip and uncurled the instinctive fist formed in anger, repressing his true position with a shudder. "I confess to having been rash and impudent in the past but I now find my character smoothed and augmented in social value through the acquaintance and now devotion to your daughter Emma."

William Toopey continued to conduct himself with absurd haughtiness, determined in his mission to somehow remove the prospect of Thomas being a frequent and unwelcome visitor to his home. Oh heaven forbid should the honour of marriage ever be requested, but the wily old gentleman had a plan in mind.

"Well sir, I have told you directly of my concerns and I am at least pleased that you have chosen not to remonstrate on the matter." Mr Toopey stroked his chin before hooking both thumbs in the pockets of his waistcoat. "I want to set you a challenge and should you perform well and retain the state of feelings my daughter has for you I shall concede that your future lays together as a couple. Are you prepared to take up the gauntlet?"

"You may depend on it," Thomas replied with curiosity.

"Very well." Mr Toopey collected an ornate but scuffed box and offered Thomas a large badly rolled cigar. After taking an even larger cigar for himself, and lighting the pair from the fire, Mr Toopey allowed himself a wry smile as Thomas coughed and spluttered with vigour. "I want you to avoid my daughter and stay out of her company until the end of June. I shall then arrange a meeting for you both in this very room and if you should still rally to the same feelings of love and devotion then I shall yield and grant my blessing to any further union. If I were to gamble upon the outcome, I would wager that any true prospects of romance would have so diminished that you will be barely able to remember each other's names. Trust me sir that there is no finer cribbage player in Salisbury than I and this is no different than playing a rubber for sixpence. I have a purse bulging with the sixpences I claimed only last night."

"And should I refuse to enter into your game?" Thomas gave him a defiant look.

"Then you may depend upon it that I shall send my daughter overseas to America, where I have a prosperous cousin." spluttered Mr Toopey. "In that case you will not see my daughter again but if you are strong enough to take the challenge then you shall be reunited again by next summer."

Thomas's face moved between an expression of anger and defeat as he failed to keep pace with his true emotions. "What a man you are sir," Thomas finally replied when his shock had subsided, "It is my belief that you are not doing your daughter a service here, but you have me at a disadvantage unless of course that we may choose to elope."

"I should impart to tell you that I have influence way beyond the spire and not to mention that you would be consigning both yourself and my daughter to a life in poverty or yourself in the Gaol should you return to this town, secured by whatever charge I wish to bring." Mr Toopey made the consequence clear with confident refrain.

"But I can't avoid Emma so easily if we are both frequenting the town," Thomas challenged.

"Your father I believe has secured a business venture in London to deliver polished steel products to the nobility." Mr Toopey remarked with more than a hint of planned cunning. "He has done nothing but boast about this fact for the last few weeks at the George and Dragon in Castle Street."

"And your point is?" Thomas inquired whilst being fully aware what of was going to be suggested.

Mr Toopey hesitated for a moment before pursuing the same monotonous line of conversation, "Let me make it plain and clear as to my business proposition, with the business being the affairs of the heart. I am suggesting that my lovely daughter is given a charitable assignment to the poor of the town. I have already raised the subject with the Rector of St Martin's church who oversees the voluntary school in the Old Malthouse to promote education for the poor children of the parish. He is very agreeable to Emma assisting there and believes it will be redeemable for her soul to see such a side of life and that she will be held in profound respect for her position in the future. And as for you sir taking a position in London will allow you the opportunity to prove your worth to your industrious father, not to mention your opinionated mother, and enhance your reputation beyond that of habitual brawler."

"Indeed you have given this much consideration," Thomas tried not show his indignation. "We are therefore both thrust into the wilderness with the promise and understanding that upon our return should we both still testify the same level of ardour and devotion then we can resume a proper courtship with your blessing."

"That is the full extent of my meaning sir, and I am glad that you have at last found the scent," said Mr Toopey with a gruesome smile. "We shall see if you both truly languish and pine for each other."

Thomas found himself backed into a corner from which he could not escape and his acceptance was soon a formality. As Thomas left the house that evening with his head bowed low and feeling weary, the conniving Mr Toopey held an expression akin to a fox watching a pack of chasing hounds drown in the river to which he had led them.

I personally bade Thomas farewell as he left by coach for London, and I noted he was totally out of humour. The weather was at least kind for the season and Thomas did find a glimmer of comfort through my promise to watch over Emma Toopey.

"I should say that there will be no doubt that I shall return to claim Emma's fair hand," Thomas winked with some exaggeration as he lent from the carriage before departing down the road.

I do often wonder if this was the moment when fate intervened to change the course of my life to follow a path to ruin and damnation. Dear reader it is now I have to confess to a turn of events for which I still feel great shame and desperate sorrow. The Journal was taken over by new owners who were more inclined towards Liberalism and taking a rather neutral stance on political issues as opposed to the previous owner, a staunch Whig who sadly ended his days in a debtor's prison. The new people in charge were very quick to sing my praises, and so very often. I was presented with more work beyond being a mere Penny-A-Liner and was soon feeling extremely accomplished in my work. So absorbed was I in my occupation that I found little time to share with Katherine, and even when I did so would hitherto overlook any opportunities for leisure or social engagement, or I would demonstrate extreme disinterest in most of her topics of conversation. The sweet young girl I had so coveted became quiet and withdrawn in my arrogant company, and was prone to tears when I left the room. I recall this now with sad reflection but at the time would lay the blame for our melancholy meetings upon that dainty girl. Even my dear sister Lilly, who was now blossoming into a pretty young woman, chose to consult with me on the matter. She spoke lovingly but stressed that she could not be agreeable with how I treated Katherine and that it was I who was not beyond reproach in the matter. I was not at all softened by this observation but instead left for town by foot with the intention of sinking several winter ales to warm my soul and deaden my senses. As I strolled purposefully down Exeter Street the sky was dark and cloudy, and so comparable with my mood. I was soon even further out of spirits as it began to rain heavily and I was forced to take shelter at St Ann's gate. Conscious of another taking shelter there too, I grew impatient for the rain to stop so I would have no reason to enter into conversation with a stranger.

"Upon my word, is it not Ralph Chatterforth?" a young and familiar girl's voice sounded.

Startled by this unexpected remark I turned to see the innocent face of Emma Toopey as she lowered the cloak that covered her head. Despite my promise to Thomas I had not ventured to see Emma since his departure, which was some three months previous and in which time Christmas had come and gone. I was so charmed by her beauty that I felt it somehow inappropriate to spend too much time in Emma's presence.

"The very same," I replied loudly and sounding rather superior before softening, "and how are you?"

"I can assure you I am generally well, feeling both worthy and independent in the work I have undertaken. I must acknowledge though that over these past few weeks I have found myself feeling lonely and often disconcerted. I should not feel this way and I do curse myself sometimes as I am constantly reminded of the situation of the poor wretches I am helping in my duties, and that their lives hold no comparison. But tell me why those children with so little are yet so happy and content with their existence and yet I am so sad whilst having wealth and a wonderful man prepared to sacrifice so much to be my husband." Emma trembled terribly.

"I do understand what you are saying and you should not feel guilty. Some people are born to a purpose and others will find it less natural but the fact that they are willing to forge ahead when called upon is both admirable and remarkable. Miss Toopey there is no weakness in reflecting on your own position as you surely need companionship in order to share your thoughts, whether they be happy or sad. There is no taint in wanting to enjoy the happiness you are so willing to share." I smiled broadly and felt as calm as I had felt for a long time.

"How glad I am to see you Mister Chatterforth," Emma moved forward out of the shadows with an appealing smile. There was a tranquil beauty in her whole demeanour that melted my heart in an instant. " I do not suppose that I could put upon you to meet with me on occasion, just to brighten my spirit and of course only with the full blessing of your companion, Katherine Milliner?"

"I could not part from here without making the very same suggestion myself, and it would be in keeping with the promise that I made to Thomas, and for which I now feel incredibly guilty for not keeping." I was unconscious to any opinion that Katherine may have on the subject and would decide to exclude her from the agreement in any case. I had also readily dismissed any further prospect of being so enchanted by Emma that I would betray Thomas.

As the rain subsided I led my petite and kindly companion by the arm and walked her up St Ann's Street. As we strolled I found myself telling jokes and offering nothing but humourous observations that caused so much merriment that Emma's infectious laugh eased her own worries and broke down the barriers of my new stern and sharp resolve. And so from that day I found a new purpose in life and anticipated every meeting with Emma as a joyous occasion to behold. I did not have the slightest feeling of guilt as surely our meetings were not remarkable beyond conversation, and I remained the perfect gentleman at first. I even improved in temper towards Katherine although this was just a feeble attempt to mask my new outside interest.

As the months passed I was plighted to be held in ever increasing regard for my writing skill by the Journal's owners and presented with a great many opportunities. Driven by the constant thought of Emma's sweet face and endearing shy refrain I could not even think of anything that might sour my mood or countenance. As May came the sun began to shine brightly and Emma and I would meet by the Avon and stroll in the warmth of the summer air. It was all so perfect until my life was suddenly pushed into dreary retreat when one otherwise fine day Emma presented with feeble hesitation a letter. I could tell that she was embarrassed through being so quickly coloured and so evidently keeping her wonderful wide brown eyes from my view. I stopped still to pay scrutiny to the writing that was by the hand of my best friend, Thomas Endstreet. The letter remarked upon the fact that Thomas was soon to return home and the final sentiment was clear in that he was so longing to claim Emma as his bride. I returned the letter with considerate conduct and reassured Emma that I held Thomas to be a fine gentleman and quite possibly the most fortunate man in the whole world in gaining such a prize. As I remained outwardly kind and meritorious, my heart was truly breaking and my eyes welled to the point of weeping. That night I could neither eat nor sleep and my mood darkened to extend a sharp vicious riposte to anyone in my company. The following day I sent a boy with a message to Emma to sadly cancel our meeting. Instead I consoled myself by dining with Katherine, whose beauty I had long since failed to recognise. Her simple declaration of the impending return of Thomas degenerated my mood quickly and when she innocently enquired if I had heard any news of Emma Toopey, I was precipitated to rather harshly end our relationship. This came with an abrupt statement that any feelings or sentiment once held between us had with certainty died. Katherine paid very little deliberation upon my comments but instead declared both agreement and relief at the turn of events. With little intermission she left both my father's house and save for one final occasion, she would no longer be part of my life.

Far from being conscious of making a rash decision over my future with Katherine, I was overcome by an irresistible mood of happiness. My mind was made up that I would declare both my affection and hitherto repressed feeling for Emma. I felt sure my sentiment would be immediately reciprocated and had already plotted how we could both elope and live on the land of my Great Aunt's farm in Cumbria. The next day I sent a message to Emma that our meeting that day could proceed as planned.

At length I almost wished the majority of the day away in order to instigate my shrewd notion, and could barely write a coherent sentence so much was my mind in turmoil. The sun shone brighter than ever as I doggedly made my way to our usual spot by the Avon near Fisherton Bridge. I swear I nearly swooned like a lovesick woman as Emma greeted me with a warm smile from beneath her wide and very bright brown eyes, highlighting the sublime dimples on her cheeks. Even now I shudder at the thought of that meeting with a tear in my eye.

We strolled casually as my heart did beat ever faster. "I am glad you were able to come today as I felt rather sad that we could not meet yesterday," Emma looked up and directly at me as I looked back with longing at her buxom shape defined in such a small frame.

"I am sure that I too was very unhappy not to be with you yesterday," I paused by the water's edge unable to contain myself any longer. "I need to declare something to you," throwing off any restraint I gently put my arm around Emma's waist and pulled her towards me before kissing her lips softly.

As we moved apart from the embrace, for a moment Emma looked so sad and then astonished. I felt sure that her eyes betrayed an inner love for me before she bowed her face from view and shied away from me.

"Ralph you are such a good man and I swear that you have been more of a friend to me than anyone else in my whole life." Emma looked back towards me and tears were streaming down her cheeks. "Now I feel so down-hearted and fear that I have given you reason to believe that our relationship is much more than an innocent friendship. Please let it be understood that no good can come of finding love between us as the consequence would be so grave."

"But I cannot be distracted from my love for you and I know I should rather have no comfort if you reject me and I declare I would rather die. I am now free from my relationship with Katherine and felt sure that you would rather be with me than Thomas." I was now shaking in desperation with a strained look of serious concern.

Emma now sobbed openly, "but I did not know that this would be so. I am keeping my heart for Thomas and that will not change. Please do not torture me further with your words of anguish for I now hold myself wholly to blame in this matter and now wish we had never sheltered from the rain that evening. I would rather have remained sad and lonely than to have now left you in such despair."

"I now understand how you are truly disposed and I am sorry to have embarrassed you and placed you in such an awkward situation," I hung my head in defeat not wishing to hurt Emma any further. "I feel we should now depart and not meet again unless in the company of Thomas or another."

"Very well," Emma said quietly as she peeped up through reddened eyes. In an instant she stood tall and kissed me tenderly on the lips before turning and walking away without a further glance.

For the weeks that followed I became absorbed in my work in an effort to ensure that Emma did not occupy every passing thought. I was as good as my word and ensured that Emma was not faced with the imposition of my presence by chance meeting or otherwise. On several occasions I nearly weakened but apprehension and anxiety over how I would be greeted deterred even a single step towards the St Martins' Malthouse. And so I remained busy from early in the morning until late at night until the events of one desperate day when I was interrupted in my writing by the Editor. He spoke of a highly dispirited and positively weary gentleman seeking my urgent attention upon a very grave matter.

Thomas Endstreet was stood impatiently waiting by the door and I feared at once that he had come to confront me for such an unforgivable betrayal, convinced that Emma had revealed the truth. I only wish that this had been the only fact of the matter.

"My goodness Thomas, this is such a surprise for I did not expect to see you back in Salisbury for another two weeks," said I trying to sound cheerful but feeling breathless.

"I declare to you Ralph that I am rendered disconsolate and do not know how to act or where I can turn for comfort." cried Thomas with the most pained look.

"Whatever has happened?" I led Thomas along the road truly believing as we strolled that Emma had declared that she no longer loved him. Surely she had rejected him on the grounds of loving another.

"I come here with terrible news of Emma," answered Thomas in a low and pitiful voice, "when did you last meet with her?"

"Indeed it must have been a few weeks ago and I can tell you she was so excited that you were soon to return." I gave encouragement whilst turning away under a cloud of guilt.

"I thank you for your kind nature and for looking after Emma. I thank you from my heart," Thomas began to weep.

"Whatever is wrong Thomas? Is this the result of a broken heart?" I returned in a suppressed voice so as not to draw the attention of passers by. Even as a child I hardly could recall Thomas ever weeping.

"A broken heart is what I have. Broken because my true love will soon depart this earth," Thomas raised his shaking hands and clasped them firmly together.

"N – n – no, please do not say this," a chill now went down my spine."What is wrong with Emma?" I demanded.

"There is a horrible disease taking over this town like the plague itself. So many have already died and now my beautiful Emma lies in feeble exhaustion with haggard eyes and pitted cheeks, withered of spirit and fight." cried Thomas fiercely.

"There is no hope?" I urged, praying that Thomas was overstating in his aggravated frame of mind.

"No hope at all," was the simple reply.

"Take me to her," I responded in earnest with no sympathy for my friend's wretched condition but rather through an overwhelming fear for Emma's plight alone.

Thomas did not need any encouragement and led me to a nearby carriage, instructing the coachman to make haste to the Toopey residence. I was conscious of Thomas's anxiety and concern as he failed to relax to any degree or even mutter many words for the entire short journey. I too was overcome by worry, numbed at the thought of Emma's plight. Upon arrival we were ushered with haste by the maid to Emma's bedside, where the broken figure of William Toopey stood hunched and in tears as my own father tended to her.

It was obvious that Emma had a severe fever and was so pale and sickly that I feared she had already passed away save for a sudden and violent cough that caused her whole body to twitch. The beautiful young girl who had so recently won my heart was now so weak and exhausted, draining of life and withering away before my eyes. How I longed to walk her true healthy self by the Avon once more in carefree summer abandon.

"Doctor, is there any hope?" Thomas spoke to my father with a trembling voice.

"Lord have mercy on her soul," returned my father starkly causing Thomas to breakdown completely into a flood of tears.

Emma's eyes closed tightly as she drifted away. Biting his lip, William Toopey helped Thomas up and led him from the room. My father packed away his instruments and moved to one side without acknowledgement to his son. Instinctively I moved closer to the bed and knelt down beside the ashen complexion of my dying Emma, instantly feeling the heat the fever was generating. "You will always be in my heart," I whispered whilst trying not to crumble. Softly I kissed her forehead. Emma's eyes flickered open for just a moment, still wide and beautiful but devoid of the sparkle of life. "I loved you Ralph, please forgive me," Emma spoke softly within a sigh before finally breathing her last breath.

Weakened by such sudden and unexpected grief my head fell forward and I buried it deep into the bedding, crying as hard and long as a newborn. My whole body was overcome with anguish for the love I should not really openly lament but I could not stop my frame from visibly trembling and convulsing.

"Be calm," the authoritative voice of my father sounded, reminding me of his presence. I instantly strove to compose myself, unsure of how to explain my reaction and yet questioning why Emma has requested forgiveness. Was it because she had not accepted my offer of elopement?

After a final look at the still peaceful figure of Emma, now at least free of pain, I left the room keeping my grim face hidden from the view of my father so he could not see that I continued to weep. On the landing a commotion broke out before me as Thomas voiced loud and passionate recriminations towards William Toopey, declaring that in his effort to keep Emma and Thomas apart that he had all but killed her as much as aiming a pistol and firing. The conversation that ensued was not a long one as Emma's' father simply stated "no,no,no," and shook his head gravely. At length I feared that Thomas may strike the grief-stricken father and so moved closer to intervene. Thomas recognised my impulsive move and looked as sternly upon me as he did William Toopey. "Damn you, damn you all," he screamed and stormed from the house. A profound silence followed before Mr Toopey drew himself up in an effort to show a brave face. My father reappeared and gave me a steadfast look before offering his condolences to Mr Toopey. "I believe it is shameful that your daughter died in this way and as a matter of course someone should be brought to account," said my father angrily.

"I trust it will be so but it will not save my Emma and so I have little fight in the matter." replied Mr Toopey mournfully.

"How can this be anyone's fault?" I cried out, "by what means can someone be to blame for a fever?"

"Well," rejoined my father after staring directly at me for a while, "to temper your remonstrance I should state that this was no common fever. Miss Toopey died from Cholera and she is not alone in the dirty cesspit streets of this town. This very day I have already tended to the deaths of many as young as Miss Toopey, and some even younger. Three in Church Street by St Edmund's, four in Winchester Street and then three in Scott's Lane. Before the summer is out I expect the death toll to be several hundred."

"What has rendered such a dire and fatal state of affairs?" I returned in total ignorance.

"Have you not heard of Salisbury's new title?" William Toopey interrupted, "the Venice Of England. So called because of the large open water channels that run through every street alongside every poor borough, and where Emma had worked so charitably over these last few months."

"I know of the water channels," I acknowledged emphatically, "but are you saying they are at fault here for spreading this Cholera?"

"The water channels have become little more than open sewers running amongst a dense and poor population. I know that you walk down Minster Street every day, have you not taken notice of the stench generated there as each house discharges its effluent into the water?" My father pressed quite fiercely.

"I do declare that I had become used to the situation there and simply tolerated the smell." I mumbled with a rueful countenance. "But if this is so then I shall not rest until I have contrived to reveal the truth behind such a downright criminal death of such a charming, gentle and playful girl."

"I thank you for your consideration here today for my daughter Master Chatterforth. I am truly touched by your concern and can see it to be ardent and true. Now may I request that you go forth with your chivalrous necessity to right a wrong but leave me to lay down in my misery and mourn the only true light that shone in my life." William Toopey's face betrayed a tortured soul way beyond my own restrained distress.

"Yes come Ralph and stop playing this imaginary part in the life of Mister Toopey's daughter. You have loitered longer than her fiancée in such a peculiar nature." My father almost pushed me towards the door and then ushered me to his carriage.

As we travelled back in to Salisbury my father was quick to further his general feeling of displeasure as I stared blankly through the window pained by the memory of the soft beauty that had now departed.

"I have noted that you are trembling still Ralph, quivering so in remembrance of a girl who was betrothed to your friend. Whatever has gone before, you must break the chains and swear to make no utterance of any event that was shared with Emma Toopey." My father almost implored before whispering in a low voice, "believe me son I do understand as I still conceal my own grief for a beauty long since departed from this world."

I ceased staring out of the window and moved around to look at my father, astonished by his remark that above all was so out of keeping with his normal harsh tone.

"My heart was torn long before you were born Ralph, and I saw in you today an image of myself. I too played the wrong hand and have suffered ever since." Father spoke slowly, "so now you must not feel shame and instead pray for Emma. And then you have the chance to be worthy and reveal to the world how these channels and canals bring death to our streets. By the words you write will surely end the suffering."

I did press for more information on my father's past but was quickly discouraged by his stern riposte. Instead I made a bold promise to declare the cholera scandal to every household that sat below the spire and beyond if necessary.

Still extremely low in spirit, I took my usual place in the Journal office and began to write a strong narrative in declaration of the scandal of death on the streets of Salisbury. Resolute in my objective to ensure that others did not suffer a loss like mine, and to bring out something positive from Emma's death, I scribed a strong piece with firmly voiced principles on what should be done and with stress on the need for an inquiry. By my own hand I had created a monument to my sweet Emma and relayed it to the Editor for immediate consideration due to the circumstance. I then took my leave on grounds of compassion declaring an intention to not return until after the funeral. Self-centred in my own grief, I failed to pass even a single thought for the condition of my good friend Thomas.

It would have been imprudent to grieve so openly at home so I locked myself away in the bedroom under the notion of being unwell. My delicate sister Lilly tended to my every need and as a consequence I felt so guilty in betrayal. I so wanted to share my secret life with Emma but was so unsure how Lilly would feel upon the matter. To lose the trust and respect of my sister at this time would have finished me.

With dark clouds making an appearance to hold court over the bleak day of the funeral, the Chatterforth family joined the respectful gathering at St Martin's. People came from across the classes to express sympathy for the charitable girl, who had been nothing but kind and honest. Looking around the crowd I observed the anguish of William Toopey that was set against the bitterness of despair on the face of Thomas Endstreet as they both stood by the open graveside. Providing fortitude and support by Thomas's side was his sister, Dorothea. She had blossomed into a very attractive woman, very much in the image of her mother as she stood with elegance and refinement despite the situation. I could not help but gaze upon her for a moment until the distraction of turning wheels became audible in the distance and the rain began to fall, causing Dorothea to look across to where I stood. Stopping to faintly smile for a moment, she quickly returned her attention to Thomas who was shaking with some force.

The funeral cart came splashing through the mud in a slow sombre movement. As it stopped suddenly there was an immediate movement to take the coffin by the waiting pallbearers as the undertaker's lad held still the horse by its reins. A stunned and yet profound silence fell until broken by the droning words of the Minister through the service. A chorus of sobbing broke out as the coffin was lowered into the boggy grave. Closing my eyes tightly I turned to walk away, feeling both numb in my thoughts and awkward in my stride. Despite every obstinate effort, tears flowed freely down my cheeks and I fell weakly to rest on one knee in the sodden long grass. A slender hand touched mine and offered enough comfort for me to revive and get back to my feet.

"At least I now have my answer and can move on," a faint female voice sounded.

I looked up to see Katherine walking away now clear in mind on my deception and able to move on in her life. On my part I made no attempt to repent my unworthiness or propound such unforgivable ill-treatment of such a fine lady, just standing to observe as she walked from the churchyard and from my life. Many years later I did hear that she took a respectable position as Governess for a wealthy family from London. By all accounts she married the eventual widower and found a new life in Italy.

"Well Master Chatterforth how you have grown into a fine and distinguished gentleman," another female voice sounded in my ear but this time with a strong confident air.

Looking away from Katherine, my attention was now diverted to Dorothea Endstreet who stood patiently waiting for acknowledgement to her compliment.

"Thank you for your kind remark Dorothea," I returned without expression. "It is good at least to have the opportunity to see you again but sad that it is bound by such a sad occasion."

"Yes I have had to pay my brother a great deal of compassion since coming home and if truth be told I can scarcely believe that a girl would ever reduce him to such a sorrowful broken wreck. I never met her but so wished I had just to contemplate the qualities that captivated Thomas." Dorothea seemed far from being forlorn but rather jealous that another woman had captured a stronger hold on

Thomas than she. "Well I am sure you are so happy to see me Ralph like a sight for sore eyes. Does you heart not beat faster in an uncontrollable and vivacious manner driven by the very thought of romance with the beautiful sister of your best friend?"

I laughed feebly but could not find any words in reply.

"Do not oblige me with an answer and I already know it to be true and certain and cannot bear to watch your uncomfortable musings for a moment longer. My how you blush in my presence like the shy schoolboy I last saw," said Dorothea, delighting in her position, "come walk with me."

We were left to ourselves to walk far behind the funeral party and I was at least able to now keep back my tears for Emma, compliant to the strong hold that Dorothea had over me.

"I am so glad that this funeral has now passed and thankfully so prompt and yet respectful," Dorothea twirled a highly elaborate and fashionable umbrella above her head as she strolled with her usual stiff deportment that extolled a refined and regal air.

"Yes and now hopefully Thomas can move on," I had lapsed into a bounder, acting so far removed from the true emotion of the situation.

"He will I am sure, but what about you Ralph Chatterforth?" Dorothea stood still by the roadside and although the rain was still falling neither her finely groomed hair or expertly pleated dress was stirred by the weather.

"What about me?" I repeated feeling under scrutiny and wondering whether my concealed betrayal was really public knowledge.

"It has been observed and relayed to me that you have found no fortune in love and remain as alone as the shy young boy I took under my wing. This is not something I can bear to see develop any further before my eyes and feel I must endeavour to change your fate for the good.". Dorothea spoke with sophisticated coolness as if it was already decided.

I stood silent under the weight of the expectation now held upon my response. "But surely you will soon return to Paris?" I replied rather timidly.

"Do not worry for I have now returned for good. I have now gone beyond what Paris can offer me and know it to be true that Salisbury is the place of opportunity. It is here in full view of the spire that I can indulge myself equally in business and to raise a family." Dorothea smiled knowingly as she delivered her assured statement.

I did not reply save for a polite nod of the head and then hastily moved Dorothea back towards the funeral party that had congregated at the bottom of Milford Hill, patiently awaiting the two stragglers. After the formality of expressing a final round of condolences, I was able to retreat home with mixed thoughts on the failed imprudent relationship with Emma that had literally been put to the grave, and was now swiftly disengaged so cruelly in my mind by the somewhat oppressive attention of Dorothea. And yet why did I not look for an instant escape from Dorothea's attention? Was it in some way perverted that I secretly craved the thought of her preying on me with such wantonness?

Chapter V - *Where I am rendered desperate by the Journal's blindness to the cause of Salisbury's cholera outbreak but others contrive to ensure the disease is beaten.*

There were many questions in my head that I dare not try and answer with any confidence when it came to the matter of how to deal with Dorothea. As I strolled to the Journal office with a brisk step I was at least able to find distraction in the main priority ahead. That was to ensure that the people of this ignorant town were made fully aware of its current inclination towards decay and degradation. My article was bound to find mutual recognition of the canals that flowed with death and no longer would people just shamble by and accept the condition of the streets. I was about to open their eyes to the truth, or should that have been their noses. As I entered the Journal office I could almost feel that there were several pairs of despairing eyes cast upon me. No word of greeting was uttered, as was the normal tradition, and so I simply marched into the premises with a heavy purposeful step. As I glanced around the room from my desk there was still no acknowledgement of my presence. The Editor appeared with my article in his hand and I waited in proud anticipation as his tentative footsteps still managed to arrest the attention of the room.

"In short Mister Chatterforth the Salisbury Journal cannot allow you to take such a liberty with your position," the rather stout Editor, Mr Binkerpick, announced loudly so all could hear.

"How do you mean sir?" I asked

Mr Binkerpick reddened and threw my article on the desk, "this sir is a respectable newspaper and not renowned for supplying the good citizens of Wiltshire with such fancy fiction as this."

"Are you charging that I have lied in this article? I stood with an impudent and fiery twinkle in my eye as a nervous whisper echoed around the room. "The words written tell the truth and are stated in good faith and with a determination to bring good health to this town in the name of all those who have died and have yet to die. This does not compromise the name of the Salisbury Journal but rather it enhances the very moral duty in serving all those who read it with the truth. And from the truth will come change."

After a long and uncomfortable silence, Mr Binkerpick refused to alter his view or stance, "I fear that your mind has been rotted by the demons of grief and if you cannot see that this writing is nothing but a comedy or farce then I have very grave concerns about your worth and ability."

"At least confirm the outbreak of cholera even if you are not ready to examine its cause," I offered more calmly with a shrug of the shoulders.

"I shall not print that because there is no cholera in this town. People get sick and die but there is no conspiracy. They should make provision to feed themselves more substantially," Mr

Binkerpick patted his fat stomach bulging beneath a stretched and stained grey waistcoat.

I could not help looking at the arrogant portly Editor with a pained expression but decided not to lengthen the altercation any further and just somewhat meekly declared that I would be exonerated and that he and the Journal would be brought to task. In truth I wanted to depart in a storm of rage but instead, after casting the final dice, left the office and my job with a noble gait and a clear conscience.

I did not have to bide my time for very long to prove my remonstrance to be of true value. The actress Florence Thistlewood, deeply mournful friend of Emma Toopey, was to prove to be the key in unlocking the chains imposed by the Journal in restraining the truth. Florence had friends at The Times of London no less and found them ready to pledge assistance in forcing Binkerpick's hand. A strong and direct article followed that condemned the provincial Journal for its censorship. At last the truth was known, although the snivelling Binkerpick simply claimed he was acting in compassion by not alerting the citizens of Salisbury to the threat of cholera. Panic was feared by all accounts.

I am glad to say that this was the start of important changes to the town's streets, with improvements to both the water supply and general sanitation. Within five years, Salisbury had pure water and a plan to fill the open watercourses was initiated. So even now I raise a glass of clear water to the memory of the beautiful Emma Toopey.

Chapter VI - *Comprising the particulars of Daniel Drumdale's devious nature and the remarkable introduction of Mick Mickle.*

Whilst the constant to the central episodes of my life has always been Thomas Endstreet, it is of great importance not to dismiss the part played by my other former childhood associates when roles were allocated in the great conspiracy still to come. During my courting of Katherine and vain attempt to woo Emma Toopey, Daniel Drumdale continued to find employment at his father's Bank. It was said that his scheming father was often required to make ingenious arrangements in order to cover for his son's unfortunate character. If he was not consoling or bribing a furious relative or fiancée of some poor innocent girl that Daniel had made salacious advances to, then it was to professionally cover for the boy's inadequate work. For most of the working day he would simply sit on his stool and stare out of the window above his desk, continually observing people passing by the Market Place. Daniel always told me he hated to see anybody looking happy or content and would amuse himself with thoughts of how he could change the course of their lives to bring ruin and damnation. To find delirium in having such an appetite for the downfall of another was such an unearthly trait, even if for the majority of time it remained within his sick imagination. Although notwithstanding other employees in the Bank did suffer through Daniel's position held so beyond reproach. It was understandable that as others toiled and with Daniel just sat yawning on his stool that strongly voiced and justified complaints became so frequent as to the point of repetition. Daniel was duly defended and reprieved by his father, leaving him free to muse on ways to make his fellow worker's days both dark and uncomfortable. By reducing the ladies to extreme low spirits or by igniting the tempers of the men, Daniel ensured good reason to terminate employment without the slightest charitable concern. Daniel Drumdale was a scoundrel who would wet his lips and find undiminished triumph through the cruel sport of manipulation.

And so to Edwin Gurden, who had always looked sickly and miserable in childhood and forever defeated by his stammer to ever truly seem normal. In adulthood he was a weak sallow fellow who demonstrated little in the way of intelligence and was always reminded by his father of the enduring disappointment he was to the Gurden family name. Forced to take a role in the background, and back room, of the Tailor's shop, Edwin felt as if he was banished to suffer for an eternity. Crammed into a little room by day and feeling nothing but sorrow, Edwin would find his escape each evening in the Taverns and Ale Houses of Salisbury. Dressed in selected ragged clothes, and disguised with a wig and extra large hat, he found solace amongst many wretched individuals who could hardly read or write. Without condition Edwin felt clever and discerning and hardly had the time to stammer at all in his alternative life. He was not Edwin Gurden by night but rather the mysterious Mick Mickle, which was apparently the best name Edwin could think of.

Finding solace in the crowded Inns, Edwin was highly generous in spending his wages to the attraction of many new acquaintances more than happy to offer a stranger's welcome in exchange for free ale. Edwin found his main sanctuary under the sign of the Pheasant, or the former Crispin Inn, on the corner of Salt Lane. For generations the site of the Inn had offered a place to meet for many people of business. And so it was still the case with transactions of all descriptions completed, accounts settled and conveyances finalised. For the most part this was good honest endeavour but in the dark corners of the room could be found a far more disagreeable and altogether immoral scheming. One fateful day, Edwin was introduced, as Mick Mickle, to George and Robert Crabbe, holding court as usual in the farthest and darkest recess of the Pheasant. The Crabbe brothers were notorious for their reckless and villainous character in most circles of Salisbury society. George was a craggy squat man known for being loutish and very ill-mannered. He had in fact only just returned to Salisbury having been transported for burglary some three years previous. His younger brother Robert was much taller but always covered in dirt and grime and of such a devious and unscrupulous manner that it was said that he helped send his own father to the gallows for a small financial reward.

The Crabbe brothers welcomed Edwin into their fold and he spent many evenings in apparent drunken exultation, oblivious to the efforts of many to consult with him on the true nature and probable intentions of his new friends. It was not long before Edwin's company was monopolised by the evil pair and it was only he that joined them each evening by a smouldering fireside that was devoid of any true embers and reeking of smoke. They were now ensured not to be overheard and the Crabbe brothers had their opportunity to entreat Edwin into their many immoral operations. Robert seized upon Edwin's desire for recognition that was devoid in any dealings with his father. With the exchange a of a few careful remarks and whispered suggestions, Robert was able to manipulate and occupy Edwin's thoughts at will. The notion of theft was dismissed as harmless fun that would bring social decoration to those who succeeded rather than moral shame. With measured precision it was decided that George would demonstrate to Edwin both the skill and imagination required to play the game. Edwin agreed to meet the brothers at noon the following day prompting Robert to yell "the game's afoot," before raising his tankard as a toast.

The next day, Edwin's excuses for venturing from the Tailor's shop in the middle of the day were readily accepted as nobody was sufficiently bothered to miss him in any duty. Having secured his disguise, Edwin met the Crabbe bothers on the corner of the High Street at the time agreed upon. Robert then led the way back towards Fisherton and was quick to single out a small shop selling articles of personal decoration such as millinery, lace and gloves. Two very young ladies were serving in the shop and trade seemed brisk.

"Let us begin the game," Robert sneered with a crooked lower lip. "Stand here Mick Mickle and observe, but not just me and George. I want you to roam your eye up and down the street and let me know instantly if you should spot a Peeler. Clear about that?"

Edwin felt very unsure but simply nodded his head.

"Good boy, I said to George you would be a good boy. And let me tell you that if you do well then by all means you shall duly be considered as engaged for a much bigger game next week. If you should falter then you will need to consider how you go, especially when it is dark." Robert inclined his head with a sinister tone and expression.

Edwin stood shaking as he observed the commencement of the game, although his sight was drawn more to the events in the shop than checking who was walking by. Inside Robert had made his way over to the two young shop attendants and proceeded to wildly fan and flap his arms as if he was having some odd seizure. The young ladies watched in fear at the scene before them with dread as to what action to take. George meanwhile had taken a position by the window with his head bowed and his arms folded before him. Stirred in an instant by Robert's distraction, George moved quickly to avail himself of a number of items from the window display. They were soon held within two very deep coat pockets. Almost seeming quite invisible to others, George briskly left the shop and moved along past Edwin, offering a sly wink in the process. The nonsensical scene in the shop now abated and Robert too departed and strolled after his brother with no sense of urgency. Edwin took an awkward stance for several minutes before a scream from inside the shop startled him to move away. The very recent theft had been discovered. Edwin walked with some haste in the direction taken by his villainous associates.

Very soon afterwards, Edwin found the brothers loitering inside the walls of the Infirmary grounds within the thick bushes. To me there is an irony here in that some forty years previous would have found these crooks within the old Fisherton Gaol that had stood there for many centuries. The Infirmary had indeed purchased the dour buildings for nearly two thousand pounds after they became redundant, I recall my father saying. Edwin had no appreciation in this regard as he recounted the tale, but rather he remembered feeling a sense of pride and achievement as Robert slapped him heartily on the back for a job well done. Edwin then accompanied the brothers to an obscure backstreet pawnbroker, where George emptied his pockets to reveal his ill-gotten bounty. As well as a pair of fine silk gloves, there were several rolls of bright valuable ribands. The ugly looking dwarf of a man who owned the shop gave a loud grunt of discontent as he held up a lamp to view the fine cloth in the dark room cluttered with mostly rusting junk.

"You may feed off my good nature again gentlemen for although there is no reward for me I will part with eight shillings no less," the dwarf winced badly from the shadows.

"Make it nine for a fair division amongst three," Robert nodded at Edwin stood lurking by the narrow and short doorway.

"Ugh, this is very peculiar business indeed," the dwarf pondered and peered over at Edwin. "In order that you may tread upon my floor in the future I will pay you nine shillings. Sometimes I show so much charity that I feel giddy and need to lie down."

The dwarf laughed and shuffled over to a hidden money box and promptly paid Robert before ushering his visitors away as a loud knock at the door heralded the arrival of another with goods to offer. Edwin was surprised to walk past a well dressed woman waiting her turn, who held in her hand a couple of silver mounted pocket-books.

It was now declared that Edwin was an honorary Crabbe brother, quickly and adeptly accustomed in their trade. Edwin felt pride in belonging, having been truly shunned by his family and held in ridicule by his friends. Before Thomas had gone to London he had constantly mocked the unfortunate Edwin without compromise and lacking any regret on reflection. Daniel Drumdale used the stooping shy Edwin as an errand boy and I simply did not see him socially for many years. Now the awkward gangling boy that had no real life as Edwin Gurden had found an identity and acceptance at last, albeit under the guise of Mick Mickle.

Consequently, it was not long before Edwin was enticed to play a much more illustrious game with the promise of great excitement and substantial reward. Without any other observer of note, Edwin shook hands with both Crabbe brothers in the usual dark corner of the Pheasant Inn. Robert did so with a capricious smile, barely visible in the weak light offered by a single flickering flame amongst a damp bundle of firewood. There was then an agreement and confirmed understanding of where to meet the following day, late in the afternoon.

The next day Edwin once again made a simple excuse to leave his chores and was held in no regard whatsoever. He was free to dress in the concealed disguise that turned him into Mick Mickle within the small yard at the back of the shop. After slipping through a narrow alleyway, Edwin took the short journey by foot but was made weary by a persistent rain that soaked his hat and wig, increasing their weight significantly. The tall man stooping and struggling against the wind and rain drew the amused attention of many passers-by. By the time he reached Silver Street, Edwin could barely manage a faint smile in greeting the Crabbe brothers as they stood sheltering in the shadows of a concealed passage.

"I find you strangely unfamiliar today Mick Mickle," Robert Crabbe looked Edwin up and down, stopping at the cheap sodden wig. The unkempt black dyed hairs were springing in all directions like the plumage of a peacock, far from looking natural as they protruded from beneath a crushed velvet hat.

"I am sorry to say that I find any kind of rain to be most disagreeable." Edwin exclaimed as he moved out of view of the street, smoothing down his wig as best he could.

"So be it," Robert confirmed as he smacked his lips, "we must now make our move with stealth."

Robert persisted with his intended plan and pulled Edwin abruptly to the corner of the passage. Through the rain he picked out a small jewellery shop across the road, owned by a Thomas Topple Esq.

"Same game as before Mick Mickle," Robert sneered as he pulled Edwin's face close to his own. "And don't you go making any mistakes or our friendship and your life will be at an end. Don't you forget that Mick Mickle, for if you leave me and my brother in the lurch then we will do nothing else but come looking for you, in Salisbury or anywhere." Robert's voice deepened with gritty menace.

"I shall be a good and faithful friend," returned Edwin.

"Good," grumbled George as he moved alongside Robert, holding a long life preserver that must have been all of fourteen inches.

Robert led the way across the street and made for the Jeweller's without looking at anybody in his path. In the gloom he stopped before the shop door and peered in through the window, spying the frail figure of Thomas Topple as he tended to a bag of precious stones. Looking back at Edwin with a frightening glare, Robert raised his coat collar as high as it would go and then opened the door with a fast deliberate motion and stepped inside with George close behind, who was holding on tightly to the life preserver.

Edwin looked about hesitantly and was immediately alarmed by three well dressed gentlemen who had gathered on the pavement only a few yards further down from the jewellery shop. The men were engaged in casual conversation. Edwin cast a wistful glance into the shop and saw that the Crabbe brothers had confronted the petrified Thomas Topple, towering over his short frame by a foot and more. George pushed the Jeweller with some force and he let out a loud cry, which caught the attention of the group of gentlemen.

"What was that commotion sir?" a tall man with excessive whiskers enquired of Edwin as he led his two associates over to the shop.

"I don't know I'm sure," was all that Edwin could muster in response.

A loud moan came from the shop and all the gentlemen turned to observe as one. George was holding the Jeweller by his collar.

"I sense a very foul wind indeed," a wiry fellow commented to his friends as they moved closer to the shop,

"I think it just a harmless quarrel," Edwin returned to try and slow any intervention, especially as he was now too afraid to raise the alarm to the Crabbe brothers and be immediately drawn in as an obvious accomplice.

Not satisfied, the tall gentleman marched into the shop and found George Crabbe beating Thomas Topple over the head with the life preserver.

"I say, stop that right now," cried the tall gentleman as Thomas Topple fell to the floor in a great deal of pain.

George Crabbe tried to charge out of the shop but was sent to the ground by the tall gentleman with a swift trip and a push. Robert Crabbe barged past as the gentlemen moved to secure George in an arm lock. Robert did not get far and was caught by the other two gentlemen. More people now gathered outside the shop, attracted by the commotion and a Peeler was called for. Edwin edged away and took refuge in an alley, where he removed his hat, wig and coat. They were thrown aside and Edwin moved on unnoticed back towards Fisherton as several Peelers took care of the Crabbe brothers.

The Crabbe brothers were charged with assault and robbery. A fortnight later Thomas Topple died from his injuries and George was tried for murder. At the trial George admitted striking Mr Topple but bizarrely tried to claim that his death was due to a very bad cold, and not from the blow. The jury did not accept that and he and Robert were both hanged on December 15th, 1849 at the county gaol, with a report stating that 'an unusually large horde of persons gathered to witness the event. Edwin was among them and overheard many a conversation about an apparent accomplice, whose identity had still not been discovered. Some called him a traitor who would be made to pay. Mick Mickle was gone for now, but would return.

Chapter VII - *A new employment opportunity at Plumeworth's Publishing Company. In which old friends find refuge in drunkenness and courtships are born from the sadness of two family funerals.*

By 1850 I was in new employment at a small independent publishing company in Guilder Lane. It had only been founded some five years previous by the rather extravagant figure of Gerald Plumeworth, proudly putting his family name above the door. Gerald was a man with many fanciful notions in his head, remaining indifferent to any who dared doubt that he would not succeed. He had set his mind on finding another Charles Dickens but in truth spent most of his time hawking the very tedious writing of his two half-sisters, Virginia and Kate Foxhead in a bewildered state of believing they could rival the Bronte sisters. I had the more mundane task of managing the publication of large factual books for use in universities. Without this trade, Plumeworth's would not have lasted beyond the year and allowed Gerald to proceed with his impractical and illusory conceptions.

Plumeworth's operated out of a quaint building that was once a small factory, offering meandering dusty corridors leading to cramped printing rooms at one end and secluded writing rooms at the other, should any notable members of the writing community of Salisbury and beyond wish to visit. Apart from when the arrogant and talentless Foxhead sisters dropped by on far too frequent occasions, the writing rooms remained vacant. My dark and dingy office was between the printing and writing rooms, and only offered a small amount of natural light through a single pane of glass in the high ceiling.

Beyond my new employment, a bond had drawn me back together with the three friends I had first found acquaintance with at the Twizzle School. Orchestrated by Thomas Endstreet, I would now meet with him, Edwin Gurden and Daniel Drumdale for several tankards of ale at least three evenings a week. We would meet at the Haunch of Venison, a former brothel that boasted beams made from old sailing vessels and a grand fireplace that had been in use since the year of the Armada. The evenings at the Haunch were mainly filled with exaggerated reminiscences and anecdotes, hiding the inherent failure in us all in finding a wife. Although of course there was true and very recent tragedy to blame on Thomas's part. Or should that be on my part.

Through it all this odd group of bachelors found high spirits through the ale consumed and the united company. I recall one exceedingly good occasion when we made plans to find the hidden tunnel that supposedly ran from the Haunch to St Edmund's church, built for the purpose of allowing the clergy to sample the delights of the old brothel. Thomas brought along a couple of shovels for our next meeting and we speedily went searching for the tunnel in a state of drunkenness. Making a great deal of noise, we only succeeded in attracting the attention of the nearby residents, who thankfully presumed we were nothing but upstarts engaged in a brawl. The tunnel remained hidden, and I still do not know to this very day if it truly existed. One thing was for certain was that my life was now only filled with mundane employment and wretched inebriation.

In the midst of a generally dull year, and through an intolerably weak state of mind, I found myself once more in the constant company of Dorothea Endstreet. The family connection was drawn even stronger as Thomas began courting my own dear sister, Lilly. This state of things can be accounted for by the untimely death of my mother, which was then followed within a month by the very unfortunate death of Kitty Endstreet, mother to Thomas and Dorothea. My own mother's death was the result of a violent fever that I still maintain was incurred by badly fouled food served at an informal string concert she attended in Romsey. By all accounts most of the guests felt ill in the days that followed, although nobody else died but my mother. It was as if she could not find the energy to fight the infection, or I do wonder if she could be bothered to fight it. For sometime before her death her normal exuberance seemed crushed and Lilly and I could often hear her crying and sobbing in her room. My father made no effort to comfort her and instead made no secret of his temper whenever she was in such a dark spirit of desperation. On one occasion he even threatened to have her committed to an Asylum under the pretence of lunacy. I will never know what caused my mother's change in character but chose to fondly remember the highly sociable lady with a love of music and literature who wanted to ensure her children saw the same joy in life as she did. The joy she saw for most of her life at least.

From the moment my father stopped the clock, I could understand that my mother's death was really a release for her. This did not stop me from weeping profusely at the grand funeral that took place at the church of St George. The Endstreet family all attended and in particular Thomas showed great patience in comforting Lilly, who was badly affected. A period of continuous mourning had seen her grow very weary and withdrawn, condemned to a low spirit within the black clothes she wore. Thomas would listen intently to every tear stained muttering and reflection, and offer unfaltering support in return through many kind words. In contrast Dorothea would comment on how she was made weary by such a gloomy affair and how she trusted that I would find fortitude with some haste in being a man of stern character. The funeral did not yield any release of emotion from beyond Dorothea's stony uncompromising manner. As I walked from the church, the sky that had been so full of black clouds in keeping with the situation was broken by a single strong ray of sunshine. I rubbed my sore eyes so dimmed by tears and beamed a smile in memory to my mother.

It was only a matter of weeks later that Lilly and I were attending the funeral of the Endstreet matriarch, Kitty. The account of the day of her death states that early in the morning she entered into an argument over an extremely trivial matter with two Farmhands on the edge of the Pembroke Estate. Following the encounter, Kitty made her way to the Farmhands' employer, with whom she was very good friends, and made it very clear that she would be very grateful and desirous for the two scoundrels to lose their jobs. Due to the cordial regard the Farmer held for Kitty he granted her wish and the men were dismissed without severance. The eldest of the two Hands was known to have a surly temperament and had been involved in numerous brawls in the Inns around Wilton. It was said he was filled with anger and rage upon his dismissal, striking the Farmer hard on the jaw before marching off to drown his sorrows in many jars of ale. This left him in a dark murderous way as he staggered into Wilton late in the afternoon. Some confusion is cast around what occurred but the case would seem very damning indeed. Kitty Endstreet was seen making her way down Wilton High Street to join some friends at the Morgan Tea Room. She strolled with her usual precocious air as if she owned Wilton itself. At no great distance away a driver was about to board his coach in order to pick up passengers from a nearby Inn for an onward journey to Yorkshire. Before he could climb on he was pushed aside by a swarthy gentleman smelling of ale, who had crept upon him. With a lively nature he took the horses forward with an almighty charge in the direction of Kitty Endstreet. As others tumbled over each other to get out of the way there proved to be no time for Kitty Endstreet and she was struck with some force and trampled under hoof on the pavement. The coach made its way out of Wilton and was found abandoned a short distance into the countryside. The swarthy attacker, whom the driver could not name, was never seen again, and neither was the angry Farmhand. Kitty Endstreet lay regally still with only a small trickle of blood on the pavement by her head as a shocked crowd gathered rolling their eyes and flailing their arms with emotional shock and distress. Kitty Endstreet was indeed dead.

So the Chatterforths and the Endstreets were rejoined in union in such a short space of time, and once again by the side of a grave. Thomas was a shattered man and not afraid to show it, but was comforted now by Lilly and I could tell he was appreciative of her kind intention. Dorothea looked upon him with some disdain as she looked to sustain her character of exceptionally strong spirit and did not shed a tear that I could see as the coffin was lowered into the earth. With the service over I trailed behind Dorothea by several feet as she retained nothing but her own company. Notwithstanding, and after a brief struggle in my own mind, I made haste to catch Dorothea and inform her of my sorrow at such a sad occasion.

"Did I not say that nobody was to speak to me?" Dorothea said sternly before I could even speak, turning her face away from view.

"I was not aware," was my innocent response, "and I shall leave you now if you wish it so."

Dorothea turned towards me and it was clear that many tears were running and had already passed down her red cheeks. "I do not mind if you stay Mr Chatterforth, in fact I would rather you did." Dorothea pulled a handkerchief to her eyes but could not hold back her solemn emotions and fell forward sobbing profusely on my shoulder. Affectionately I put my arms around her and held Dorothea's shaking defeated body as tight as I could.

Chapter VIII - *Relating to the courting of Dorothea and the particulars on the success and enterprise of the Endstreet family business.*

So the cast was set and without any struggle in my heart or lingering concern in my thoughts, I began to court Dorothea

Endstreet. In truth I was still unsure if we were bound by love but rather just a convenient companionship. Still numb from the death of Emma Toopey and bewildered in the ending of my relationship with Katherine, the strength of our relationship gained credence with such rapidity. Likewise, my sister Lilly had no sense to spurn the advances of Thomas Endstreet and their coupling too defied true logic and meaning.

After her mother's death, when it came to family matters Dorothea was not content to take a place in the background but rather began to take hold of the cutlery business as her father's health deteriorated and Thomas's interest, along with any sign of vocational ability, never truly shone through. With the growth of the railway more visitors came to see the cathedral, therefore providing a succession of customers for any shop with goods to sell. Dorothea opened a cutlery shop on the High Street itself and was very quickly acquiring a small fortune. Lilly was given a position in the shop by Dorothea, who expressed open enthusiasm for my sister's undoubted ability to sell the goods, whilst often remarking out of her earshot that Lilly's pale beauty was always guaranteed to divert the attention of every gentleman walking by. Dorothea ensured Lilly was seated with proximate positioning by the large open window like the silverware on display. The decision was profound indeed and the shop was often crowded in the extreme. Thomas's role was to simply carry the stock, either to the shop or for the benefit of a customer to the train station.

At least I was able to take leave from the Endstreet business and continue in a position at Plumeworth's Publishing House. Albeit that my position had now changed to that of Literary Editor. Despite the very little chance of success, I certainly had my hands full in dealing with the many deluded clients that Gerald Plumeworth rounded up from various coffee houses and informal society concert gatherings. Despite the appalling number of tales I was bound to read and then offer editorial judgment upon, I was never openly dismissive to any of our clients, although many would start in high spirits only to end in a downcast manner, conceding on their own lack of ability. I collected a good wage, as supplemented by the continued business in text books but Plumeworth's was never destined to be in any kind of great profit and I would not controvert the dreams of my employer by suggesting any change to his plans.

In this time Daniel Drumdale had taken Edwin Gurden under his wing, although this was principally on account of Daniel falling in love with Emily Snogdrake, the daughter of the town's most eminent Physician. Emily was beautiful indeed but very much lacking in intellect and was in the habit of giggling incessantly whenever she was nervous, which was very often when in any male company. Emily had a twin sister called Hetty and they were inseparable in attending all social functions. Daniel therefore made the necessary arrangements for Edwin to accompany Hetty in order to gain more time alone with Emily. I submit that Hetty did not have Emily's beauty, despite being her twin and was in truth twice her size. Hetty would not giggle when nervous but rather fan her face with great speed. What with Edwin's stutter, Emily's giggle and Hetty's fanning, a night in their company was a trying experience indeed.

I am glad to recollect some very happy times, especially the calm summer evenings of 1851 when the four reunited Twizzle pupils and their partners were to enjoy many fine picnics in the meadows. After a short journey by cart, it was a wondrous joy to be able lie upon the grass under the shade of a large oak tree and debate the rights and wrongs of the world whilst enjoying a bottle of fine wine and an array of exquisite fruits and other fine refreshments. We would then take a stroll in different directions to spend time with our respective partners. I could never help staring as Thomas led Lilly by the hand towards a field of hay, still reflecting on whether their union was of sound judgment. The incredible passion of Dorothea proved to be a suitable distraction from my concerns and I would soon turn my back upon Lilly and Thomas. Our intimacy was very advanced indeed and even the thought of our kissing would enrapture me. Under the Sun's warm and excessive glow we would kiss and roll upon the floor as soon as we were alone. I was utterly defenceless to Dorothea's charms and we were soon making love with only the spire in the distance as a witness. It was I who was the pupil in this matter and Dorothea was quick to acknowledge that her stay in Paris had furthered her own education when it came to the art of lovemaking.

"I am convinced that only the French, and the Parisians in particular, put the art of lovemaking above all else," Dorothea would state on many an occasion.

We would all regroup to toast the end of each evening with more wine before travelling back to Salisbury. I did not venture to ask how passionate the encounters between Thomas and my sister were becoming for fear of the answer. Daniel and Edwin always returned together with the Snogdrake twins several steps behind, giggling and fanning for all their worth and with a great deal of grass entangled in their hair. When our spirits were exceptionally high, we would stop the cart at the Green Dragon Inn for some ale. It was said that this was the very place that Charles Dickens had described in his wonderful serial 'The Life and Adventures of Martin Chuzzlewit', although it became the Blue Dragon in the telling of the tale. This is what we were told by the landlord on many occasion as he always drew attention to one of his customers as proof, a bandy legged tailor who was described by Dickens along with the Inn.

I recently returned to the old oak tree under which we sat, high upon the hill beyond Alderbury. All of our names are still etched there, not withered by time or the weather, unlike those that had scribed with such purpose at that time.

Chapter IX - *Takes me to London and the pomp of the Great Exhibition. An unexpected sighting that is mysteriously dismissed by Dorothea.*

Dorothea's mind was never far from business, and she placed great emphasis on making further advancement to augment the climb to the upper class echelons of Salisbury society. A golden opportunity to enrich the Endstreet name was presented when the Great Exhibition was held in London, which did not just showcase the manufacturing industry in Great Britain but rather the whole world. It was said that Prince Albert, consort of our Queen, was responsible for the notion and an incredible hall made of iron and glass was constructed to house the event in Hyde Park. Dorothea ensured that Salisbury's principle exhibit was several fine cutlery cases bearing the Endstreet name. A fact that was not just reported in the Salisbury Journal but The Times as well. In September of 1851, Dorothea commanded that I accompany her to the Great Exhibition before it was closed for good.

On the day of our journey to London, Dorothea was in congenial spirit as she perceived my own trepidation as a novice travelling on the railways and to our capital city for the first time in my life. I was to truly witness the squalid streets made murky by the heavy foul smelling air that I had read so many accounts of. After paying little over 36s for two second class tickets and securing a place for our luggage and umbrellas, my anxiety waned and I began to observe the surroundings with absorbing interest. The opportunity to travel directly to London by train from Salisbury had only been made available some four years previous. It took the train barely four hours to reach London as it followed an initial route along the coast. The view was quite stunning, although I do confess it took a stern resolve on my part to withstand the sheer numbness I had to endure in sitting upon a solid wooden bench that jolted continually as much as the ride in any horse drawn carriage I had known. Dorothea assured me that the seating in first class was of a different constitution, whilst stressing that she had forgone a position there in order that I may accompany her to London.

Upon reaching London we were taken by carriage to Hyde Park, seemingly joining a succession of other carriages transporting men and women of commerce and Industrialists to witness the renowned fair in the now infamous Crystal Palace. It was clear that Dorothea had engaged her thoughts upon the assured opportunities offered by the Exhibition and as a matter of course in our journey through London she barely gazed out of the window or gave any consideration to my own musings other than to declare that she found the smell of the city detestable and the merits of the buildings too dull and familiar. I indeed did take in the sights but must confess that it was during a moment of observing my own reflection as the skies darkened overhead, that I was drawn to a very familiar figure seemingly doing business on a street corner with two very stout ruffians. Rising slightly from my seat to make a closer observation, I confirmed my certainty of espying Thomas Endstreet. And yet he had made no mention of journeying to London. Dorothea roused suddenly, stirred by my uneasy position.

"Ralph, please contain your boyish excitement as not a gentlemanly thing to do in jumping around like a jack-in-a-box at every peculiar sight you may come across," Dorothea spoke with a disdainful tone.

Slightly abashed I sat back with some constraint before taking a deep breath and finding the presence to speak up without any obvious apprehension. "I was only trying to catch your brother's eye as I did not expect to see him in London this day."

Dorothea huffed loudly before taking a more genteel position after seemingly considering her response. "Thomas still has many friends in London from his time here and does visit frequently, but obviously not today." The final remark was punctuated with a churlish chuckle.

"Then he must indeed have a twin," said I forcefully after feeling rather goaded.

"Then he must indeed," replied Dorothea before tapping the roof of the carriage with her umbrella, "coachman, make more haste please."

I could not resist a final glance back, only to confirm the presence of Thomas Endstreet as he walked from his rough acquaintances carrying a large money bag and holding a sneering wide grin.

The exhibition itself was a wonder to behold, with the most weird and wonderful contraptions I had ever seen, and collected from the far flung corners of the colonies. Dorothea made innumerable attempts to introduce herself to every individual of wealth and influence she could find, and believe me there was an abundance. At times I stood by in frustrated boredom as Dorothea recounted the same overture regarding the Endstreet tradition in cutlery through every repetitive meeting. She would also continually affirm that Salisbury was to hold its very own Great Exhibition the following year, when the Endstreet brand would be most prominent. However, she closed deal after deal as many gentlemen fell victim to her charm.

Exhausted, we retired for the evening to a very clean and respectable guest house. I was quick to lie upon my bed very early in the evening, only to be awoken a couple of hours later by a noisy argument in the street outside between a man and woman, that was frequently interspersed with hellish yelling. My patience was finally worn and half dressed I ventured to the window to observe, but the disagreement had now abated. The woman scurried back towards the guest house with rain beginning to fall as the man stood still. My view was clear and make no mistake it was Dorothea and Thomas Endstreet.

I did not venture to mention the matter to either Dorothea or Thomas. To say the truth, I was now truly enjoying my life after such a period of indifferent fortune and in principal did not want to consider averting the situation to a poor state once more. There was no profit in venturing to question or challenge the Endstreets for fear of drawing hostile and uneasy intercourse that evidently would leave only myself in an uncomfortable position. Better to stay quiet and avoid consternation. I therefore chose to prudently ignore the incident and any other strange affairs that I may observe for the time being.

Chapter X - *In which you will see the fall and rise of Thomas Endstreet, blighted by an addiction to gambling.*

The winter did not seem long in coming that year, typified by long dark and stormy evenings. The season passed along and I took heart from many romantic nights with Dorothea by the fireside, which were often supplemented with several glasses of hot punch or port wine. The Endstreet family business was booming and Dorothea was of the most cheerful and amiable bearing. As a couple we would delight in kissing for much of our evenings together, hardly pausing for conversation.

I did not see a great deal of Thomas during the winter, as he spent more time in London. He did return rather hastily several weeks before Christmas when Lilly was taken ill, but now seemed so different in character and appearance. His tone was very remorseful as if spirits or demons were haunting him and had chased away his once playful mischievous nature. No longer a man of many words, Thomas now rarely smiled and had grown a thick beard to match his unkempt hair. It was so obvious that there was a very uneasy air between Dorothea and Thomas and many people often remarked that whilst she dressed in the finest and most expensive of dresses, he was reduced to wearing little more than second hand ragged shirts and trousers that always seemed to carry the dust and smell of London. One quiet afternoon as Lilly rested in her bed, I finally did question with Dorothea over a casual cup of tea as to why Thomas's standing had receded so badly when the Endstreet name and business was thriving so royally. Dorothea sighed heavily as I was fixed with a stern look, and I thought that she would not utter a word on the subject. However after a moment's pondering she moved her chair close to mine in order to speak in a whisper.
"I am sure there is no disguising the fact that Thomas has brought himself into a shameful situation," said Dorothea almost complacently. "It is not that I am hard-hearted in failing to aid him, but the prudent measure is for him to consider his actions and find his own dignity by reclaiming his position as a gentleman. Father is in agreement that we will provide him with shelter and food and water but that he must clear his own self-inflicted debts or find final penance in a debtor's jail."

"Thomas has fallen into debt," I remonstrated loudly.

"If you please, this is to go no further," Dorothea demanded quite angrily. "My brother is a man so easily bored and during his time in London was attracted by the thrill of the gambling-house. These Hells, so outwardly welcoming with their handsome gas-lamps and green baize doors can simply entice a gentleman to his ruin. Thomas was curious at first, attracted by the company and the opportunity to endlessly smoke and drink. However he was soon unable to show any constraint and began to attend less respectable establishments. His debts began to mount and his efforts to clear them became more and more fruitless. Now Thomas has a self-imposed mission to restore his standing after he was refused assistance from the family. Recent circumstance has seen the debt increase further and so Thomas was to spend more time in London, corroborating in an underhand business venture with the scoundrels to whom he owes money."

"But what of my sister? Surely she must be told and be allowed to disown him?" I stood up and almost cried out.

"No," replied Dorothea, drawing herself up to meet me, "I made a promise to Thomas that should he be successful in his purpose, then Lilly shall not hear a word of his wrongdoing. She believes that he is working hard in London for the Endstreet business to forge a future for them both and her love for him means she is willing to suffer his current and unfortunate demeanour. I fear that all will be at an end should you reveal the truth. Thomas is your best friend and you must trust him to right his wrong."

"I scarcely know who to trust anymore," I sat back down with sudden thoughts of how I had betrayed Thomas in my love for Emma Toopey. I surely owed him his chance of redemption.

Lilly recovered her good health quickly, but I now mulled and feared for their relationship as I found myself mistrusting my best friend. I now felt uncomfortable whenever I was in the presence of a man I had known for most of my life.

I am pleased to report that the good name and character of Thomas Endstreet was restored by the spring of the following year, marked by his arrival from London one fine day in April. It was not long after Lilly had remarked to me over breakfast that the Thomas she once knew was now seeming more dead than alive. This had left her very low in spirit and fearing for their future together. At this time she had only seen Thomas once since Christmas and on that occasion he bore the scars and bruises from being in a terrible fight. The only thing that retained her heart was the passionate and loving letters that Thomas dispatched on a frequent basis. I too was longing for his company as I was a man now spending most of his time in the company of ladies, both at home and at work. I now saw very little of Daniel Drumdale and Edwin Gurden, who were socially inseparable from courting the Snogdrake twins. In truth we four former Twizzle students were only ever reunited as a group when Thomas was present and at this time he was very much absent.

Everything then changed that fine April day when both Lilly and I were at the Endstreet residence in Wilton, enjoying evening tea with Dorothea. It was commented by Dorothea's father that I was looking rather wan in appearance and that I should look for a hobby or challenge to break my dull routine of a life. It seemed that no member of the Endstreet household knew how to be anything but direct without any sense of tact or sensitivity. Dorothea smiled at the suggestion before endeavouring to make my well-being her priority. With perfect timing came the sound of a carriage drawing up outside, and we all looked as one to see who was visiting. Out of the carriage stepped a man so dapper that it took me the time of him making several strides down the path to realise it was Thomas Endstreet. Handsome of face once more, devoid of beard but now sporting a finely groomed moustache and with his hair expertly cut to a decent and very tidy length, complete with long dark side whiskers. He was wearing a most expensive black suit that was the epitome of modern elegance and was whistling loudly as he went.

"Here he is," Dorothea muttered complacently as Thomas strode into the room. "I'm afraid to say that we had all got to the point of giving up on you."

"My dear sister, how honoured I am to prove you wrong," Thomas bowed down to kiss Dorothea on the forehead before stooping even further to whisper in her ear. He then drew away to laugh with an immensely loud boom as Dorothea stayed both mute and unmoved.

"Oh Thomas," Lilly squealed despite her tear soaked eyes, "please say you are home for good."

"You need not be afraid of my deserting you ever again for I now truly have no cause to do so," Thomas spoke gently as he embraced Lilly.

Thomas now turned to me and shook my hand heartily and spoke with a strangely earnest manner. "Thank you sir for your friendship and patience. I can now say without any reserve that my life is in order and I will never venture back to the wretched place where I have been. I now seek nothing but the happiness that the love of your dear sister can give me and for the strong bond that your friendship bestows."

Dorothea remained quite still and hardhearted as I relented to hug her brother, "I am so pleased on this great occasion and I have truly missed you dear friend. I would hold you tighter but fear creasing and ruining such fine togs."

We both now laughed with great gusto as Mr Endstreet went to fetch a bottle of his finest port. Now that Thomas had returned, surely my dull life would swiftly change for the better. In fact he was barely home for two weeks when all of our lives took a new course.

Chapter XI - *Several acts of marriage are agreed and performed.*

The first move came from Thomas himself as within his new found passion for life there existed a very strong desire to be married. Lilly was very humble and flattered by Thomas's offer, although upon agreeing to his proposal was not able to restrain her tears. The duty of then asking my father's permission for the union was performed in a general air of silence within a purposefully darkened drawing room. My father gave the impression that he was pained to be asked the question and ensured he repressed Thomas's fervent curiosity to know the answer. Finally he acknowledged an almost reluctant approval with a nod of the head and a wistful smile. Thomas vigorously shook my father's hand, stirred inside with relief and excitement but confining his desire to leap in the air with joy. When joining Lilly he then acted with feigned complacency as if the meeting had not gone well before heartily hugging my dainty sister with such force until she was figuratively nearly drained of all her blood.

The announcement was quickly made to all close family and friends at a hastily arranged dinner party, with the event set for July at the Church of St George in Harnham. I was announced as Best Man. However, Dorothea seemed very indifferent to the whole affair and in fact made it quite plain that she was of a highly disinterested demeanour. I never before witnessed her take such a role in the background, shrinking from notice. Her rancour was then augmented further when Daniel Drumdale chose his moment to make a joint announcement on behalf of himself and Edwin Gurden. It was stated that the cheerful disposition of the evening could in fact be trebled as he and Edwin were to marry the Snogdrake twins on the very same day in August at the Church of St Lawrence close to Old Sarum. As the room resounded with applause and cheers I watched Dorothea slip out of the door as if she was being tortured with pure envy.

I followed after Dorothea but she must have walked with some speed for she had gained the far corner of the garden before I finally spotted her. I approached with a little caution but with intent on soothing her disposition.

"Do you come just to humour me or finally act like a gentleman?" Dorothea spoke without turning, somehow knowing of my presence even from several feet away.

"You seem very out of temper," I remarked with some astonishment.

Dorothea finally turned and even in the fading light it was clear that her eyes were red and swollen from weeping. "Look before you sir and decide if you wish me to live my days as a defeated spinster or whether you wish to finally propose an honourable position and take me as your wife."

I was confronted with a demand that required compliance or damnation. "I scarcely know what to say," I replied whilst hardly drawing breath and desperately trying to find the right words.

"Do you have a fear of marriage?" Dorothea drew herself up "I am sure it would now be beyond reason that your hesitation is due to falling out of love with me."

"I am of course in love with you and would scorn to be anything else," was my submissive response.

"Then what action must you now take and what words do you now wish to convey?" Dorothea now stood directly in front of me as she spoke in a hurried and breathless manner, her eyes wide and radiant and her chest heaving.

Thomas and Lilly had now ventured into the garden through thoughtful concern for our absence. "See there," I heard Thomas say and turned to see him point and then lead Lilly over. They were promptly joined by Edwin, Daniel and the Snogdrake twins.

"Are you both all right?" Thomas enquired as the group neared us.

"We are fine for I believe Ralph is about to attend to a very important matter," Dorothea rejoined with a gentle voice.

After a long silence, during which I confess I did consider an act of defiance, I finally crouched down on one knee. I heard the ladies gasp in the still air of the evening. "Dorothea, in keeping with the immense pride of our two families and for the sake of my heart that you rescued from loneliness, will you do me the honour of becoming my lady wife?"

"Certainly sir," Dorothea replied, "you have done a very beautiful thing for which I truly love you."

"Bravo," Thomas shouted before presenting himself to shake my hand and hug his sister. The others needed little persuasion to follow and the engagement was now formally sealed in front of our friends.

Matters were quickly and satisfactorily arranged, with Dorothea's father rendering his approval and the date set in September for a wedding at the Church of St Mary and St Nicholas in Wilton. In truth I had no time at all to pause and consider my decision, and in particular if marriage to Dorothea was a true representation of my heart's desire.

The numerous wedding celebrations were not long in coming. First to July and the altar of the Church of St George, where Lilly made her way holding my father so fast by the hand as the bells pealed so loudly. Thomas was stood in waiting by my side, very patient and without a hint of exhibiting any nerves. As they took their vows, Lilly was captured by the emotion of the occasion and wore an expression of devotion. Thomas by contrast now seemed almost removed in his thoughts to other matters, pausing to speak and even then in an often low and incoherent tone. Close by Dorothea sat with a knowing smile that betrayed to me a concern over Thomas's distraction. Despite the warnings and assurance, it could have been feared that Thomas had once again been unable to repress his desire for gambling. However if it had been necessary to make a guess, rather than an inappropriate wager with regard to the situation, I would have been quick to say that Thomas was possessed by a new sin. For now his behaviour was not so extraordinary as to impeach me to question further, but ultimately a perversion of events would bring the matter to a head.

The marriages of Edwin Gurden and Daniel Drumdale to Hetty and Emily Snogdrake respectively offered a very quaint and unusual affair. As the Snogdrake family were of country stock, the whole wedding party made their way to St Lawrence Church on a well scattered layer of blossom to ensure a happy path through life. The wedding carriage was drawn by a grey horse for further good luck. I am still sure that the Snogdrake mother was by far the largest lady I have ever seen but at the same time she had the most cheerful voice and always ensured merry laughter in whatever company she kept. Dorothea dismissed her as being of an uncouth manner and unduly familiar with people she did not know. This remark was said in a whisper to my ear but Mrs Snogdrake was stood nearby and her immediate expression suggested that she heard every word. After a quick glance, Mrs Snogdrake stuck out her tongue in

Dorothea's direction before it could be observed by anybody other then myself. A wink of the eye and a kindly smile followed before the twins' mother returned to entertaining the other guests. I scrupulously tried to keep a straight face but it proved extremely awkward and in the end I sniggered and then bellowed with laughter. Dorothea raised her eyes in astonishment and was clearly not amused.

The novelty of attending these wedding celebrations soon turned to the reality of my own marriage on one very stormy Wednesday in August. And so to the Church of St Mary and St Nicholas in quaint Wilton. Never had a cloud been seen for many weeks and then on my wedding day we were all abandoned to continuous rain amid dark skies and forced to hurry into the shelter of the church for a hastily convened ceremony. It was indeed a magnificent church and had only been consecrated some seven years before, now dominating West Street in Wilton as it proudly occupied the site where a medieval church had once stood. The church was also extremely popular and it was only due to Dorothea's friendship with the Pembroke family that secured the date. As well as being church patrons, many of the family were also secured as our wedding guests. How unfortunate it was that we were all subject to the inconvenience caused by a number of leaks and the occasional draught that caused a great deal of uncomfortable fidgeting. Again Thomas Endstreet, my best man, seemed listless in his demeanour and seemingly spending the whole ceremony peering through half shut eyes. Since his own marriage to my sister, Thomas had been very erratic in his behaviour from playing the languid and docile companion to the argumentative and unpleasant bounder. For now I would not interfere in Lilly's private affairs, however on this very special day it was the ire of Dorothea that was to be invoked.

Let it be understood that Dorothea was highly disposed to all forms of superstition, having strong misgivings should anything go awry. We had to marry on a Wednesday as accordingly it was the best day of all in the same rhyme that declared the Sabbath out of the question. The rain was seen as dismal luck and the leaks were discouraging but then Thomas forgot to drop the ring, and in so doing ensure that all evil spirits were shaken out. With the vows exchanged I resorted in a feeble attempt to drop the ring myself but without relief to my bride's growing fatigue. Thankfully Thomas remembered to pay the clergyman for his services before his final misdemeanour was revealed, chilling Dorothea to the bone and causing her to swoon. It is of course of the uppermost importance that the congregation should throw rice or grain after the departing couple, and thus ensure fertility in the marriage. Thomas had been tasked with supplying large quantities of grain to uphold the tradition but had left all the bags at the Endstreet's residence. As the rain came down with renewed force, the ladies began to exchange remarks in whispers and many gentlemen coughed with excessive frequency. I raised my eyes in anguish towards a pious looking Thomas, who simply shrugged his shoulders in response, regardless to his forgetful action. Within a moment, and so swiftly, Dorothea's face went perfectly blank as she gazed in silence before a loud and fitful sigh heralded her swoon and subsequent fall into the mud. Now I was never one to be disconcerted by the blackening of superstition but perhaps these incidents were of very real significance to why I sit and write this tale today.

There is no disguising the fact that the honeymoon in Brighton was a much muted affair. It was a lovely spot where we stayed, with the distinct smell of the sea stealing into the homely room at the Inn every morning and evening. We took many walks and dined in fine establishments, but beneath it all there was no true romance, only pleasant company, In truth my favourite memory was from the frequent occasions when Dorothea would take to her bed for fear of swooning from a frightful chill in her head. She blamed the constant breeze from the sea. I would wander across the road and lie beneath a tree to shade from the sun, where quite by chance I caught the pleasant air of a piano being played. I remember the first time I crept to observe the origin of the sweet music with great curiosity. A young lady was sitting down at the piano as an elder relative stood nearby, totally enraptured. Then the young lady would start to sing in a soft and lilting voice and time would stand so still for a few blissful moments. From a distance the young lady with long brown hair would stir my imagination until my eyes closed tight and it was Emma Toopey sat playing the piano and I was the captivated audience stood by her side. The performance was repeated every day and on the final occasion I sat hard against the tree to sob unseen.

Chapter XII - *Thomas Endstreet goes astray under the influence of Samuel Bunstaple, and takes me with him. Dorothea concocts a plan for our benefit and cure.*

Thankfully Thomas was there to greet Dorothea and I upon our return to Salisbury train station, from where he accompanied us by carriage to our new home in Harnham, not far from the mill and almost under the shadow of the spire itself. Lilly was already waiting there with Daniel Drumdale, Edwin Gurden and their new Snogdrake brides. By now the house was perfectly dark as I carried Dorothea over the threshold to shouts of laughter and vigorous applause in recognition to the true start of our married life together.

In truth it felt like the only inhabitant of this dreary cold house was I alone for the first few weeks that passed. Dorothea swiftly busied herself once more in the ways of business and in particular turned her attention to Salisbury's very own Great Exhibition that was to take place in October at the Guildhall. Finding myself released immediately from the expected confines of marriage, I was encouraged at first to spend more time at the new home of my sister, Lilly, and her husband, Thomas. From my doorstep to their doorstep was little more than a mile and the evening air often provided good therapy as I roved by foot with only my thoughts for company. After a few days, the very cheerful countenance of my sister quickly diminished and there were often traces of tears on her face. Thomas was no longer there to greet and welcome me to his home, as he had previously done with such warm hospitality. At first I was told he was either drinking ale at the Rose and Crown Inn or apparently retired to his bedroom, unable to face visitors through illness. I knew my sister so well and pressed for the truth but Lilly assured me there was no reproach on my part for the heavy atmosphere and delicate situation that had manifested so quickly. As a loving brother I was once more concerned for my diminutive sister, so obviously fatigued by even a mere reference to her husband. As I offered comforting words, Lilly mused with a heavy heart and a sullen nature on how Thomas had seemingly reverted to juvenility. For the most part of the week he was very agreeable and exhibited an honest tender heart in the attention shown to his wife. The Endstreet business was often neglected, but under Dorothea it was a thriving firm that really did not require Thomas's employment. He was however content to reap all the financial rewards presented and able to enjoy an outlet of continuous entertainment on frequent evenings. This however did not include Lilly but rather a new companionship that bestowed such a variance in character upon Thomas that he was often unrecognisable as the same person from one day to the next. Thomas would sometimes return home late in the evening almost asleep on his feet and entirely affable but the next day the morning would present a new image. A mostly fractious man full of melancholy spirit, who would tremble as he lay in bed, often just staring at the ceiling and incapable of doing anything. Such occurrences had deteriorated to the extent that Thomas would lie in an immovable and silent state from morning until late in the evening. It transpired that during my recent visits Thomas was either with his new companions or concealed in his bedroom, unrisen for the entire day. Upon the evening of Lilly's tearful confession to me, Thomas laid fast asleep upstairs. Lilly assured me that the very next morning he would be restored to a normal character with no memory of the sorrowful dark position of the previous day. And so he would remain until the next meeting with his mysterious companion the following week. I was determined to confront Thomas immediately but was assured by Lilly that it would be fruitless to do so in his condition. Notwithstanding, Lilly asked if I would help discern what was affecting Thomas so badly by gaining intelligence of his weekly meeting with his new companion. I readily agreed to follow Thomas covertly and loiter with intent to dispel the mystery and return my sister's marriage to a happier position.

On a specified evening of the week following I dressed so as to appear a stranger to those who even knew me well, wearing a long black coat that was matched in colour by a thick scarf and a small hat. I made my way to Thomas's house and loitered by the hedge that divided the garden from the Harnham meadow. I recollect that the weather was very foul indeed, comprising of a blustery autumn wind with squally persistent rain. Thankfully I did not have to wait long for Lilly to appear at the Drawing Room window and point towards the path as indication that Thomas was about to venture forth. Instinctively I moved further in to the shadows and crouched very low. In a short time Thomas appeared and made quick progress away from the house and towards the Rose and Crown. He was resolved to make great haste in walking strongly against the wind with his coat firmly buttoned over his chin. He did not stop once for breath or thankfully glance over his shoulder as I conducted an equally swift and vigorous pursuit. Finally we approached the warm glow of the Inn by the river and I slowed my step only to be surprised as Thomas walked by and went off in another direction. Only a short distance beyond the Inn he suddenly sprang over a short wall and rushed toward the front door of a small dwelling. Thomas's speed made it difficult for me to keep near him, but I was able to covertly move into a position to observe his next action. After a knock at the door applied with a kind of musical beat, a short man wearing a bright cloak appeared and welcomed Thomas warmly. As the man paused I was able to observe him fully under the light of the gas lamp and almost immediately recognised him as the poet, Samuel Bunstaple. A leading light in the Salisbury Romanticism circle, I knew him as a flamboyant figure from my profession in publishing. I was however surprised to see him as it was widely accepted that at that time he was residing in Tuscany having suffered for art with a decline into mental illness, during which he had already tried to claim his own life. It was said that he had stripped himself of his own clothing in full view of several ladies engaged in painting landscapes as part of a class and then thrown himself to the mercy of the Avon. At that very moment it began to rain heavily as the ladies only dared peep through their hands. He was saved by the art teacher, a very large lady who scarcely deigned the sight of Samuel's naked body as a concern and stripped down to her own considerable corset before plunging into the water and quickly bringing the wretch back to shore. Samuel supposedly did not even nod his head in any kind of acknowledgement of gratitude but rather began to laugh hysterically as he writhed naked on the wet grass in full view of the astonished young ladies.

So there stood Samuel Bunstaple, unembellished by any previous misfortune and most surely the catalyst for Thomas's recent odd behaviour. I was immediately agitated as to what might be taking place in the house and rendered it necessary to gain closer inspection. Without much deliberation I climbed over the small wall and ran down the uneven paving, tripping twice as I went. Swiftly I moved around the house and secreted myself below a large window, which was slightly ajar at the top. I could hear the very cheerful voices of several gentlemen deliberating quite openly about the attributes of a lady referred to as Madelaine. The discussion was indeed graphic about every part of the lady's anatomy, and interspersed with raucous laughter. It was with astonishment that I then heard a lady's voice, making equally lewd remarks. I quickly gathered that this was indeed Madelaine, particularly as one gentleman remarked that he would have to make love to her within the hour. Crouching down on my knees, I peered into the window. I could see three gentlemen who were smoking pipes and sketching without any artistic prowess on parchments. I recognised one of the gentlemen as a medical practitioner who was known to my father and another as an Innkeeper. I turned my head to see what these gentlemen were drawing and was immediately confronted by the sight of a lady devoid of all clothing, laying casually on an old and shabby lounger. A nearby lantern illuminated her voluptuous figure in very fine detail. For a moment I paused to admire this considerable display of beauty, even replacing the stunning Madelaine in my mind with an image of Emma Toopey with I as the fortunate artist left to capture her beauty. The far door to the room suddenly opened and I was forced to shrink back down out of sight. I raised my head very slightly to observe further and saw that Samuel Bunstaple had entered the room and from his speech appeared to be intoxicated. He informed the others he would be in the next room if anyone wanted him. Bunstaple turned short upon Madelaine and made some very lewd remarks, but she was not cowed or embarrassed at all and instead giggled and laughed inanely. Taking a moment to gaze one more time at Madelaine's fine figure, I then crept along to the next window.

The room into which I now peered was much smaller and very

simply furnished with several armchairs. It was illuminated by two gas-lights, but it was still very difficult to see clearly due to extremely thick tobacco smoke. My eye grew more accustomed to the view and I was soon aware of the presence of numerous gentlemen that included both Thomas Endstreet and Samuel Bunstaple. The general behaviour was extremely boisterous as many glasses of spirits were proffered without a second thought. Bunstaple's voice was the most prominent as he recited several of his own irksome poems. Highly satisfied, he then encouraged the others to recite their own work and I began to wonder if this was just some highly irregular poets' society. As one small gentleman with a very ruddy complexion attempted a recital that was close to a whisper, I watched as Bunstaple drew something up from the floor by his chair. It was a wooden box that was quickly opened to reveal a long white ornate pipe held on a simple stand. Bunstaple withdrew the pipe and filled it with a substance, taken from some nearby scales, prior to lighting it and then drawing to inhale with total nonchalance. He relaxed back in the chair with an expression of utter cheerfulness. The impious Thomas Endstreet then proceeded to use the very same pipe and stimulate the same mellow mood. In no time at all every gentlemen in the room had taken their turn and where all regaled in a calm peaceful air. The only noise now prevalent was the cackling coming from Madelaine in the next room, which grew to such a din that I was almost curious to go back and see what was occurring. But then it went quiet and I was bold enough to stand and look directly at the enthroned Thomas Endstreet now devoid of most senses through numbness. In the silence a fat gentleman had come and stood unnoticed by my side.

"And who might you be sir?" remarked the gentleman causing me to turn around in haste and shock.

"Ah," was all I could muster followed by a very long pause.

"It is inexcusable to spy on people in this way sir, so I demand to know your motive." The man's ruddy cheeks glowed brightly as his face moved in close to my own.

"Dear me, whatever is going on out there?" Samuel Bunstaple had moved over to the window, alarmed by the commotion even in his induced state.

"I did not mean to create such a disruption to your evening but was rather just trying to find my brother-in-law, and good friend, Thomas Endstreet." I finally found a confident voice, "I'm sure I saw him venture in this establishment, but could not raise anybody at the door."

"Do you know this here prowler, Thomas?" Bunstaple called over to Thomas.

"I do indeed," the swaying figure of Thomas appeared, "and I am so curious to know why Ralph Chatterforth is here. A man of such prudish morals who had the misfortune to marry my sister."

The seemingly tranquil evening was now broken by a hearty roar of laughter from Bunstaple, which was echoed by the large gentleman by my side. Even the artists in the other room were now stirred to such a degree as to turn there attention away from the delights of Madelaine and hurry in to the next room. After ruminating for a couple of minutes, Bunstaple told his portly friend to accompany me into the house.

It was even more obvious on gaining entry to the house that it was very much at the disposal to all of Bunstaple's acquaintances for whatever bespoke entertainment they desired, no matter how depraved. As I walked through to see Thomas, the highly voluptuous Madelaine appeared in the doorway of the room in which she had been displaying her well built figure. She was now wearing a thin robe that clung tightly to her portly shape and offered me a cheery smile by way of a welcome.

"I take it that you are now cognizant of the opportunities here to enhance and revive your senses in order to view the world in all its artistic delight." Bunstaple wore an expression of unmitigated contentment. "Am I right in thinking that Mr Chatterforth?"

"I care not Sir what takes place in this house but wish only to assist my dear friend and in so doing save my sister's heart from being broken beyond repair." My response was abrupt as I glanced purposefully towards Thomas, who returned a vacant prolonged stare.

"Very good Ralph," Bunstaple clapped his hands in mock glee, "and so you shall take our dear friend Thomas home this fine evening in the fullness of time."

"And what do you intend in the meantime if we are not to leave this very minute?" I pursued with some trepidation.

"I simply put it to you that you join us in our merriment rather than interfere with proceedings with any further ado." Bunstaple procured from another gentleman the small box containing the pipe. "If you have a hidden passion in your soul Ralph, whether it be an ardour for a woman you never married or for a simple desire to experience new hope in life, then I present you with the key to unlock that passion. It is known simply as opium, brought from India and holding the power to inspire and enlighten every sensual ability that man may possess"

I went to reply in indignation but my tongue failed me. Bunstaple had roused a curiosity in me in terms of the suppressed feelings that had been with me since Emma's death, and from the day I had been married were beginning to haunt my thoughts with alarming regularity.

"I fear that I may be ill," was my feeble reply.

"Nonsense, no more than should you have too many jars of ale, is that not right Thomas?" Bunstaple shouted to my friend, who still lay half asleep on a chair nearby.

"Ralph I promise that you will find the experience enlightening and very interesting," Thomas said calmly after stretching his arms in the air. "I say that we will both leave here in much better heart than when we arrived."

So I took my bow as a newcomer to the influence of Opium,

deciding that I could then understand why Thomas was now behaving as he did and rather selfishly needing a release from my own mundane life. Once inhaled the drug was highly effective in releasing my tension and relaxing my mind. It was as if I had left my body in the room to allow my soul to find hope and pleasure in a bright and colourful dream. From deep within I once again found Emma Toopey, sat in her chamber brushing her hair with the window open and the warm summer air streaming in. Lost in the moment I was told later that I simply sat in the corner of the room nodding my head and smiling, engaged only in my new world. Even as I walked home with Thomas, the elation remained and I readily agreed not to share my discovery with Lilly.

The next morning brought a feeling of anxiety as I awoke late from my slumber and had to apologise profusely for my timekeeping to Gerald Plumeworth. I then found a melancholy hung over me for the rest of the morning as I felt sombre in reflection away from the comfort of the drug. Such was the immediate influence that it had on me, that I found it easy to lie on Thomas's behalf and defend his behaviour. Now it was I too that yearned to return to Bunstaple's place and join his exclusive club. This is how it went on for some time as week after week I escaped the confines of my pitiful existence on a journey induced by Opium. It was a world where everything sparkled and my dreams blossomed to the verge of reality. But morning after morning came the downside, and the overpowering heavy weight of my true life became a burden I was finding it increasingly harder to face. I continued in employment with obvious reluctance as my dour symptoms progressed to become visible through a lack of pride in my appearance. I really wished my life to only exist in the confines of my bedroom in the day and in the solace offered by Bunstaple's place by night.

During this time, Dorothea had proceeded in her active arrangement of the Endstreet display at the Salisbury Exhibition, maintaining a heightened haughtiness and general air of superiority to anyone else in the vicinity. When the Exhibition was at an end, Dorothea spent time in Paris and London in order to finalise several highly profitable business opportunities. For now I, her husband, had the fortune to escape Dorothea's attention. It was such a convenience that I was able to take such a bold approach in my increasing use of Opium, seemingly escaping any murmurs of discontent in our small community.

However it was not long before I utterly depended upon the drug and had no care for the financial costs. But both I and Thomas did not entertain the fact that our behaviour in company away from Bunstaple's acquaintances would soon awaken a rather startled impression tempered with idle gossip of a descent to madness. A decline to the use of a frequent vulgar tongue in public as we two addicts became nothing more than woeful actors forcing our crazy Opium induced thoughts and pitiful humour on any victim we might seek out in both the Inns and Coffee Houses around the town. Without any contemplation, upon a mixture of Opium and ale we would simply make endless speeches that rambled on and on, punctuated by frequent fits of laughing and chuckling when there was no joke to be found. We both grew pale and very thin as food was ignored for the sake of constant refuge in the wretched unreal world that was now indistinguishable from reality. My desperate sister Lilly had long given up imploring for a return to sanity and had retreated to our family home to spend more time with Father.

One dark November evening, I stumbled home after a memorable evening at Bunstaple's, which had left me in my now accustomed demeanour. As I made my way towards the Drawing Room with swollen eyes, a throbbing head and a harsh cough, I was greeted by the sight of Dorothea sitting in absolute aloofness. I paused by the door looking around the badly lit room until I could focus on the severe and grizzled face of my wife. Forgoing any initial conversation, I simply made way to a nearby chair and thrust myself upon it.

"Once you have been cured of this madness, we will never talk of this again," Dorothea finally spoke as she uttered these words with total contempt.

"What do you mean?" I replied, trying not to laugh.

"I mean that my husband is now the social equivalent of a dog, and that this fact is known throughout Salisbury society. Even worse, your staunch friend and my so-called brother is your equal. But no matter as I have the means at hand to resume you both to sanity. An excessive treatment to remedy the situation." Dorothea nodded an expressive approval of her plan.

"I am sorry that you are out of temper this evening," I faltered but then spoke boldly, "I confess I have found a new interest in life, but it should be of no trouble to you. Whatever your proposition, I therefore decline the offer and ask you not to interfere in my affairs."

"It is quite clear that there is nothing to discuss," Dorothea replied impetuously as she rose to her feet whilst clapping her hands loudly.

I shudder now as I dwell on this recollection. From the hallway appeared three solemn looking men, who tramped towards me with purpose. It was clear that they were eager to apprehend me as if I were some common criminal and took positions to surround me. In short my position was hopeless with no opportunity to resist. Unwanted restraint was put upon me as Dorothea moved forward in confrontation with a fearsome expression.

"Ralph, this is not a punishment but simply a course of action that must be taken," said Dorothea. "I have arranged for you to be committed to Laverstock House in the care of the renowned Physician, Oliver Hardrake. You have been registered as an insane person with clear instruction that discharge will only be granted with a total return to sanity."

"No," I shouted and struggled against the grip of my captors, but to no avail. "I demand that you spare me such an ordeal as I am of sane mind and have no place in such a pitiful asylum."

Dorothea's only response was a nod of the head and an expressive glance towards my captors. With my arms held firmly in place behind my back I was then swiftly and forcibly escorted from the room and with equal expedience taken from the house and bundled into the back of a secure carriage. I was handled as if I were nothing more than a heavy package and landed heavily in a heap on the floor. The doors were shut and locked to leave me lying in total darkness, dejected and brooding. The carriage moved off almost immediately at a pace that made it clear that I was to be traversed to the asylum as quickly as was possible. As I cowered in the corner, alone with my thoughts, I felt feeble and weak and longed for the carriage to simply return me home, or that I might awake to find that this was all a bad but vivid dream The alternative was the lingering misery awaiting me and the end of this hasty journey.

For the two months that followed I was held like a criminal in a prison, confined to a room so small that it was easily covered in two paces from the bed to the wall. I knew perfectly well within a short time that I had no choice but to capitulate and prove that I could control my supposed lunacy. At first I was left trembling and sweating as if dying without the comfort of Opium. I begged for release from my agony, that carried a sickness greater than any illness I have ever known. Nobody came to help me. Then came a torrent of fear and self-loathing, which was so dark and agonising that I would have almost welcomed death. My mind was pressed with a constant heaviness as it became difficult to blend night and day or sleep with subdued waking consciousness. Meals were simple and rationed, consisting of either bread or gruel, although the large jug of water by my bed was constantly replenished. I was inspected daily by a forthright physician, to whom I was not allowed to speak under threat of being gagged and bound. Time soon began to hang heavily and I feared rapidly descending into real lunacy, which distressed me to the point of weeping Then little by little I found hope for redemption as sense and reason took hold of my thinking. Day by day I began to feel confident of recovery.

I saw very little of the other lunatics save for the odd glimpse on my morning walk to take some air. In fact it is the face of one hideous old man sat in a corner screaming and pointing at nothing at all that haunts me more than any spirit could muster. I often hoped to catch sight of Thomas Endstreet, assuming that Dorothea had made similar arrangements for her brother. In fact I later learned that Thomas was interned at the more agreeable Fisherton Asylum, and held in much less restraint.

It was a welcome occurrence when I was suddenly moved from my little room to a well furnished bedroom that looked into a small paddock. I was promptly informed by a jovial white-headed man that I had responded well under observation, much to his apparent astonishment. Under the circumstance I was to be allowed a period of reflection and quiet indulgence before an anticipated release back to the care of my wife, and all in time for Christmas. I humbly accepted the kind offer and was forthwith provided with plentiful and wonderful meals to re-build my strength and restore my withered stomach to a more portly shape. During that time of repose I found a joyful splendour as I was left alone intent with a pile of books.

Chapter XIII - *New employment at the Salisbury Assizes, Dorothea is rendered desperate for a child but I ensure that the course does not run smoothly by finding distraction in a brothel.*

It was a cold and windy winter's night when I was conveyed by carriage back to Harnham, arriving home in style on Christmas Eve and in marked contrast to how I had left under such constraint in the relative warmth of autumn. I found Dorothea sat on the Drawing Room sofa in silence by the fire, which shone brightly near to a large Christmas tree.

"I am very disturbed by my recent experience but on reflection realise that I was very much mistaken in my behaviour," I spoke with a humbled spirit. "Please may you forgive me Dorothea?"

"The course that you took was inexpressibly painful to me and to your sister, Lilly. You compromised us both," returned Dorothea with an air of conceit. "Further, you encouraged my brother to a similar inclination, bringing dishonour to the entire family. Now we must look forward and not allow our marriage to be blighted any further. At length I expect you to be a devoted and attentive husband until your dying day, rendered in obedience and admiration whenever in my presence. Notwithstanding, I will return you and your family to ruin and damnation if I am not wholly satisfied."

"I'm sorry that these words are spoken with such a bitter voice," I observed with a little contempt before returning to a softer defeated tone. "I understand and agree with your remarks and hope that we may never have another quarrel. I assure you that I will do everything to be a venerable gentleman and a loving husband." I stood with my head bowed.

"It is of course delightful to hear you speak with grace after such imprudent behaviour. I believe your regret to be genuine," Dorothea looked straight at me. "Sit yourself down and remain in silence for the rest of the evening. I may then decide that we will make love for your first duty will be to render me with child. I intend that we have several children so you will demonstrate yourself to be a true and worthy gentleman in this regard."

I sat and reclined on the other end of the sofa, trying desperately to find some affection for my wife but failing despite my true repentance. In the silence I found solace in the distraction of memories, recollecting the sweet nature and perfect beauty of Emma Toopey. Her face remained such a powerful picture in a dream and then as a vision as I undertook the task of making love to Dorothea.

Whatever contradictions remained within me regarding my fateful circumstance, I fervently welcomed the spirit of Christmas like a long lost companion intent on providing both blessed relief and distraction from the impressions of the past and the very uncertain path into the future. On Christmas Day, Dorothea and I took leave of our own house to enjoy the festive hospitality of the Endstreet family home in Wilton. Hosted by Dorothea's father, we were also joined by several of her Aunts and Uncles and by Thomas and Lilly.

We arrived at the Endstreet Estate just as dinner was announced and I felt a little embarrassed as I found myself seated opposite Thomas and Lilly. After an initial silence I shook Thomas warmly by the hand and then hugged my frail and delicate sister as tears rose freshly in her eyes. Lilly did not have a reproachful word for me despite my selfish action whilst supposedly rescuing Thomas from his decline into degradation. Thomas's shame had become my own through a weak resolve and it was only as I looked at Lilly that I was really overcome with guilt. I had been so absorbed in my own affairs that I had dismissed my dear sister's welfare so lightly. We all acceded to enjoy the felicity of the season before making rather merry with undiminished humour and temper. From that opening awkward reunion we all three became good company through the pleasure of good conversation during a fine dinner, when the wine was not spared. Dorothea sat near her father and was constantly peering at us with apparent distaste for a very obvious abandonment to enjoyment.

When the table was cleared, I was able to speak more openly with Thomas whilst Lilly took some air with Dorothea. Whilst agreeing to draw a line under our recent liberal shortcomings, we did briefly share tales of recent experiences through the treatment contrived to cure our addictions. I did consult Thomas on the subject of Samuel Bunstaple, wondering if the infamous poet was still daring to run such a wild establishment. Thomas informed me that Bunstaple has in fact disappeared in mysterious circumstances following a great fire that had destroyed his home and left several charred corpses. The story had made the front page of the Salisbury Journal and even featured in The Times no less, with sightings of Bunstaple being reported in both London and Paris in support of the suggestion that he was not one of those that had perished. There was little doubt that the fire had been started deliberately and yet all the evidence pointed so strongly to Bunstaple being the perpetrator that he was either guilty with wanton abandon or portrayed by another to be so. I turned these things over in my mind and with dread considered that Dorothea may have taken such action in removing any temptation from Thomas and I. She was certainly a lady of influence and yet I dare not fully consider that she was capable of such an evil undertaking.

The following year saw me in new employment once more following news that Gerald Plumeworh had lost patience for my continued absence and had taken on another apprentice in my place. I did not protest his decision, and suspected that Plumeworth had learned of the depravity of my association with Bunstaple through the town's literary circle. We parted on good terms with a firm handshake and the exchange of kind words. Considering my recent actions, it was with some irony that my new profession was as clerk of court at the Salisbury Assizes, responsible for minuting proceedings. It was a position of some importance being that this was the Assize Court for the whole of Wiltshire. In truth I was offered the job after a far from satisfactory and very short interview when no hint or indication was given that I was to be successful. For my part I uttered very few words of any consequence and presented a mood sure to discourage any empathy. There was complete mystery in the course of the following day when I was notified that it would indeed be extremely desirous if I could start work with immediate effect. Thomas Endstreet then divulged that it was surely more than just circumstance or coincidence that Dorothea had conversed with the principle Judge the previous evening. I was therefore by intimation obliged to my wife for a new career and it would appear for sustaining every aspect of my existence. Now reduced to a grovelling repressed man stripped of independent spirit, I timidly accepted my lot.

This was now to be the state of affairs as accordingly Dorothea continued in her role as a powerful lady of business and I complimented her with a somewhat inferior position. And it cannot be denied that in the general remarks of Salisbury society I was held in the same regard as a tame domesticated pet. In general our way of life was very formal, with little discourse over dinner or during frequent games of cribbage. The one endeavour upon which Dorothea was truly dependent on me was in our lovemaking and the prevailing necessity to bear a child. Whether this was a brisk affair by the side of the fireplace or a rousing exertion in the bedroom, it was the one area of my life that still retained passion. The only other release from my general despondency was descending upon the Inns of Salisbury each week to quaff several jars of ale with Thomas Endstreet, Daniel Drumdale and Edwin Gurden.

Fortifying myself with assurance through drinking ale was such a contrast to my daily toil of existence. I found a dignity that was the perfect medicine to my wife's overpowering influence that had undiminished power over me and the town in general. As far as I know in private there was not another person in business in the whole of Salisbury that was well disposed to Dorothea. In public was another matter and everyone tended to be obsequious to the point of almost bowing and scraping. The fear was daring to cross the town's undisputed matriarch and being met with swift and surly retribution. The Endstreet brand now held an improbable supremacy over Salisbury that stood as tall as the spire itself. Thomas reaped the rewards and offered my sister Lilly a rather splendid house that had an air of comfort through a design of modern elegance. I could not rock the boat for the very consequence of denigrating Lilly's position. A situation that was rendered with even greater perfection by the winter when Lilly gave birth to a son, Toby. By the following spring Edwin Gurden was the father of a daughter, Josephine and Daniel Drumdale was soon to be a father come June.

For Dorothea there was still no hint of motherhood and I was subjected to initial looks of contempt and eventually wickedly taunted for a lack of virility. I was by all accounts an unnatural husband and the poorest kind of imitation of a true gentleman. Bewailing her misfortune in this matter, Dorothea struggled to comprehend how she could obstinately mould all aspects of her life with total control and yet could not succeed in producing a child through reliance on another. In private she was frequently reduced to floods of tears that were duly repressed in my company. With an inconsolable wife at home I sought greater freedom in finding further cheer and pleasure in the town. With Thomas and Edwin occupied by the joys of fatherhood, I was left to drink merrily with Daniel Drumdale. It was true of Daniel that at this time he found the pregnant figure of his wife to be somewhat repulsive. His impiety was extremely forthright and he declared that he would not be of intimate acquaintance with Emily Drumdale until she had given birth and no longer resembled a large pig.

In the course of things and upon a frequent state of inebriation,

Daniel was tempted by the allure of a renowned Brothel on Winchester Street. Daniel received a letter of introduction from a gentleman of good connexion who would drink ale regularly in The Pheasant, and Daniel even became so addicted to the experience that he became as popular a client as any other and was granted the privilege of overnighting. Anonymity was retained in all declarations as Daniel enjoyed companionship with at least five of the many common prostitutes on offer. At first I resolutely declared my intention to not even set foot on Winchester Street itself during any given evening, let alone take the path to the door of the Brothel. It was only after interchanging a great number of harsh words with Dorothea one very fraught evening that I found myself occupied in submissive discourse with Daniel about the prospect of at least viewing the Brothel.

"I would say that you would be a blind and foolish fellow to then not wish to sample the many treats on offer," Daniel scoffed as we shaped a course from The Pheasant to Winchester Street.

"I do not know if I can truly go that far," said I shaking my head nervously and with a rueful face.

On the hour of eleven in the evening I was led into the lodgings that housed some twenty women. Whilst I was riddled with hesitation and misgiving, Daniel greeted several of the prostitutes with extraordinary confidence and a gentle fondness. He told me to take a seat on a rather threadbare sofa before turning his back upon the room and leading a short girl with bright red hair to a chamber up the stairs. I knew perfectly well of his intention but was still strong of will in my own resolve to reject any such pursuance. A procession of gentlemen began to arrive from all walks of life in Salisbury and beyond. One gentleman from Shaftesbury even sat next to me for a while and openly declared that he was head of a highly respectable and virtuous family, that deemed it as matter of great religious importance that he visited the Cathedral at least once a week. After spending the afternoon in prayer he felt lonely and restricted in the rather dull Inn where he lodged and would slip away to find comfort in the Brothel. On the first occasion he had only wished to take some evening air but had been tempted in by a mature lady who spotted him loitering on the street. The lady had apparently roused a passion in him that he now struggled to control and which had led to the gentleman both praying for forgiveness of his sins and for thanks for his salvation in equal measure. The man was soon gone, enticed by an old hag of a prostitute who was as ugly as sin itself. To my mind she resembled an ape in a dress with excessive facial hair and several unseemly warts.

I continued to recline listlessly on the sofa as my state of inebriation wore thin and I contemplated that it was time to leave. Daniel had been gone some time and I began to doubt if he would reappear before dawn. It was staggering to witness so many women of easy virtue passing through the lobby to collect their customers. Often they arrived in groups of two or three at a time in order that the eager gentlemen were not kept waiting long for their unspeakable moment of fun. And so it went on until midnight and broke into the early morning. I made it clear that I was only present in accompaniment for a friend and had no inclination to partake in the services under offer and in fairness it was from then on never intimated by any of these ladies that I should render myself to their charms. Just as I had finally run my patience and stood to leave, the most delightfully pretty girl came in from the cold. Instinctively I helped remove her coat and was greeted with a warm smile beneath the largest brown eyes that could ever be imagined.

"My pleasure to be of assistance," I said with some formality.

The girl curtseyed as if I were her master.

"Allow me to introduce myself, I am Ralph Chatterforth," I continued, "here in a capacity to accompany a dear friend."

"You are a gentleman and a very kind gentleman at that," the girl replied with an accent that came from the countryside. "My name is Kate."

The front door opened once more and two very loud and drunken men bounded in. The taller of the two threw his coat across the sofa to reveal a rather ill-fitting velvet waistcoat that bulged over his large stomach. Kate visibly flinched as she was reviewed by the newcomers.

"What a deyv'lish fine young creature we have here," the tall man pulled Kate towards him with a rough hand. The other man threw himself on the sofa in a state of exhaustion. "I can wait no longer to see what beauty lies within, so come young creature let us make love this instant. Let us go to yonder chamber." The man had a look of contempt and a sneering tone to his voice that I instantly despised. He squeezed Kate's hand tightly and began to pull her towards the stairs.

"No," I shouted with a severe look upon the man, "I will be obliged if you would return the lady to my side."

"I am hungry and in need sir, so do not cross me," the man bellowed in reply.

"Stop!" Said I.

"What the devil is your problem sir?" The man returned to confront me, leaving Kate to cower in the background.

"My problem sir is that you take with some brashness a young lady that was by my side," I spoke with some disdain.

The man paused for a moment and then rocked his head back with such a hearty laugh that his slumbering companion awoke. "I am no thief you odd fellow."

At that time an older lady appeared, openly displaying her large mature charms squeezed tightly into a red bodice. "Well Nathan Rooney, why am I not surprised that you are at the centre of all this bluff and commotion. Come and I will fix you something special and no mistake. Bring your dim brother too for Irish Mary will shortly be available."

Rooney slapped the woman's behind and growled like a wild animal, "I swear I may take you before we reach the bed Greta,"

"I do not doubt it" Greta cackled and thankfully led Rooney away, supporting him up the stairs as he adjusted her scant clothing at every opportunity. Rooney's docile brother needed little encouragement to follow after.

I was now alone with the demure Kate, who looked so innocent with her flushed red cheeks and unblemished pale skin. She did not speak but simply walked over to embrace me, resting her head gently to my chest. The odd thing was that it was I who was trembling and needed to be somewhat reassured. As she looked up at me with those large brown eyes, my heart began to beat so fast that I feared I may swoon like a delicate lady.

"You are such a fine and distinguished gentleman that I will actually be proud to share my bed with you and not take another customer all night," said Kate.

I looked at Kate's beauty more closely and for all the world swore that I saw Emma Toopey. "I would be a fool to decline, but shall reward you without question," I demanded.

Without any further hesitation I allowed Kate to lead me up the stairs and every time she stopped to turn around and look at me with her beautiful eyes, I shuddered and contrived to imagine that I would be making love to Emma Toopey herself. The bedroom was small and cold and badly lit. The thick drapery did not help in this regard. Still in a nervous state, I felt obliged to avert my eyes as Kate removed her clothes but in truth on returning my sight could only make out a hazy figure in the gloom. She moved forward and gently encouraged me to remove my own clothes, and I became overwhelmed with a strong savage passion. As we quickly became entwined and prostrated, Kate showed me so much warmth and affection that I could not have envisaged such amazing lovemaking, even through a dream. I swear until this moment that despite the fraught situation between myself and Dorothea, I had not bestowed even a remote intention to seek infidelity. And yet as I lay there with the slight figure of Kate by my side, I felt no dishonour or guilt. Instead there was a feeling of victory and utter satisfaction.

By the morning the house had fallen silent, only broken when I clearly heard a strong footstep climbing the stairs. Daniel Drumdale then entered the room without a single knock before moving forward on tiptoe so as not to disturb Kate. "Come quickly, we must go," he said in a low voice. "Leave the girl some money for her service and leave her be."

"I – I – should say goodbye," I protested.

"Hush," returned Daniel, "she is already history. You must dress and come with me."

I dressed as quickly as I could muster, fumbling as I did so through a sense of aggravation. After leaving five pounds on the bed by the sleeping Kate, Daniel drew me with haste from the room and then from the house itself.

"It seems so cruel to leave in this way," I muttered.

"I advise you to remain detached in emotion if you are to ever return to this place or your treachery will be realised at once." Daniel returned. "I truly did not expect to find you within a mile of this place this morning, and especially to be induced into taking the services of a common prostitute. Who'd have thought it, the earnest and upstanding gentleman that is Ralph Chatterforth is now truly a man of the world." Daniel's eyebrows elevated as his face contorted into a sneering approval of my actions. "Now with due respect to the time of day you must think of good reason why you did not return home last night and deflect attention from the fact that you used a prostitute almost under your good wife's nose."

Without speaking I nodded my head in strong assent under the realisation that I had indeed committed a hideous act. Daniel's constant use of the word prostitute pulled me back to reality and a feeling of such downright discomfort in what had truly occurred last night. On top of it all I would need to apply every ounce of cunning to invent an ingenious tale to cover my absence when confronted by Dorothea.

"Forgive me my dear, for I felt a duty to stay with poor Daniel, who was in such a drunken state that I truly feared for his actions. I felt it wise to find a room in one of the town's Inns and confine his desperate behaviour far from the delicate position of his lady wife." I stood before Dorothea like an unruly pupil facing the Headmaster with cane in hand.

With a grim face Dorothea sat back in her chair but spoke not a word.

"I simply had no way of getting word to you," returned I fervently, "but pray please do not mention this to Emily Drumdale as I fear she will suffer in her current state."

"Why do you speak so hastily Ralph?" Retorted Dorothea, "it is as if you are here to beg."

"It really is no matter at all," I replied, "I just entreat you to understand that I was feeling great pain in being parted from you, such is my faithful devotion."

"I don't believe I have ever heard such an awkward speech in all my days," replied Dorothea sharply. "I now suspect something more behind such snivelling."

"I would not deceive you," I whined, "I just could not face you if I had."

"Do not prolong this any longer then," said Dorothea impatiently with some sharp gestures. She promptly rose from her chair and left me standing awkwardly as my exasperated wife then swept out of the room. I had somehow survived.

I made a decision to stay away from Daniel Drumdale, the Ale Houses of Salisbury and therefore from Kate the Prostitute. With great reason if I kept away from temptation then I could avoid my own destruction as surely my luck would soon run out by taking any other path. As for Dorothea, she never again spoke of the occasion that marked my imprudent act and I in return tried to make amends with a show of ardour.

Chapter XIV- *Certain consequences of my dalliance and a special arrangement is contrived.*

Emily Drumdale bore Daniel a son in June as it was confirmed that Lilly was already carrying another child. The joy felt by Thomas Endstreet was not shared by his sister, who took the news as if a family loss had been announced. Dorothea now pined more than ever for a child of her own. It was even of little consequence when Hetty Gurden lost a child before birth in the autumn, for Dorothea still felt that it was she that was being neglected and somehow punished from experiencing the formality of motherhood. To compensate we both busied ourselves in work, assuming that fate would soon present us with a healthy child. I was finding immense satisfaction in my new employment, having the opportunity to hear about the circumstances and position of so many different sections of Wiltshire society. In many ways it made me appreciate my own lot and I was able to banish the rebellious spirit within and face each day with smiling good humour. To confound it all, then came such a revelation that all immediate hope of having a family was seemingly abandoned.

In short I Ralph Chatterforth brought a disease into the household that would have caused moral outrage throughout Salisbury if it were ever made public. Stating the facts as dryly as I can, both Dorothea and I displayed such painful and unsightly symptoms of a private nature that it was as if hounds of hell had fed upon on us from under the bed clothes as we slept. With such scabs and sores there was no chance of disguising or denying the fact that I was infected with a venereal disease and the initial realisation of my own disposition left me in a continual tremulous state. Despite some hope that Dorothea may not have been infected, and that I could simply flee to a new life abroad without suspicion being aroused, I was immediately cowed in front of my stern unyielding wife who had almost simultaneously discovered, through some considerable pain and embarrassing blemishes, that she was cursed with the same outcome following my own depraved folly.

"You will oblige me sir to confine your explanation to nothing but facts," Dorothea raged as she walked to and fro in the bedroom, scratching occasionally after several strides.

"I must confess to having entertained a common prostitute on Winchester Street. I feel nothing but sorrow and shame for what has happened." I murmured apologetically. There was no point in pretending that anything else has occurred. "I have no peace of mind in confessing my actions as I have thought a great deal about it since that foolish night. I venture that I must have declined into madness and beg for you to forgive me."

Dorothea stood still whilst turning her eyes on me and then frowning. She then spoke in a manner that I just could never have imagined in the midst of this dire situation.

"It will always remain that this miserable wretchedness was your work, and I find your audacity hard to bear." Dorothea spoke with a disdainful voice but her face betrayed a cunning thinking within. "Still what is done, is done and now we must look to repair the situation as best we can. Your conduct is beyond reproach and you will now obey my every command to restore this house to the true warmth of a loving and complete family. Do I make my position clear sir?"

"Yes my dear," I assented with a nodding head as I dare not controvert any request she may have. At the same time I was left wondering if Dorothea had somehow arranged this unpalatable situation all along such was her restrained benevolence.

Dorothea remained immovable and passionless in regard to the reasons as to why and how I had brought this unsightly disease into our lives. It was I who was totally unprepared for the unsightly lesions and inflamed joints that heralded a horrible decline in health. The Great Pestilence that the Salisbury Journal would hold up as undeniable proof of the moral and social decay of England itself. London was being called 'The Whoreshop Of The World' and by no means was our family alone in being affected by the plague that was frequently being passed from prostitute to wife. Although touched in no small measure by the physical affliction of the disease, it was the social embarrassment that was of far greater concern to Dorothea. Determined to retain an upright position in Salisbury society, Dorothea bore no emotion to her physical plight but rather made plans to protect the situation with an impassive air.

Dorothea made an appointment with an eminent doctor, paying him handsomely for his services and confidence. This came with a stern warning of the fact that Dorothea could ruin the doctor's career should he choose to speak or even hint as to why he was being employed. This sinister short and very odd looking man readily yielded to such persuasion, content to solicit a great financial reward.

"With such a generous commission I will remain nothing but confidential," said the stooping sneering midget in a high back hat. "I have every hope for your prospects of a quick recovery." He raised his eyes to me in condescension.

Sat in a small backstreet hovel that just about passed for a surgery, I felt so meek and insignificant as the doctor examined me with a persistent jolting twitch of his badly disfigured chin and laying his hands upon me with unnecessary firmness. The whole experience was positively awful and I felt stripped of all dignity. Thankfully neither I nor Dorothea were subjected to using mercury as I had heard it said that this was the way to certain madness. Instead we were prescribed a concocted medicine to bring comfort and relief to the throbbing sores and the constant chill that stayed under the skin.

In due time my ailments began to lessen but I still carried the guilt of seeing Dorothea continue to suffer as her face grew so pale and her eyes so red. Every night brought dreadful unrelenting nightmares and Dorothea was forced to take sanctuary in the confinement of the parlour by day, unwilling to be seen in public. My sister Lilly grew suspicious and would prevail in trying to visit but thankfully I made a good hand of dissuading her from seeing Dorothea in person, explaining that she was simply stricken with a bad cold.

When Dorothea was once again in a condition to face the world, I concluded in my mind that this was an end to the matter. It had somehow been of good fortune that the disease had passed and that Dorothea held no grudge or anger for my carelessness or infidelity. It was then just before Christmas that I found myself sat opposite Dorothea in the lounge and I distinctly recollect that she was in extremely good spirit, looking remarkably radiant in a beautiful ivory coloured dress. Leaving her brown hair to fall over her shoulders and with wide excited eyes, Dorothea announced that she had a fine notion to share with me, which would profit our lives in no short measure, upon which her mood changed quickly.

"You must endeavour Ralph Chatterforth to provide me with a son. In truth I have never really had the desire or want to go through the pain of childbirth. It is such an unladylike disposition that is nothing but a common and vulgar spectacle. At one time I was prepared go through the experience in order to attain my heart's desire, but you have proven totally inadequate in providing me with a child to bear." Dorothea relayed her thoughts with a sneering tone. "You will doubtless be surprised that I have not most assuredly found a way to punish you severely and cast you aside, as I should, like a broken toy. Believe me that was my first contemplation, but you were saved by the very fact that I would have had to bear so much shame and ignominy."

"I still hold the deepest regret for my actions, and know I have disgraced myself." I returned with sincerity and a shake of the head. "But what do you want of me? How can I provide you with a son when I have so far failed to do so and you no longer have the desire to go through childbirth?"

"I have made up my mind that you shall no longer share my bed," Dorothea said firmly. "I cannot endure your flesh next to mine ever again. Furthermore it must be concluded that the infection you have so willingly shared with me will finally ensure that I will never be able to carry a child. I have hence applied a business-like thinking to the matter and decided upon the perfect arrangement."

The severity of Dorothea's expression as she made this startling announcement was one I had only ever accounted previously when observing her during trade dealings, where my wife was feared and reviled in equal measure.

"I will be happy to oblige in assisting with your plan and in so doing keep your name and reputation but please tell me what I should be prepared to do?" I enquired with a little haste.

"Mr Chatterforth." Dorothea returned rather formally as her eyes gleaned within a frightful stare upon a face that did not flinch for a moment. "Do you remember when we travelled to London for the Great Exhibition and you enquired as to what business my brother, Thomas, was conducting there at the time?"

"I do indeed." I replied with curiosity as to what facts were now to be presented.

"Thomas's business involved brokering certain transactions to benefit the delicate circumstances of all concerned parties." said Dorothea turning her head slightly to look away from my gaze. "In short Thomas would help find good homes for the poor children born in the slums of London into a life of destitution. With the utmost humanity he arranged for newborns to be taken from disease ridden hovels to the homes of wealthy couples unable to bear children of their own. The pauper parents would receive a financial reward in return and Thomas would only take a small commission for his providence. Thomas worked with several influential and charitable business partners, with the right connection in the city."

"Whilst admiring Thomas's virtuous undertaking I cannot truly contemplate that you are propounding that we enter into such an arrangement. Are we really in such a dreadful state that we must buy a child fresh from its mother's womb?" I spluttered whilst gesticulating through shock and disgust. "I find this whole notion to be completely absurd."

Dorothea remained steadfast with her eyes fixed upon me. "My decision is made and you shall be submissive in this matter. I have already taken the liberty of speaking to Thomas and secured both his confidence and assistance. To betray me and refuse this request will lead to your ruin and damnation, make no mistake in thinking it will not. So what answer do you make?"

It was clear that nothing else could be done as I stood momentarily in silence, contemplating my situation. "I have no choice but to concede but my answer must be qualified in that I am acting under duress and notwithstanding feel wretched in doing so."

Dorothea turned her head disdainfully towards me, "If that is all then I shall lose no sleep over your anxiety of mind but will immediately make preparation for the arrival of our son."

After uttering these final words on the matter, Dorothea left the room and closed the door behind her. I took a seat and like a frightened child shrank back in the solitude of the dimly lit room, alone to pass all manner of thoughts through my mind. I tried to make sense of what I had become and why I had not the strength or inclination to recoil from any involvement in the plot already set in motion.

Chapter XV- *Containing the further progress of the plot and acquaints the Reader with the villainous Bilge and Cardoon.*

Christmas came and went without any further comment or remark on the iniquitous preparations that lay ahead. I was left to sleep alone every single night, no longer able to share the joy of a woman's tenderness. Time did not change Dorothea's position in this regard and any pleasantry towards me was only ever acted out in public. Our few private moments together were now cursed with awkward silence or spiteful outbursts of temper on my wife's part. This situation was evident a great many times through to the spring of 1854, when the prompt finally came to truly begin our hapless conspiracy.

Dorothea announced to me one Sunday evening in March over dinner that she wished that I would now fulfil my pledge and move things forward with great rapidity. The comment had no sooner passed when a message was sent to summon Thomas, who made his way with great precipitation and immediately declared his vow of secrecy on the matter.

"It is truly an extraordinary request, but one I am willing to accept on behalf of my dear sister and best friend," said Thomas in a tone that seemed to mock.

"Will this not represent a great deal of trouble on your part?" I inquired with an embarrassed squint.

"Not the least trouble at all dear fellow," Thomas rejoined. "I could not bear to think of my sister having to endure this constant hardship in such an unhappy circumstance. It is impossible to imagine that you shall not be a father and Dorothea never experience the delights of motherhood. I am just sorry that you were sadly not competent in the matter of procreation."

"How dare you make such a statement sir and I demand you withdraw it immediately with an apology," I demanded.

"Why, is this not the truth then?" Thomas said in reply, whilst staring at Dorothea to prompt an explanation.

"I am afraid my husband is ashamed of his shortcomings," Dorothea rejoined and looked straight at me. "I suggest poor Ralph that you make this one confession here and now or face public humiliation and damnation."

Dorothea had made such a clear statement that it was instantly understood that I must accept the blame and declare as much to Thomas in order to continue my now accustomed life of wealth and standing. I feared that otherwise my dalliance with a prostitute would be declared openly and I would be cast aside.
"It is the truth," I muttered in defeat.

"God bless you for your honesty Ralph," Thomas cried and put an arm around me. "Do not have any fear that this matter will be discussed beyond this room. Instead by Christmas you both shall have no cares beyond watching over the child that will be with you, demanding your affection."

Thomas explained part of the plot that he had already concocted with great promptitude, stressing that Dorothea must soon take to wearing a cushion beneath her dress to confirm to the world that she must be carrying a child. The deception would be well executed by the use of numerous cushions growing in size over the coming months, until December when Dorothea would take to her room and await the arrival of a son. Although of course this was to be no natural birth but rather a delivery conceived as a matter of business.

Seeming almost proud of his commission, Thomas then turned to me. "I will need to speak to you separately regarding the transaction itself, including collection and safe passage between London and Salisbury. It will be more pleasant in this regard to discuss the situation over a jar of ale, and not place any further concern upon Dorothea."

"Certainly," I replied with a grimace.

"Good, then I shall make the arrangement," declared Thomas, who soon left without sharing any further thoughts of his scheming.

I was left alone with Dorothea and her deep contented breathing as we exchanged no words and sat in the darkness to reflect simultaneously with very different emotions.

It soon became very apparent that Thomas had given immediate consideration to indulging both the confidence and assistance of other parties in hatching his somewhat mysterious plot. Without expressing any regret in exposing our confidence, Thomas confirmed that he had already shaken hands on a deal with none other than Edwin Gurden and Daniel Drumdale, and that they had both stated their delight in being able to help a dear friend such as I in a time of dire need. An appointment had then been made for two days time to be convened at noon at the King's Arms in St John Street in order to complete the details of the delicate business transaction. Thomas declared that I should be delighted at such a quick and profitable outcome but my frightful expression surely displayed nothing other than a deeply troubled mind that could not see the propriety in such a situation.

At this present time I have a very sober recollection of making my way to the King's Arms on that fateful day, filled with such apprehension that I was inclined towards a desperate state indeed. Thomas was already holding court as I entered the dark and squalid Inn, drinking ale with Edwin and Daniel as he almost burst with arrogance in the role of his sister's honourable saviour. Thomas immediately declared upon the confidence of our two companions as they tried in vain to mask their smirking faces behind nearly empty tankards. He then proceeded to order more ale and ushered us all to the corner of the room so other patrons would not be obliged to listen or pass comment on our discussion.

What followed was a short conference that advanced the plot with great alacrity. In short, Daniel would take responsibility of all money matters through a specially arranged bank account and Edwin would facilitate the transportation of the child through his connections in the criminal backstreets of Salisbury by reprieving the sinister alias of Mick Mickle. With a puckered brow, Thomas then confidently declared that he would devote his time to brokering a deal in London by considering only the most worthy of proposals, and would only pay attention to those suitors that made a favourable impression.

"I will execute my duties with considerable promptitude whilst applying absolute diligence in purchasing the highest quality of goods," Thomas spoke haughtily as if declaring his actions as an act of chivalry and with very little thought for my true misfortune in this matter. "A toast gentlemen if you will, to our bond of duty in delivering Dorothea and Ralph their first born child."

"To Dorothea and Ralph," Daniel and Edwin spoke as one and clashed their tankards together with Thomas's, splashing a great deal of ale into the air and to the floor. Timidly I pressed my own tankard against the others and in doing so raised such a cheer that everyone in the Inn stopped to stare.

Within an hour Thomas ensured that many more tankards of ale were dispensed and consumed, with a hearty request that we should all make merry in a mood of celebration. Little by little I began to find solace through the effect of the strong locally brewed ale until it took no deliberation at all in dismissing my turmoil to make happy through inebriation. More and more ale was procured as full and empty tankards moved to and fro from the corner in which we remained through into the evening. I hesitate now as I can tell you no more of that evening because any sober recollection was soon at an end. The only gratification was that I somehow made it home safely, although I awoke very late the next day feeling both unwell and very uncomfortable. I was overcome with guilt under the weary strain upon my head that came courtesy of such a drunken period of unconsciousness. My appearance was frightful and preposterous as I stood up from the bed fully clothed in the same attire from the day before. I looked ridiculous and felt inclined to be sick but yet I somehow found a cause for merriment, laughing boisterously and with so much vigour that tears ran down my cheek.

Dorothea threw open the door in agitation and tore into the room shouting with scorn, "Ralph Chatterforth."

I proceeded to laugh with even greater feverish delusion.

Very soon afterwards Thomas took leave to London by himself, insisting that it would not be right for me to join any negotiations at such an early stage. In the meantime Daniel had made provision for an erroneous account to be opened at the Bank under a suitable alias which was then handsomely funded by Dorothea, including provision for a token commission for both Daniel and Edwin. My friends would indeed make a profit from my plight.

Edwin retrieved his pitiful disguise to re-enact the vagabond figure of Mick Mickle and seek out the seedy ale-houses of Salisbury where only the idle and villainous kept company. The shadows cast by Mick Mickle after the hanging of the Crabbe brothers was seemingly not mentioned, nor the reason for his awkward and ungainly reappearance. At first Edwin simply made a habit of frequenting these Inns so as to be recognised and accepted, sat in a corner night after night enjoying the ale. The next step was to avail himself of these uncouth crooks and find a trust amongst thieves.

Edwin soon re-found a great deal of security in his alias and chose to seek company with a curious fellow who made a habit of sitting alone by the fire with his back towards everyone else. He was of a large build and beyond fifty years in age, always wearing a hat despite the stifling heat, It was clear that the man was respected by the other rogues and in fact somewhat elevated in status judging by the continual homage that was paid towards him. As Edwin approached with apprehension and finally came to see the man's face he could not help but vent an expression of shock at the sight of several deep and unsightly scars. Two ran down either cheek in almost perfect symmetry and another dug deep into a leathery pock marked chin.

"I feel obliged to introduce myself sir," said Edwin with a hesitation that implied fear.

"Don't call me sir." retorted the man with a scowl, " and it is for me to know who you are."

"You know who I am?" simpered Edwin.

"Look about you," the man's face altered to resemble some ghastly apparition. "These people all have exceptional eyes and ears in order that they might survive and not succumb to jail or the gallows. Every man here knows who you are Mick Mickle, former companion to the Crabbe brothers who fled liked a frightened animal rather than try to help save his friends from the noose."

"How are they disposed towards me?" Edwin tried hard not to stutter and was very afraid of the old man. "Do I find good company with you sir?"

"Do not call me sir," the old man shouted and nearly climbed from his chair.

"I am sure that I shall not insult you again," Edwin returned.

"Indeed or it shall be followed swiftly by your last breath. Come here!" said the man beckoning for Edwin to draw nearer. As he did so the man grabbed hold of Edwin's right hand and pressed it against the scar on his chin. "This was a gift from Robert Crabbe after I dared to speak against him in the Pheasant some five years ago. He vowed to take my life should I ever cross him in Salisbury again and so I was forced to leave and take my chances in Bristol. It is my good fortune that he died courtesy of your cowardice and so I have no gripe with you. However you ought to watch your back Mick Mickle as the Crabbe's still have friends who may wish to bring you to account."

The days and nights passed on and Edwin kept a respectful distance from the stranger in the hat who always held court in the same Inn, the same chair and the same position by the fire. He did host frequent but short conversations with many who frequented the Inn. Most were strangers and some were regular patrons. The man was not an intimidating size but simply demanded respect by his demeanour, and each visitor would listen as he spoke. Edwin continued to observe discreetly whilst keeping watch on those around him for fear that a friend of the Crabbes' may seek him out. Edwin's nerves could not take much more and so he decided to run the risk of approaching the man once more and seek guidance on a transaction.

The man's name, as was informed to Edwin by a simple ragged urchin rewarded with a shilling, was William Drudge, better known as Bilge. Notorious in the west of England in tales of theft and murder and for somehow having the good fortune to always avoid justice. People sought him out for the company he kept and it was said that Bilge could arrange anything if the price was right. Always he would gain a handsome commission and stayed removed from the act itself to stay beyond implication.

Edwin took a deep breath and approached Bilge with some misgiving once more as he sat in gloomy rumination.

"So it is Mick Mickle again," Bilge said, "what course of advice do you seek from me now?" Bilge smiled to allow the glow of the fire to illuminate his rotten yellow decaying teeth.

"I seek your assistance in a matter for which you shall be greatly rewarded," Edwin returned.

"Go on," said Bilge with a scornful stare.

"I need to arrange safe passage from London of some goods for a wealthy acquaintance," Edwin continued.

"Ah," said Bilge fully opening his eyes, "You mean to say that you have found a place in Salisbury society. How can that be?"

"The business was brought to me entirely by chance," replied Edwin doggedly. "I was fortunate to find honest work in the market and a business man sought me out upon hearing that I could help him."

"What are the goods he wishes to transport so secretly?" Bilge growled.

"I am not at liberty to disclose," said Edwin taking a long breath.

"Then why should I wish to help?" Bilge observed, filled with obvious curiosity.

"It should be enough to say that there will be the princely sum of one thousand pounds available to you in commission," Edwin stated with confidence.

"Well that news I like indeed, but at least tell me the size of the goods?" Bilge asked whilst betraying a greedy eagerness to complete the transaction whatever the challenge.

"Let us say that it will be a package no more than the size of a small baby," Edwin just about completed the sentence without reverting to his juvenile stutter in all the excitement.

Bilge betook himself to present a more than adequate accomplice who would listen to the proposition and agree a price if all was agreeable. It was clear that Bilge was curious to unwind the mystery behind the proposal and declared to Edwin that he would introduce the abettor in person. In a short time he would set forth a place and time of meeting on the condition that the wealthy benefactor would be present.

"If he does not show then the deal is dead at the outset," Bilge said with a sharp hiss as he looked steadily at Edwin. He then reached out and very deliberately grabbed Edwin's right wrist with a strong grip, "Cross me and you shall not be able to walk away from the meeting."

Edwin simply nodded and dared not speak, quickly moving away as Bilge released his hand. As he neared the door Edwin looked back at the daunting figure of Bilge sat by the smoky hearth holding court with another nervous figure seeking assistance. Edwin took a parting look at the dreary room as he paused to consider the true danger of his role, considering if it would be wise just to secure a retreat and confine the alias of Mick Mickle once more to history. If Thomas Endstreet had not returned from London that evening, such a cloud of doubt would have remained with Edwin and the whole sordid affair may have come to a halt there and then. I regret at this present time to say this was not the case and that Edwin's faltering resolve was diminished and indeed strengthened by the infectious persuasive countenance of Thomas.

It was only two nights later that Bilge summoned Edwin to his side and divulged the time and place where the arrangement was to be made. Edwin was to bring his wealthy friend the very next day at noon to the door of the Cardoon Loan and Life Assurance Company, who held small premises in Crane Street that were positioned with some irony across the way from the Workhouse. Within the hour Edwin had reported the conversation to Thomas and I.

"I cannot help but speculate that I will simply be robbed and then murdered," I cried in fear, "and that Edwin will be murdered too. I truly do not have the strength nor the courage to see this through"

"Good Heaven," replied the imperturbable Thomas, "do you not think it unwise for these ruffians to murder you before any money has been presented. Uneducated they may be but stupid to such a degree would have led to a noose long ago. I swear that you shall not come to any harm"

Thomas was of course right, but I still felt a great unease with the whole situation.

The next day Edwin, disguised as Mick Mickle, led the way down Crane Street and singled out the rotten rain beaten door that led to the office of Cardoon Loan and Life Assurance Company. It was still before noon and so we devoted a number of spare minutes nervously stood outside, jigging from one foot to another. Upon noon, Edwin very deliberately lifted and sounded the large brass knocker. A tall, very thin, gentleman greeted us and expressed gratitude for our punctuality. We were led through two small rooms that contained pile upon pile of paper and no furniture. Next was a winding narrow staircase that came to another room just like those below. At the back of this room was another that was dimly lit and furnished with a table and several chairs. Bilge sat in a corner almost masked by darkness. Another man sat by the table in fine clothes, drinking brandy.

"I am obliged to thank you for meeting with me," the man was well spoken and seemed well tempered. "I am Mark Cardoon."

"Mister Cardoon you may depend on us to bring you honest business in a discreet manner," Edwin said humbly.

Bilge immediately laughed so hard that it caused him to cough rather violently by the end.

"The words on your lips are not true sir for if this was an honest transaction then you would not need to sound out Bilge." returned Cardoon.

"That is true sir," Edwin said with his head bowed and with an awful stutter.

Cardoon now fixed his stare upon me. "I say sir; please tell me why you should wish to engage my services. Do not worry as I shall not pry upon your identity."

"Undoubtedly I require you for a difficult and unusual task," I replied looking straight at Cardoon and showing a nerveless tone of voice. "Due to a very unexpected turn of events, I need to arrange safe but secret passage for my child from London to Salisbury in the month of December."

"Why should it be December and not this very month?" asked Cardoon.

"The child is not yet born," I replied sheepishly.

"It is your bastard child?" cried Cardoon, laughing.

"Yes," I replied, causing Bilge to laugh heartily once more along with Cardoon. In the midst of such an awkward situation I had no option but to lie.

Once the incessant laughter had abated, Cardoon stood to confront me with a serious air. "I intend to help you and give assurance of nothing but a first class service. My commission will be one thousand pounds just like Bilge here, with five hundred paid in notes by this very same time next week to this office. On delivery of the money I will introduce you to the coachman who will transport your yet to be born child. I'm even thinking of calling him the Stork. The other five hundred will be settled on completion of the job"

Bilge contributed another wheezing laugh and hacking cough, "I am happy to have the same conditions so you should bring my five hundred pounds too next week and the other five hundred when the job is completed."

After a short silence I showed impeccable gentlemanly manners and shook Cardoon's hand and Bilge's too, "I accept your condition in good faith and will be here with one thousand pounds next week."

"Not even a thought of barter so I can indeed deduce the importance of this matter as well as the fact that you have such wealth that payment of such a sum is viewed as nothing more than loose change." Cardoon spoke dryly with a roguish glint in his eye that concerned me.

I made my bow to both Cardoon and Bilge and walked out with an external confidence that did not betray my nerves within. Edwin could not mask his own excessive shaking but to his credit traversed the stairs without stumbling. In a whisper I entreated him to walk slowly and as we finally strode out into the street I turned around to find Edwin so out of breath I feared he would faint.

Thomas was fine with the arrangement and dismissed my concern that Cardoon and Bilge may have some villainous plot in mind that could ruin us all. The release of one thousand pounds was arranged by Daniel for the following week and the matter stood without further comment until once again I walked with Edwin by my side to meet Cardoon at his office in Crane Street, complying with his hitherto demand. As a security against somebody trying to steal the black leather case holding the money that I gripped so tightly, Thomas followed behind as we made our way from Blue Boar Row. Indeed all was fine until we neared our destination when a wretched man in rags swaggered over from the front of the workhouse and desperately begged that I give him three or four pounds to save his family from damnation. I declined whilst keeping the discourse pleasant but the disagreeable-looking fellow became aggravated and grabbed hold of the case with some force and with almost ample strength to take it away. I pulled the case back towards me as Edwin froze still to the spot and Thomas hurriedly made his way to help. Without warning a perfect stranger of a man disengaged the wretch's grasp and sent him sprawling to the floor.

"Go on your way," said the man in a rural dialect.

The wretch obeyed and ran down towards the river. Thomas

stopped running and now calmly walked by, bidding me a good day as if a total stranger.

"Thank you, I am indeed obliged to you sir," said I to the stranger.

"Indeed but I had good reason to help," the man stroked his shaggy black moustache. He wore a long blue coat that almost reached his boots and stunk of stale tobacco smoke.

Before I could inquire of his reason the door to the office of Cardoon Loan and Life Assurance Company was opened. "I see you have already met the Stork then," cried Bilge.

The man now known as the Stork shook me firmly by the hand as a preliminary to Bilge ushering us all through to the small cramped office up the stairs. Cardoon once again sat waiting in the gloom.

"Straight to the point of money," Cardoon said, "I take it you have it all in that case?"

"I do indeed sir," I answered, "you will find it all in order."

"May you oblige and open it," Cardoon responded as he brought the solitary gas lamp in the room to the front of the desk. "Place it here."

I did as requested and the numerous bundles of notes were soon on display. Cardoon sat staring at the case for some minutes with a look of satisfaction.

"I guess we are in business," Bilge interposed rubbing his hands at the prospect of holding his cut.

"We are," I assented as Edwin stood idle and mute by my side.

Bilge and Cardoon looked at each other as if they could not believe what was happening and a long pause followed.

"W-w-w-w-what next?" stammered Edwin.

"We will carry out the task for which we are entrusted" Cardoon spoke to me directly in reply before turning to the Stork, "our friend here has a highly suitable carriage and is known to make frequent and sometimes highly irregular trips to London. You have just purchased his services, albeit that we must now wait in patience until December. Once the time is upon us you can have Mick Mickle send a message to Bilge at The King's Head who will afterwards consign the news to the Stork. Notwithstanding Bilge will confirm the details of the conveyance by the very next evening."

"I will be gladly at your service," said the Stork advancing his craggy face into the light, "will it just be you to take with me apart from the child?"

"No, I will be accompanied by my brother-in-law too," I answered.

Cardoon changed in his manner as his face altered horribly, "maybe that ought to be extra."

"No," I returned rather firmly causing Edwin to jolt in fear, "we stick with the agreed fee."

"Aha! So it will be that if we push too hard you will indeed snap in your temper," cried Cardoon, "I like your spirit sir and will respect our original deal. However I sense that there is more to this arrangement than you are letting on and will tell the Stork here to be in dutiful observation at all times. Should he impart news of some greater magnitude or mischief then I cannot swear that I will not use it to further advantage when the deed is complete."

"Upon my word you will not find such a game to play," I replied indignantly to the obvious threat of blackmail.

"Aye, aye! Do you hear that my friends?" Cardoon almost whispered, "it is either a bluff or a challenge." He then pushed forward a bottle of wine set upon the table and laughed, "we shall now not trouble ourselves with anything other than sharing a drink to toast the undoubted success of our arrangement."

Cardoon took a swig of wine from the bottle and passed it round to all present in turn. It was sharp and bitter in taste but was the seal to an unwritten and illegal contract, now set in unyielding motion.

Chapter XVI - *A family matter with the death of my Father and finding unexpected comfort with a lady travelling to Plymouth.*

In truth I was abashed whenever I took the time to contemplate the reality of the commitment now made. For a while I could not make up my mind whether to flee and hide in another town far away but in truth I simply beheld the comfort of my life to be of more importance than my pride. I still traced this whole diabolical catalogue of events back to the death of Emma Toopey, for whom I had held a higher love than I was ever allowed to express. All thoughts of romance and the passion of my dreams were now hidden so deep within. Nobody else had the least idea of my secret save for my father who had witnessed that final tender moment I shared with Emma as she lay in doleful stillness on her deathbed. It is befitting that I state this fact for it was in the August of 1854 that I must record the sad passing of my father. He died as the result of a hideous infection that came from examining the wound of a mason working on the Cathedral. I will not forget how I felt on hearing the news from Lilly, which was bestowed with all the tenderness of my dear sister's kind heart. Lilly held my hand with a gentle sisterly affection as the tears on her cheek betrayed the sad declaration before a single word was uttered. As confirmation came in a whisper I realised that through my own errant deeds that I had not seen my father for some six months. I felt such shame that his fever had brought a withering death over several weeks and yet he had beseeched Lilly not to bother me. I tried to seek repose but instead broke down crying in my sister's arms in submission that I had failed my own family. It is a memory that I dwell on with nothing but pain.

In the midst of Lilly and I holding each other tight in mourning, I caught sight of Dorothea standing in the doorway. My wife was wearing a cushion beneath her dress to fool the world that she was with child and far from her face being sullen she instead smiled broadly, making no attempt to offer words of condolence or step forward to comfort her devastated husband. I actually have no doubt that she found some pleasure in my exhibition of sorrow as she turned at first to move away with quiet footsteps so as not to be noticed. Instead she looked back one more time and realising she had caught my eye, seemed to taunt with some delight as she winked with great exaggeration.

In the days leading up to the funeral I saw nothing of Dorothea, instead choosing to stay with Lilly and Thomas. My spirits were low but I did find solace in seeing Lilly so doting and happy with her children. I am conscious even now of the turmoil in my mind and can recollect the burial as if it was yesterday. As the coffin was lowered into the ground at the church of St George, I could not look down but instead watched the faces of the small crowd gathered to pay respect. The sound of the clergyman's voice sounded with distinct crispness on a warm sunny day through an otherwise solemn silence. As the final declaration was made, Lilly began to sob and hold my arm ever tighter. I somehow managed to retain composure as I observed the contemptible and unnameable behaviour of both Dorothea and Thomas as they stood on the other side of the grave. In summary, they were whispering and laughing as if attending some quaint garden party. Each would take it in turn to lean forward and speak before causing the other to snigger. Their pitiful and childish show had no respect for the occasion and was looked on with some scorn by the others present. As we walked away from the church on impulse I found the courage to protest vehemently to Dorothea about her behaviour as Lilly was led away by Thomas.

"You speak with such little experience of how a lady must deal with her emotions whilst carrying a child," Dorothea cried whilst fanning her face and blushing out of character. "I find your affection so lacking my husband and fear I must retire to the bedroom immediately as I now feel quite unwell."

So ended my attempt to shame Dorothea as my remonstrance had been of no use. It was now that I was observed in a bad way as the other mourners showed concern at my supposed pregnant wife holding her hand tight to the bump created by a very large cushion. An affronted couple led my actress of a wife to a nearby chaise. I saw no prospect in responding in such an aggravating circumstance and instead took myself down to the Rose and Crown Inn to drink several glasses of ale.

I was happy to wallow in solitary pity but found my attention drawn by a pretty girl staying at the Inn to break her journey to Plymouth. I say this to remark on every significant event of the time, and it was here that I found temporary reverie after engaging in conversation with this girl who had such a good-natured, albeit very pale, face. It is with a smile that I recollect how I introduced myself in a state of inebriation as a down trodden husband banished to a life of misery. The girl did not have to overcome any shyness whatsoever and came to sit by my side.

"I shall be happy to be in your company sir for I too am part of a cruel loveless marriage," said the girl with an air of boldness as she held out her dainty right hand. "My name is Dora."

"Charmed I am sure Dora," I kissed her hand very gently as my heart beat faster, " I am Cedric," I lied without pausing to consider.

"You're quite a lover I suppose?" Dora said coyly

"Why yes," I replied astonished.

With such an immodest introduction we then moved on to engage in such open and honest conversation to finish most of the evening. After an hour I even confided that Cedric was not my real name and replaced it with Ralph. In turn I learned that Dora was really Janet and that she was married to an extremely rich landowner who treated his tenants, cattle and wife with the same equal contempt. His tenants were forced to endure such hardship in order to pay an ever increasing high rent; his cattle were poorly kept in small cramped fields and his wife often beaten in a drunken rage whenever the brute found fault in her housekeeping. This vile man apparently had so many mistresses in Plymouth that he barely had time to share his own wife's bed. Occasionally Janet was sent to London to stay with her husband's Aunt so that he would be free to do as he wished in his own home. Janet was now returning to Plymouth after spending two months in the capital, where she was little more than a maid to the overbearing and conceited Aunt.

I found myself comforting this pitiful girl and she readily accepted consolation. Janet ventured to suggest that I could stay with her for the night as her room was situated at a height that would be easy to climb from the garden below. I really ought to have politely declined and left Janet at this point to return home but did not have the strength of purpose. She left to retire to her room and I went outside to make my way down the street and through to the back of the Inn, cutting myself on brambles as I went. Finally I looked up to the small window above and could make out the sweet expression on Janet's face as she held a small gas lamp before her. After looking around to make sure I was alone it was a simple task to climb the ivy as Janet pulled the window open. She welcomed me into the room with open arms and a tender kiss that melted away any lingering doubt upon my impulsive action.

Of course we found ourselves on the bed and made love so passionately that it is still a joyful memory to behold. When I awoke in the morning I found Janet already dressed and ready to leave. With a sweet innocence she lent over and kissed me on the cheek before leaving as the morning light began to creep under the curtain. I looked on in silence as she went, comparing her departure in my mind to the day that Emma Toopey left me in dejection by the side of the Avon. Just as I had made a resolution to keep my feelings for Emma within my own thoughts, I would now commit this meeting with Janet in the same vein.

Now through the evening that I had found my passion with Janet I had thought little or nothing about returning home the next morning. Any separation from Dorothea, or even the shortest of partings, was now a time of pleasure. I had a true void in my heart that left me numb to the pain of reality, with a wife that was nothing but an agitation. As the door to our house opened I found myself laughing uncontrollably on impulse, determined to mock Dorothea like a giddy, naughty, child. This was the result I suppose of me dreaming about how life should have been and wishing to cast the bland truth to damnation. However it was not she but just a maid. Dorothea had not been home too, spending the evening with Thomas and Lilly.

Chapter XVII - *In which the past catches up with Mick Mickle but on this occasion he is saved by an apparent stranger.*

So the months slipped away and nothing was altered save the change in season. By the autumn, Sevastopol had finally fallen and huge bonfire was lit in the Market Place as Salisbury rejoiced and celebrated a momentous victory for England. In the background and away from the jubilation, the stooping figure of Edwin Gurden made his way to The King's Head under the guise of Mick Mickle. Once at the Inn, Edwin quickly spied the ragged figure of Bilge sat in a dark corner by himself, supping the last dregs of his ale. Instead of going to join the slovenly crook in an instant, Edwin made his way to the bar and had two glasses filled with fresh frothing ale. It was a wise move as Bilge was now so exulted in greeting Edwin that many would have thought them good friends. It proved to be quite prophetic that the only interruption came when Bilge abruptly dashed over to talk to the Landlord. Edwin stood in a very uncomfortable manner as he was left and wondered what business Bilge had with the Landlord that could not wait until later. He watched as the Landlord immediately sent a boy on an errand, clearly as a result of the conversation. Once Bilge returned and the ale was drunk, Edwin received assurance that the necessary arrangement would be made by the next evening as promised. With this remark Edwin shook Bilge heartily by the hand and begged his leave. As he left, Bilge made a hasty retreat to join a crowd by the bar and then simply disappeared.

"Curse my life if it ain't the traitor Mick Mickle," said a sneering unkempt rogue as he blocked Edwin's way near the door.

Edwin was so taken by surprise and scared beyond belief that he was close to soiling his clothes. His stammer was so bad that he could not utter a single word in reply as the man gave a toothless smile that was almost hidden beneath a wild grey beard that was covered in the remnants of a recent meal. The man grabbed Edwin's chin and twisted his head sharply to one side, laughing as Edwin winced in pain.

"Years have passed since we last met Mickle and yet your skin is as smooth as silk. No hard times for you I fancy." The man pulled Edwin to one side as another man of similar appearance held up a lighted candle to their captive's face. His eyes grew even wider with fear as the second man pushed the sharp blade of a knife up against his arm.

"P-p-p-lease Sir," Edwin pleaded, "I deeply regret if I have offended you somehow but I truly believe that your thoughts of me are unjust."

"Unjust," the first man repeated, "do you not think it unjust that our dear cousins did hang at the Fisherton gallows? And they did so because you betrayed them Mickle."

Edwin looked from one man to the other and could see a family resemblance between them despite their sullied beards. Furthermore their personal appearance was oddly familiar and it did not take long for Edwin to perceive a connection with acquaintances from his past. It was a recollection that left Edwin cold to the bone. He had been accosted by relatives of George and Robert Crabbe and there was a real wildness in their eyes.

"Come a little closer Mickle and meet your worst nightmare," the first man's greasy expression indicated how he was ready to harm or even kill his meek captive. "Aye it is true that I am James

Slymetoe and this be my brother Martin, so happy to be back in Salisbury to avenge the memory of George and Robert Crabbe."

"But they were my friends." Edwin pleaded as James pulled him towards the door and outside into the rain by yanking his coat collar with Martin pushing the petrified captive from behind, frequently jabbing the sharp knife into his back as well.

It is needless to say that no other villain in the place was interested in helping Edwin as he was shoved towards the Avon that flowed as a torrent between the Infirmary and the King's Head. In a moment Edwin was tumbled down to the water's edge by a violent shove from Martin Slymetoe. My old school friend was broken and so full of fear as James Slymetoe took a hurried step and aimed a wild hard kick into his stricken victim's chest. Edwin screamed in pain and tried to roll away as Martin aimed another kick to his head. The blow glanced him but sent Edwin's wig flying into the water; his disguise was no more.

"Look at this!" cried James, "He ain't what he seems this treacherous coward. Two faced for sure."

"For sure, Bilge said there was a queerness about him," Martin laughed as Edwin's body convulsed, both trembling in fear and shivering as the cold water of the Avon soaked through to his skin.

"Be quiet you idiot," James scolded his brother before relenting, "although it is of no harm that this wretch knows who sold his head."

Edwin recovered his senses for a moment to fully contemplate that Bilge had betrayed him. But worse was the fact that this knowledge was seen to be of no concern, as Edwin instantly surmised that he was to be killed.

"Who are you really then Mickle? And what game are you playing with your rich friends?" asked James as he took the knife from Martin and cut Edwin's left cheek with a flick of his wrist.

"I am nobody, t-t-t-truly nobody," Edwin stammered as blood ran down his face.

James thrust his face towards Edwin and bit hard upon his ear. As Edwin screamed for mercy in such pain, the villain clamped down hard with his teeth until he had severed the top part of the ear away. More blood gushed and Edwin now cried like a baby.

"Why he just don't know what to say," cried James, "he's as mute as a snake."

"Yes sir, and soon you shall be equally as dumb," a stranger's voice murmured.

"Off with you," shouted James Slymetoe in anger as he turned to survey the stranger.

The stranger was tall and wrapped in a large black cloak, his face obscured to all but his eyes by a thick scarf that also muffled his speech. From beneath the cloak the stranger was holding an old pistol and aiming it straight at James Slymetoe. For a moment the two men looked at each other in silence before the stranger fired the pistol. Smoke bellowed into the cold autumn air as the stranger reeled backwards from the force of the shot. James Slymetoe also fell backwards in to the river as he was filled with gunshot. His dead body soon floated nearby. Before Martin Slymetoe could respond, the stranger fired a second pistol and sent the hapless crook to his death into the same cold river as his brother. With no other consideration, the stranger pulled the bleeding Edwin to his feet and hurried him away from the King's Head and down towards Crane Street. At length as they reached a nearby bridge, angry shouting and anguished screaming could be heard through the still air. The stranger's eyes darted pensively as he looked back down the river at the gathering crowd retrieving the dead bodies of James and Martin Slymetoe from the Avon.

"Come quickly Edwin or we will be lynched by the mob," a familiar voice declared.

The brazen saviour then hailed a carriage that was waiting nearby and hurried Edwin aboard just as the mob made a resolute move towards them, screaming and yelling with such anger in the process. It was the last that Edwin could remember of that night as he soon passed out as a result of the incessant loss of blood just as the carriage made its way through the night.

Edwin awoke in a large comfortable bed, roused by the loud knocking on a door. His eyes opened to see my sister Lilly holding a sliver tray, upon which was a steaming bowl of porridge. Thomas was also present and sat by Edwin's bed.

"Why I do believe the patient is awake," Lilly declared.

"I dare say he did smell the porridge as he has just this minute stirred," returned Thomas.

Edwin jolted in sudden shock, kicking up his feet from beneath the bed sheets and causing Lilly to start. The awful memories of the night before flooded Edwin's mind like the darkest of nightmares. He instinctively reached up to his right ear and felt that it was heavily bandaged, and as he brushed his palm against a swollen cheek there was the unmistakable evidence of a ragged scar.

"It is my due to say that you are a very lucky man to be alive dear friend," said Thomas as Edwin's panic subsided and the patient paused to look around, uncertain of why he had ended up in the Endstreet house.

"Upon my confusion, whatever happened?" Edwin cried. "However did I end up here?"

"Why my dear Edwin, you were set upon and robbed by scoundrels," Lilly responded. "It was only by pure chance that Thomas was passing and found you in a heap on the floor, bleeding."

"It is the truth Edwin," Thomas confirmed without looking towards his bewildered friend.

"I must urge you to rest dear Edwin. I have already sent word to Hetty and told her that she must not worry as you are recovering well and have been tended to by a doctor. She will be here to see you this afternoon," said Lilly. "Now Thomas if you will be so good as to let Edwin sleep." Lilly rose up to leave and signalled for Thomas to follow.

"Just a moment dear," Thomas held up a hand to delay his departure, "I just need a very quick word with poor Edwin. It is gentleman's talk."

"You are obliged to be brief," Lilly returned before leaving the room.

"I must be quick as Lilly will be waiting for me take my leave," Thomas whispered. "Doubtless you have realised that it was I who saved you last night after you were set upon outside the King's Head."

"I did not know that," Edwin shrugged his shoulders. "How did you know to be there in order to save me?"

"In short I did not trust that crook Bilge and so kept close to you in case something untoward might happen. And happen it did," replied Thomas. "He sold your head despite his hatred for the Crabbes."

"But I did not notice you throughout the evening," rejoined Edwin.

"I was in disguise too," cried Thomas, "so that not even my sister would have recognised me."

"I am so gratefully disposed to you Thomas," Edwin said tearfully, "but I saw you murder two men. How did you come upon those pistols?"

"Those pistols have been in the possession of the Endstreet family for over sixty years. I am told they once belonged to the highwayman William Peare of Cricklade, who was hanged for his crimes in this very town," answered Thomas. "I had no idea they would work until I fired that first shot."

"Please leave Edwin be now," Lilly had returned and was stood in the doorway.

"I am just coming now," replied Thomas. "Do not worry about Bilge for I will be paying him another visit and ensuring we are given the service that was agreed upon," whispered Thomas as he lent over Edwin, "sleep well."

Edwin did not reply and soon fell asleep, remaining so until late into the afternoon when he was awoken by his tearful and distraught wife, Hetty. As she sat by his bed, Hetty showed so much concern that any observer would have thought Edwin was about to take his last breath. Edwin was finally able to express how comfortable he was and assure Hetty that he would soon return home. Thankfully she left in better sprits, taking a carriage just before nightfall. A short time later, Thomas ghosted through the night in the same disguise he had worn the previous evening and once more he carried the pistols that once belonged to William Peare of Cricklade.

Thomas hurried down into Salisbury by foot and did not seek to engage in conversation with anyone he met on the way, hiding his face behind a scarf. With a great bitterness pushing him on, Thomas was soon at the door of the Cardoon Loan and Life Assurance Company on Crane Street. Cardoon's office was well lit through the gloom, prompting Thomas to make his move without a second thought. He expertly picked the lock and crept into the building before slowly and cautiously making his way to the stairs.

For a moment Thomas paused and listened. He could hear someone talking in a surly tone and then the horrible hacking cough of another. Thomas hauled his scarf up around his face and pulled out the two pistols before stealthily tiptoeing up the stairs.

Thomas pitched straight into the small room where Cardoon and Bilge were in conference. Their conversation terminated abruptly as the two descended into shocked silence at the sight of their unexpected visitor. Thomas moved forward slowly and with caution, holding the two pistols in front of him.

"Stay perfectly still, d'ye hear?" growled Thomas in a deep uncouth voice that mimicked a gamekeeper he had once known on the Wilton estate.

"Who are you?" thundered Bilge, "what business do you have with us?"

"I've come to kill ye," returned Thomas, "pure and simple."

"But why?" said Cardoon trembling.

"You have crossed my friends and even tried to have Mick Mickle killed down the river here," replied Thomas before saying with a voice of command, "now stand up the pair of you."

Cardoon and Bilge rose to their feet with an uneasy manner, wondering what desperate fate awaited them.

"You two agreed a matter of business with my friends and were paid handsomely," rejoined Thomas. "They trusted you and yet I knew you were a couple of bad un's. Nothing but wretched murderous villains; why should I show any mercy and spare you?"

"I-I am so sorry for what we have done. It was nothing but pure greed I must confess. The price on Mick Mickle's head was more than we had ever been paid. I now know that it was the wrong thing to do," Cardoon said submissively.

"Fetch the money you were paid by my friends and the bounty you got from the Slymetoe brothers." Thomas waved his pistols at Bilge.

"Please, you have it in your power to spare us," Bilge cried. "We can still right a wrong and complete the arrangement."

"We would obviously forego any further payment but I regret to say that we have already gambled and lost the money paid by your friend and by the Slymetoe brothers." Cardoon added ruefully.

"Wot is to stop ye crossing my friends again?" snarled Thomas.

"We would not dare," said Bilge sensing a reprieve.

"If you do I have the means to track yer down and I promise you I will seek revenge like a vicious dog protecting his master. I will tear ye both to shreds," replied Thomas, stamping his foot to the wooden floor with a rage.

"We are already in your debt sir and you have my word that we will do everything to help your friends," confirmed Cardoon.

"Very well but I will be watching," Thomas replied and took a step back towards the stairs. "Bring the coachman and his carriage to the Green Croft on the edge of Milford at dawn on Saturday."

"I know it well and you can depend on the fact that the Stork will be there and waiting to take your friends to London," Cardoon simpered.

Thomas showed no emotion as he looked sternly from face to face of the two crooks before him. "If you lay down the slightest challenge or problem, then I shall kill ye both before darkness falls on Saturday."

Cardoon and Bilge drooped their heads in submissive defeat to the barrel of a pistol and in an instant Thomas had gone.

When Thomas relayed the new consideration to me in front of Dorothea, I instantly recoiled at the danger that now presented itself. Dorothea in contrast only held disdainful agitation for my concern

"Why must you be so frequently flurried? Why must I have a husband that grows to be more of a coward by the day?" asked Dorothea with a huff. "It is not so painful to be so much trouble to my dear brother. I only ask that you do this and provide me with a family that you have otherwise threatened to destroy by your unholy actions."

"Look here Ralph, do not fret. Our stratagem is still sound, if altered only slightly. We shall attain our bounty without any harm to your good self. You have my word as oath on the matter." Thomas declared as Dorothea busied herself in stitching a small blanket in preparation for the bought child she would declare to be her own and with I as the father.

I stood there in dumb bewilderment as Thomas slapped my back in encouragement and was left with the desperate conclusion that I must still go through with this crazed and insane plot. The nights that led through to Saturday were mainly sleepless on my part as I turned with frequent anxiety in my lonely bed.

Thomas had informed my concerned sister that I was to accompany him on a very important matter of professional business in London. Lilly was very uncertain about this hasty venture, but on the grounds that I would be leaving Dorothea at a time when she was about to give birth. The concealment of a cushion beneath her clothing had certainly allowed Dorothea the good fortune of fooling

Lilly, and therefore the same held true for our friends, acquaintances and every passing stranger.

Chapter XVIII - *An account of the journey to the slums of London to claim a son, brokered by the rather unsavoury Grittle and his overbearing Aunt.*

On the morning for which Thomas had fixed our departure I was awoken early, before morning had broken, by a loud scraping noise. Soon afterwards the bedroom door creaked open and it quickly became possible to distinguish the figure of Thomas as he appeared out of the shadows of night. He quietly beckoned for me to get up and requested that I meet him at the front of the house promptly. In truth I wished that sleep would simply steal itself upon me and send me into a happy dream, free from reality. Instead I climbed from my bed resolved to face whatever fortune lay ahead.

At the front of my house, Thomas was waiting in the back of a small rusting chariot. Holding the horses to the front of the carriage was none other than Daniel Drumdale.

"Is it not grand that we can call upon the aid of our dear friend Daniel to transport us both at this ungodly hour to Milford," Thomas said. "Better such luxury than the alternative, which would be to walk the streets like a vagrant."

"Thank you Daniel," I added whilst anxiously looking around and then placing my small trunk in the carriage before climbing in to sit next to Thomas.

Thomas gave the signal for Daniel to proceed as if this was the most regular of events and the horse was set towards the town following the direction of the spire. The air was cold and sharp but as I chose to sit in silence, Thomas whistled with an apparent glee. At least the light of morning finally crept in slowly as we neared the Green Croft. Presently, and not long after six o'clock in the morning, the chariot came splashing to halt in the mud. Alongside stood a black heavy coach, with the word 'Salisbury' emblazoned on the luggage cart at the rear, just visible above a bright red wheel. Stood next to the wheel was the Stork, smoking a pipe and looking very miserable.

Thomas and I alighted quickly to shake the Stork's hand in turn without uttering a single word. Our trunks were transferred to the Coach as we bade Daniel farewell. Lost in bewilderment I soon found myself staring through the window as the Stork, grumbling loudly, took the reins and drove the coach away towards London. At the same time but in the opposite direction, Daniel moved the cart off too.

As we moved through the countryside I chose to marvel at nature, finding enjoyment in everything from the sodden green grass glinting in the early morning sunlight to the sound of the birds warbling and trilling with carefree abandon. But I was soon reminded of my own position with the frequent sight of the fallen autumn leaves that covered the ground and muffled the sound of the heavy wheels of the coach. Motionless and decaying to nothing, their purpose in life fulfilled.

"Ralph, am I right in thinking you have lost your zest for life?" asked Thomas rather abruptly.

"You do speak the truth, of that there is no denying," I replied honestly. "I am really suffering and have been so for sometime. My mind is so heavy with doubt and self-loathing."

"Ah, and all because of my dear sister I fancy," Thomas cried.

"I don't think it right to speak ill of Dorothea for the fact that she is your sister," I observed.

"Why ever not as she is truly a vile creature," returned Thomas. "Whatever man was destined to be her husband was sure to have a hard bout of it. It is such a shame that it was you dear friend that fell into her clutches before you could find the true love of another. I speak as a man of great experience having truly lost my heart on two occasions. First there was Emma Toopey, God rest her soul, and now your delicate beautiful sister, Lilly. But you my friend have been snared by Dorothea like a rabbit in a trap, with no time to look within your heart."

The mere mention of Emma Toopey sent a shiver down my spine, but the truth of Emma's heart rendering confession of love on her deathbed would stay with me as a secret for the rest of my days.

"Why do you submit to help in this pitiful cause if you hate your sister so?" I asked

"Because it will make her happy. I am prepared to be made a convenience of to ensure a quiet and profitable life. Dorothea is a strong woman of business in a man's world and will see me in comfort for the rest of my life as long as she is content," returned Thomas. "My advice to you is to follow my lead and make an end of it."

"I cannot submit to this and act like a fool for the rest of my life," I answered emphatically.

"Good gracious, you have no other choice!" exclaimed Thomas, "You are seeking, and will find, a pardon in supplying this child. A pardon for your exploits with a common prostitute. Now think carefully, for once Dorothea has her child you will be free to lead an independent life away from being on show as her husband, just as I must be on show for being her brother. Make the most of your opportunity and seek out true love if you must, but be discreet."

I was almost too overcome to speak with the realisation of the advice that Thomas was giving me. Of course! Dorothea did not have to dictate the course of my life but rather she would be the provider of my good fortune, believing that she was in control and yet it would be I that was the true puppeteer.

After musing with an ever growing smile, I shook Thomas by the hand. "I now see how my position will be truly altered on our return."

Thomas pressed my hand firmly, "I am glad we understand each other."

We only came to rest but twice on the journey to London, such was the haste with which the Stork wished to be there by just after nightfall. Brooding indeed for most of that day, the Stork spoke very little apart from showing his impatience to reach our destination or to express his hatred for Mick Mickle and the mysterious masked murderer who watched over him.

"I am obliged to see this through so my friends do not end up in the Avon with a bullet in their backs," cried the Stork just before we began the final leg. "I tell you though that once I am discharged from this plot I will seek out the impostor Mickle and then his guardian with the pistols. I shall seek them out and end their days."

"How shall you find Mickle?" I returned before telling a lie, "I have not seen him since before his last meeting with Bilge."

"It will be easy," the Stork laughed, "he is the most wretched cheat in all of Salisbury. The word is out and with a price of thirty shillings too, so you might as well fix a signpost right to his door."

"I heard it was ascertained that the scoundrel was dead," said Thomas. "I only heard this from a stranger as did not know this Mickle at all, apart from knowing he was a crook. We only found ourselves in such an ill-conceived union with the man in order that we would inadvertently reach the right people that might help us in our situation. Despite having a dreadful suspicion that we would somehow be wronged, it was concluded that Mickle was our only hope. By the end he robbed a large amount of silver from my friend's house when we refused to pay him more money."

"So how did you know to be at the Green Croft this morning if Mickle double crossed you and fled?" the Stork asked, moving up close to Thomas.

"His accomplice," returned Thomas. "I have never heard his name nor seen his face, but this man was the one who handled all the business discussions. He always spoke from behind a scarf and all I can tell you was that he had piercing eyes and talked as if his throat held on to a constant handful of gravel. Mickle was no more than a servant to the man. It was he who assured us that Mickle was dead and that we were to be at the Green Croft this morning as the deal had been concluded at the agreed price."

"Then the situation is obvious," said the Stork, "all this handiwork is down to this stranger. It might be that he has murdered Mickle himself, for which I will thank him. I will then kill him."

"How will you find him," I asked.

"With these eyes and more cunning than you will ever know," was the Stork's answer, and with his final words until we reached London. Whenever I chanced to look at him I swear I could spot a hint of suspicion in the Stork's face regarding Thomas's false assertion about our connexion with Mick Mickle.

We made it to London in good time, just as darkness fell, but the coach came to stand in the middle of a slum that was somewhere south of the Thames. It was on Thomas's prompt that we came to a halt having previously provided the Stork with specific directions to this pitiful part of the Capital. Thomas left me in the coach alone, under the pretence of seeking out the friend who would provide us with lodgings and also broker the deal for the child. With my attention distracted as I awaited Thomas's return from the small dark alley into which he had just disappeared, I was surprised by a small child in rags who had stealthily climbed into the carriage.

"Can you spare a crust of bread kind sir?" the frail urchin muttered.

"Oh Lor!" cried I in surprise as if a rat had climbed upon my lap.

The startled boy fled just as Thomas returned, "whatever is afoot?"

"Just a young guttersnipe looking for food," the Stork replied on my behalf from above. "Reckon your friend here would die of fright if you leave him on his own for an hour in this place. Reckon he knows nothing of life without a servant to guide him." The Stork laughed loudly as I pondered that maybe there was some truth in his comment.

Thomas readily capitulated on the remark too in a loud voice before climbing up to enter into a whispered conversation with the Stork. No sooner had he climbed up than Thomas was down again and ushering me from the carriage. Peering timorously as I alighted, a ghastly pungent smell of effluent engulfed my senses and brought me close to vomiting. This was a repugnant neighbourhood in a desperate district of London. Several men were deep in discussion nearby as countless dogs roamed aimlessly. A loud roar erupted from a nearby Inn, which preceded two men falling through the front door and onto the cobbled street as they fought viciously; gouging, punching and scratching as if their lives depended on it.

"Maybe my friend we should get you inside," said Thomas as he took down the trunks and then thumped his fist twice on the side of the coach. It was the signal for the Stork to depart and within minutes the coach rattled away as it traversed down the street and was soon out of sight.. "Do not fret, it is well planned and the coach shall return by this time tomorrow when we shall travel through the night and be back in Salisbury before dawn with a son to present to Dorothea."

Thomas led me down a filthy narrow alleyway that was so dark that I did not see a small dog by my feet, tripping and falling to the floor as a consequence. Thomas helped me up and pulled me onwards, warning that it was not wise to loiter. We soon stopped before a large black door of what appeared to be a derelict house. Thomas sounded the huge brass knocker as I looked around cautiously, twitching at every sound that echoed down the passage behind. The door creaked open and a very tall man dressed in rags stooped to usher us in, chaining and bolting the door the moment we were inside. The man held a candle in his hand as he took us down the hall and up a flight of stairs and then into a room full of old wooden furniture that was mostly rotten and riddled with worm. A large fire and small gas lamp provided the room with light. A very plump lady in a stained grey dress sat rocking on a high backed chair, observing Thomas and I with a scowl as we entered.

"Here they are my dear Aunt," exclaimed the man, "thought you best view them before I show them to their room."

"Anything appear a-miss Grittle?" bawled the woman.

"No," replied Grittle, "I have been paid as agreed and taken the liberty of putting the money in your room within your special box."

"And you are sure they are not thieves who will venture to rob us when the job is done?" rejoined the old lady.

"I am sure Aunt, and this one seems to be frightened of his own shadow." Grittle pointed a grimy finger so close to my face that he nearly poked my eye.

The old lady laughed heartily, "You are a good boy Grittle. The agreement is therefore done and as a bargain I dare say."

Grittle looked at his Aunt with pride as she sat in a regal manner with her arms folded and her eyes fixed directly upon me. "So are you to be the father to this child," she said after a pause.

"That is true," I replied.

"And yet I sense you are not happy about this extraordinary thing," said the old lady. "And why is that? What are the circumstances? Under the influence of a strong woman will be your answer."

"If that is what you believe than that is what it is," I replied with some assertion.

"Oh it is the truth for you are put upon and no mistake," the old lady laughed. "Grittle, give the two of 'em some bread and soup and then a brandy as a nightcap. I will see you gentleman off home tomorrow with the precious child. Until then sleep well and stay out of my way," she said whilst picking up a walking stick and pointing it towards the door as a signal for Grittle to usher Thomas and I to our room.

Grittle moved unsteadily, still stooping as he walked and almost dropping his diminishing candle on several occasions. He pushed open the door of a back room and we followed after him with our trunks. The walls and ceiling were covered in mould and dirt, but it was the stench of damp and grease that was most oppressive. Two rusty old iron beds stood at the far end dressed in discoloured and heavily stained sheets that looked like they were made from sacking. There was also a table with a small candle set in the middle within a glass bottle, two chairs and an unlit fire. Grittle lit the candle from the wick of his own and then thankfully started the fire that was already stacked with wood.

"Ain't it grand," cried Grittle, "make yourselves at home and I shall go and fetch the soup from the saucepan bubbling in my own room and see if I can find some crusts of bread lying about."

As Grittle moved away Thomas immediately drew the chairs next to the fire that thankfully caught quickly as was already bright with flames that offered welcome heat.

"Now if you please why are we staying in this hovel?" I shouted in anger.

"It is on their insistence for they think we will cross them somehow if we are not here to be kept an eye on," returned Thomas. "I grant you that I have not stayed in worse than this before, but it is just for one night and we will be on our way before the sun sets tomorrow."

- 164 -

"I really do not think I have the strength of disposition to spend a night here," I said in reply, fearing for my health. "I am sure we will both have fevers by morning."

"We will be fine, you will see," replied Thomas with a rueful look as Grittle returned with a tray that held two pewter bowls of foul smelling soup with several stale crusts of bread scattered around.

In short the soup could hardly be eaten despite our hunger, although the bread was adequate sustenance. Grittle then left us with a bottle of brandy that thankfully numbed the senses and helped our travel weary bodies find sleep through the night on the damp uncomfortable beds.

And then the next day finally came, bringing with it the stark reality that this contrived plot would soon be concluded. Either that or Thomas and I would be done away with and sent to a watery grave in the Thames. That was my thought on the matter and not one that Thomas entertained without irritation.

After a ghastly breakfast prepared by Grittle of sausages and more stale bread, I bestowed on Thomas the need to take some air, however foul that might be in this particular part of London. So we ventured for a walk to pass the time before the arrival of the child, when we could return to the sanity and sanctuary of Salisbury.

We paced the gloomy narrow streets that were monotonous in their similarity. Long lines of grey cobbles that meandered across murky thoroughfares and by the side of dark, dull houses. Row after row of grey houses with not a hint of nature; no fields, trees or plants to glisten in the morning sunlight. In the air was the smell of the sewer that caused a continuous frown on the faces of the people we saw who dared to unbolt their doors for a moment and step outside. Gasping for dear life, Thomas and I almost marched towards the river and thankfully happened upon a more affluent district after walking for nearly an hour. Now the houses were much bigger and more colourful, built with elegance and resplendent under the blue sky.

I spied a coffee-house at the bottom of small steep hill and undertook to Thomas that we would stay there for long as we could before returning through the slums to our unfortunate lodgings.

"At least this is a more agreeable place in which to bide our time," I said as we took a seat in the quaint coffee-house and ordered some drinks.

"It is charming," replied Thomas, "just charming."

"I wish to be candid," I returned, "How did you come to know the rather odd Grittle and his sinister aunt?"

"Through a business acquaintance in the city, although it was an acquaintance I made in spite of my gambling debts." Thomas pondered for a moment, "Grittle and his aunt run a baby farm, seeing a business opportunity to broker children born into poverty for a better life. All around them are poor destitute mothers wanting to see their wretched children given a chance to live into adulthood. And for this chance they are also paid handsomely, with Grittle, or rather his aunt, taking a commission."

"Are these mothers not in the right state of mind to see the merits in nurturing their own children? Surely they must?" I spoke in horror.

"Obviously not or tonight we would not have a child to take home with a mother holding a substantial purse of money in its place," replied Thomas.

"I still have a recurring dreadful fear about what this really means," I cried with obvious doubt.

After some time, and with my rueful refrain not forgotten, we finally strode out of the coffee-house to prepare to walk back to the lodgings well before nightfall. This time Thomas walked ahead in silence after lighting a cigarette, as I followed closely feeling somewhat helpless. With a weary heart, I walked back into the gloom of the slums as my throat was again overcome by the stench that left me gasping. Any conversation with Thomas was kept short on the odd occasion that we stopped for a rest and in the end I was actually quite pleased to be welcomed by Grittle back into his pitiful house.

As night began to fall, I found myself stood in the poorly lit hallway alongside Thomas and with our trunks on the floor. Grittle was standing by the hallway door holding a diminishing candle, simply smiling at very opportunity and with a nervous twitch to boot. A sudden loud knock on the thick oak door startled us all. Grittle moved forward to open it and in scurried his aunt in a black hooded coat, holding a ragged bundle to her chest. I shivered as she resembled some ghastly Ghoul.

"Gentlemen, here is the merchandise which you came to London to purchase," the old hag said in triumph. She then laid down the bundle on a small cabinet to reveal a tiny baby within the patchwork blanket, still smeared in the blood from its very recent entry into the world. The old hag smacked the child with the back of her hand and it instantly wailed. "Healthy as you can see."

"Thank you," Thomas stepped forward to comfort the child and gather it up in the blanket. "And with good time as the Stork will be back on the street by now," added Thomas a he glanced at his pocket watch.

"Is it fair to ask if the mother was in good sprits when she handed over her child?" I asked whilst resisting Thomas's attempt to pass me the baby.

"My dear, she was full of joy," the aunt laughed, "taking nothing but pleasure that her son would enjoy a good life. She thanked me with tears of happiness upon her face."

"I don't doubt it at all," Thomas returned, "now come Ralph for the Stork awaits and we dare not miss our carriage back to Salisbury"

"Now take this in case the child should get hungry but only let it have a little at a time if it really needs it". The woman handed me a bottle that I assumed held bovine milk.

The purchase complete, Grittle ushered Thomas and I from the house, closing the door with rapidity as soon as we were back on the cobbled alley. I was at least pleased to see the carriage waiting at the spot where it had left us the night before. The Stork looked down on us in silence as Thomas forced the child into my arms so that he could load our trunks. Immediately we were given another demonstration of the powerful action of the child's lungs as it wailed loudly. Thomas almost pushed me on board with a plea to comfort my son. It was in itself a comment made so that I would realise what I was holding. A son; my son. I had always dreamed of having a son, but never in such a way as this.

Such was the suddenness of it all that soon we were out of London and back in the countryside, with the carriage travelling at speed. The child slept peacefully in my arms and even during the occasional waking moment did not stir with any agitation. Thomas too fell asleep, smiling as he did so. He then took his turn holding the child as I tried to get some rest myself. Even the Stork managed an amiable mutter as he took a look at the child during our first stop.

The child was so limp and quiet that I soon began to fear for its health. Thomas suggested giving the boy a little milk so we signalled for the Stork to stop once more. I took him from his blanket and lay him on the seat but he did not even whimper. Gently I smeared a few droplets of milk on the baby's lips and then watched and waited for a reaction. Thomas and the Stork stood by, earnestly hoping but the boy simply lay still hardly able to keep its eyes open. I gave it a little more milk and began to wonder if this whole convoluted plot was doomed to failure after all. How ironic that the child's mother had sold him into a better life and yet he may not even live to see morning. I gave a little more milk and then some more. Finally and thankfully there was a sign of revival as the child opened its eyes wide and began to wail. It was a cry that raised a cheer from three very relieved men. A little more milk settled the boy down and I went to wrap him back inside the warmth of the blanket. It was then I noticed the most peculiar thing, a large birthmark on the boy's hip that had the distinct shape of a four leaf clover. It was as if it had been drawn on him such was the sharpness of the image.

"It is indeed a lucky child," said Thomas.

The journey passed on down dusty roads that ran through the plains of English countryside hidden by the darkness of night. The child remained placid but thankfully, and despite the horses toiling badly, we made Salisbury in good time just before sunrise. Daniel was waiting diligently with his cart at the Green Croft.

Thomas and I bade the Stork an amicable farewell, but he made a final statement before departing. "Farewell gentlemen and I wish you both well. I doubt that we shall meet again unless you do have an allegiance with the masked stranger, for which you will pay for with your lives. Heed my warning."

I do confess to feeling very concerned at this very disagreeable parting exchange but my inner fear was quickly countered by concern for the sickly child, who once more was very listless. Thomas bade Daniel to take us back to Harnham at speed and he duly obliged, showing no patience whatsoever. On arrival I instantly spied Dorothea looking out from the Drawing Room window and almost immediately Mrs Goodfettle, our recently hired Housekeeper, came to take hold of the child. I anxiously escorted her inside and then upstairs to the Nursery, alongside Dorothea but neither of us acknowledged the presence of the other. Waiting to welcome us was a very plump lady with an extraordinarily fat red face, who filled every inch of the stout wooden rocking chair in which she sat next to a roaring fire. Mrs Goodfettle advanced to pass the limp child into the thick fleshy arms of the portly stranger.

"Take this man's eyes from me," the woman said with hostility whilst looking in my direction.

I tried to edge a reply in but was ushered away in unison by Mrs Goodfettle and Dorothea.

"Perhaps somebody could explain what is going on," I cried once on the landing as the door was shut on the Nursery.

"Hush, Hush!" Dorothea replied in agitation, "Let us pass to the Drawing Room and I will explain."

"Well?" I returned on entering the Drawing Room, where Thomas was sat dozing on the sofa by the fire.

"Well sir, I shall be plain with you," Dorothea replied. "The lady has been hired into a position at my behest during your absence. She has foremost been hired as a Nanny, but will fulfil a vital role as a wet nurse to our son. The child needs fuel to survive and I assume I do not need to enlighten you on the service the Nanny will provide in feeding him sufficiently."

Indeed I required no further explanation and began to relax in the knowledge that the boy was in good hands. I took a seat next to Thomas feeling exhausted from the effect of the journey. Dorothea and Mrs Goodfettle left the room with no more to say and I closed my eyes with willing ease. Soon Thomas and I were both snoring loudly as we sat side by side on the sofa.

I awoke some hours later and found myself alone. Still feeling sleepy and whilst rubbing my eyes, I went back up the stair case in the direction of muffled voices coming from the Nursery. Mrs Goodfettle was stood by the door, "Here's good news for you sir, the boy is going to be fine. The Nanny's a good 'un and no mistake."

I offered a smile in reply and with curiosity looked into the room, where the plump lady was busy preparing the crib whilst Dorothea stood nearby cradling the child and sobbing like I had never seen before. "The Lord bless you," Dorothea cried over and over again.

I retreated out of view and bumped into Mrs Goodfettle, who had been collecting sheets and blankets to make up the Nanny's bed in the Nursery.

"It is thought better that the boy and the Nanny should rest for now and not be fatigued any further," said Mrs Goodfettle. "The boy is still quite yellow and weak but has been well fed. A doctor has been whilst you slept and was happy enough. Took him outside for a while for some air and the boy didn't arf enjoy it. He's bonded with Mrs Chatterforth straight away. Reckon you'll do well to get any kind of attention from the mistress right now sir, if you don't mind me saying."

"It's no great matter at all," I replied without concern, knowingly raising my eyebrows at the irony of Mrs Goodfettle's harmless observation.

Feeling at a loss in my own house, I endeavoured to go for a walk and clear the muddled thoughts in my head. At first the bright winter sun dazzled my eyes as a sharp cold wind stung my unshaven face. Stroking my chin I vowed to grow a beard from that day. Dorothea hated the notion of men wearing beards. Uplifted by such a childish jape, I strolled down to the cathedral with a spring in my step and instantly felt comforted by the majestic spire reaching to the sky, towering above the town. I stood wistfully for sometime by the cloisters looking up in awe to the top of the spire before moving inside and taking a seat in the Nave. In solitude I renounced my sins in a whisper and felt such solace. I prayed for my son and for his real mother. I finally left to return home as night fell, with an overwhelming feeling of contentment, and also hunger as my previously repressed appetite returned.

Chapter XIX - *In which I become a member of the exclusive Dragon Gentleman's Club and encounter two bounders, Punting and Daffrey. An imprudent wager leads to public humiliation but the tables are soon turned.*

Throughout the weeks and months that followed, Dorothea divided her time in equal measure to either the world of business or tenderly caring for the child. Incidentally he was baptised Arthur Thomas Chatterforth, taking the names of Dorothea's beloved Grandfather and of course her errant Brother. When Dorothea was not present the plump Nanny, who went by the name of Gertrude Stimple, would frequently keep me from seeing Arthur like a dog guarding a bone. The fact that Dorothea was perfectly civil to me in public, holding up the notion of a happy family, cannot be disputed. In private I was shunned by my wife without a single intermission and left only to cultivate a rather splendid beard and find fortitude in my work at the court. I observed with ignominy as the seasons passed and Arthur grew stronger up to the day of his first birthday, a year on from the frantic journey that brought the boy from the slums of London to the clean country air of Salisbury. This was also the day that I cast my humility aside and made a personal pledge to live more freely and damn the consequences with a mutinous spirit. I would no longer stand for Dorothea draining the colour and life-blood from the depths of my soul. Here now stood Ralph Chatterforth, the defiant revolutionary.

It became widely understood that I was a man of little substance in the Chatterforth household and my self esteem had plunged to the very depths. So secretly and fortuitously I moved out of the shadows and established a new circle of friends by joining the ranks of a very exclusive Gentleman's Club on Exeter Street. I became a member of the Dragon Club that has existed for over a hundred years and so named as Exeter Street was once known as Dragon Street. I obtained an advantageous place after being referred under recommendation by a magistrate called Sidney Stroker, a long established club member and newly found friend. Sidney was a good deal older than I and held a very forthright view on any subject you cared to mention. I would often share a jar of ale with him after work in a nearby Inn and be entertained as this incredibly stout man with thick grey whiskers spouted his opinion on all manner of things in a loud aristocratic voice.

"Chatterforth, it is inexcusable that as a true gentleman you do not hold a respectful place in your own household," blustered Stroker on a wet and windy evening as we found refuge by a roaring fire with two large glasses of brandy.

"I have grown accustomed to the situation, and so much so that it no longer seems extraordinary," I replied.

"It is a matter of honour my friend," cried Stroker, "and despite your undaunted courage and restraint, I pledge that I will help you recover your integrity so that you shall walk the streets of Salisbury with your head held high. Permit me to recommend you for immediate acceptance as a member of the Dragon Club, for which incidentally I sit on the committee."

It seemed only prudent to accept the offer, although I truly expected to be found unclubbable despite my backer's assurance. The Dragon Club was known to have strict limits on membership and very long waiting lists. However, the committee meeting was held the following week and I was deemed to be personally acceptable on a subscription of three pounds and three shillings.

And when my initiation came I realised quickly how much better my life was to become. The principle room was exquisite, with lavish furnishing and a well-stocked collection of wines and spirits. One corner was set aside for reading and offered a large supply of newspapers and literature. The other members all seemed so happy and pleasant in their retreat, although the majority where white-headed old gentlemen and very few were of my age.

With all the arrangements completed I was advised of the club rules, which principally ensured allegiance and trust amongst members. To betray another member or to not offer assistance to another member when requested would lead to instant dismissal. In the course of that first evening, Stroker introduced me to a number of other members, including two young landowners called Noah Punting and Arthur Daffrey. Both were seemingly very polite, witty and intelligent.

With this agreeable new situation I felt liberated, finding release from the indescribable suffering that went with being Dorothea's husband. She had long stopped enquiring on my whereabouts, making it easy to stalk out of the house on any evening to venture down to the Dragon Club. I need not make any pretence on my actions as I was never questioned. Without the unpleasant sight of Dorothea's sour face looking at me with constant scorn I was able to engage in cheerful discourse in a wholly genial atmosphere.

I recall feeling rather flushed and giddy on most evenings after always drinking more that I intended. In fact this was true of a lot of the members with one committee meeting being adjourned 'due to the intoxicating state of those present.' Late in the evening the lamps would be dimmed so as not to attract the attention of a passing Peeler. With the flow of liquor came a stream of joke telling, which was often very rough and met with hearty laughing. Throughout the banter was pleasant and would often end in outrageous wagers when an inane challenge was presented for the nominal bet of ten pence.

And so to the wager that was forced upon me by the eminent but, on this occasion, highly inebriated Noah Punting. It was late on a Friday evening and a great deal of liquor had been quaffed, as it was on the occasion of every Friday evening at the Dragon Club.

"In recompense for the princely sum of ten pence, I have a daring challenge for you Ralph," said a triumphant Punting in clear voice as the other Dragon members present gathered round.

"I pray it will not be too difficult as after all it will be my first such undertaking," I answered.

"Such a noble and fine fellow you are Ralph," interjected Daffrey. "I am sure that Noah will be generous in his consideration."

"Quite so," continued Punting with a mischievous smile. "The matter I place in your hands is very simple. Shortly a Peeler will pass this building as he walks down Exeter Street. You are required to return to this room before midnight wearing the Peeler's chimney pot hat. Deliver the hat and claim your reward."

For a moment I ruminated on the task ahead but knew that I had no choice but to accept the wager or risk damnation and expulsion from the club I had come to love. I exchanged a hearty shake of the hand with Punting and then went down the stairs at full speed with a loud cheer of encouragement ringing in my ears.

I stood at the corner of the street trying to stay calm as I prepared to take action as the other members of the Dragon Club stood at the window above, watching the whole event as if it was a show at the theatre. As the dark figure of the Peeler approached my expression became pained as my heart beat fast and my breathing became hurried. My eyes were fixed upon the distinctive crown and brim of the man's hat. As he neared, the Peeler looked steadfastly towards me and I decided to turn away in an effort to hide my face. The man's footsteps became noisy as they sounded on the stones and I feared he would stop at the corner to confront me. Instead he passed by and into the darkness beyond as the lights of the Dragon Club were dimmed away. I made after the Peeler with a casual gait, carefully treading with light footsteps so that he would not be aware. He suddenly stopped and seemed to look back with concern up the street as I quickly moved back into the shadows. The Peeler began to walk again and I decided to move up so that I was only a pace or so behind. By good fortune the Peeler stopped again to kneel down and tie his shoelace. I judged that this was the time to act and after a cautious glance for assurance that I was alone, I moved forward and pulled the hat from the Peeler's head.

With great anxiety I ran back towards the club without any tendency to look back. I could hear the Peeler's bustled efforts to catch me as he pounded down hard on the cobbles in a pursuit driven by anger. He shouted for me to stop several times in between blowing loudly on his whistle, but totally in vain. The sanctuary of the Dragon Club was in quick and easy reach, and after a parting glance I charged through the door and ascended the stairs to the waiting members. Despite feeling highly ridiculous, I placed the Peeler's hat on my head and ran at speed into the room. A loud cheer greeted my arrival from the gathering of beaming and laughing gentlemen. Daffrey moved forward and took the hat from my head and led me to a small side room just before the Peeler entered, with two more Peelers close behind. Daffrey bade me to keep quiet as we both waited patiently in the dark confined space. I could hear a mumbled conversation taking place in the member's room but the door was far too thick to make it coherent.

After a short while the debate concluded and there was a low double knock on the door. With a little embarrassment I stepped through into the light as Daffrey put the hat back in my hand, fearing the consequence of my childish actions.

"If you have now caught your breath sir, I should be much obliged if you will accept payment for the wager," said Punting as he stepped forward and presented me with a very shiny ten pence piece.

"Thank you Mr Punting, but can I assume that everything is taken care of?" I returned whilst looking around the room to ensure there was no sign of the Peeler.

"Everything? Why of course," replied Punting with a slight grimace. "Although I am afraid you will have to make amends to tide things over, but nothing too wretched."

"I cannot help but perceive trouble sir," I exclaimed in alarm.

"It is but a small sacrifice Mr Chatterforth. Another challenge as it were, and one the committee feels that you are more than a match for," sighed Punting. "First the Peeler is waiting for the return of his hat so please hand it to Daffrey, who can take it down to him. He is waiting at the foot of the stairs."

I handed the hat to Daffrey, whilst fearing greatly for what surprise lay ahead. Daffrey sped away to return the hat, more in haste to return quickly in order to hear of my fate.

"What is my punishment?" I cried.

"It is rather simple, so do not worry," returned Punting. "Tomorrow we are to meet the Peeler on the market square. All he asks is that you spend three hours, and not a minute more, in the stocks."

"Out of the question," I shouted, "you are out of order sir and this is out of the question."

"Mr Chatterforth, without this rather small contribution nothing can be tided over. The sooner the problem can pass out of this club's hands, the better. To not take this punishment on behalf of the club would prove to be a catastrophe for all those currently present. Would you really wish to betray all your friends in such a way?"

The other members proceeded to mumble in derision, fixed in their resolution that I should accept the punishment or face damnation.

"I am afraid Ralph that you have no choice," argued Stroker persuasively.

"Perhaps then I had better go through with it," I replied through gritted teeth whilst looking straight at Punting.

"Good decision sir," answered Punting, whilst trying not to laugh. "This business must be done and I assure you that I will be there tomorrow to publicly and unreservedly offer support during the whole ordeal."

I left the Dragon Club for home that night in low spirits and fully aware that I was nothing but a pawn in Punting's juvenile japes.

And thus the next day came, so I took my position by the stocks in the market place at the agreed hour, wearing ragged clothes that belonged to the Gardener. I was in turmoil and fervently prayed that the whole event would pass quickly and without incident. The Peeler was there waiting and seemed very amiable and he simply placed me in the stocks with a muttered comment about my chance to reflect on my actions. And then I was bound and unable to move as passers-by laughed and pointed at my wretched disposition. I tried to bow my head but could not and so closed my eyes to shut out the embarrassment. Now, the fact was that several incidents conspired to ensure that my time in the stocks was extremely eventful. First and foremost I had the incredible misfortune to be seen by the visiting Royal party. No less than the Queen herself and Prince Albert walked by. I immediately remembered reading in the Salisbury Journal that the Royals would be passing through Salisbury on their way to Plymouth, and would be staying at the White Hart. They had evidently decided to take a stroll after breakfast and I had the misfortune to be a landmark on their route. Even worse an urchin chose to throw an egg at my head at the very moment they passed by.

"An unfortunate ruffian," the Queen's Attendant said imperiously in dismissing my worth.

I closed my eyes again and felt the force of two pieces of rotten pieces of fruit hit my face, as several others pounded on the wood.

"Will you not have the good grace to look at me Chatterforth," a familiar aristocratic voice boomed.

Awakened from a stupor I roused to open my eyes and was greeted by the sight of Punting and Daffrey standing before the stocks.

"I wish you had arranged for me to be flogged Punting as it would have been done by now. This whole situation gets worse by the minute," I remarked in a low whisper.

"I have never heard such nonsense!" exclaimed Punting, "this is far more honourable and I will ensure your bravery is commended at the Dragon Club. Daffrey, how much longer must this fine fellow be kept here?"

"One hour and ten minutes," Daffrey replied referring to a gold pocket watch.

"Gad it will soon be all over unless you wish to stay longer Chatterforth?" interposed Punting.

"I do not see that fitting any purpose at all," I replied with anger. "Now please leave me to endure this final hour alone and with what dignity I have left."

"Still more than an hour," said Daffrey with a chuckle and holding up his watch again.

"Now that it is clear that you are perfectly comfortable we shall take our leave Chatterforth," rejoined Punting. "But please permit me a little fun."

Punting took hold of a large overripe tomato and threw it straight at my head. Daffrey cheered loudly and the scoundrels walked away laughing. I closed my eyes again as the remnants of the tomato ran down my cheek. Another familiar voice caused me to open them again.

"Ralph is that truly you?" said the voice, "this is an extraordinary thing."

Stood before me was Thomas Endstreet, whom I had not seen for several weeks.

"I hope that you will understand that this was not my fault," I whimpered. "I will put my trust in you if I can rely on your secrecy in this matter."

"Upon my word you have my secrecy, now tell me what has occurred to place you in such an awkward situation," said Thomas as he knelt down to be near me.

I explained the full course of events from joining the Dragon Club to the wager with Punting. Thomas jumped to his feet and stood mulling over my story just as the Peeler returned to check on me.

"This is the very same Peeler from whom I stole the hat," I remarked.

"Indeed," replied the Peeler, "and quite amusing it was if the truth be told."

"Then why insist that he is put in the stocks sir?" asked Thomas.

"It was not on my insistence as I was more that happy just to get the hat back and let bygones be bygones," returned the Peeler. "It was Mr Punting who wanted this poor fellow to be punished with a stay in the stocks."

Thomas solicited and gained my immediate release from the stocks by the Peeler. I felt nothing but feeble and weak as Thomas led me to a nearby carriage. As I quietly mused and speculated about Punting's motive in humiliating me so openly, it was Thomas who decided that retribution would be sought.

"My dear Ralph, I can understand your unspeakable discomfort after such a terrible disposition," observed Thomas. "With sufficient scorn in your mind it is time to find honour through revenge."

"I am sure that you are right, but I have no thoughts on how to attempt such a task," I returned.

"And that is sufficient reason to leave the plotting to me," proceeded Thomas.

With this agreeable proposition I found strength through the notion of a precise course of action but I also felt anxious at the severity with which retribution might be gained. Once back home I lounged in the luxurious house provided by the wealth of my wife as she toiled in a place of business. I was sure that Mrs Goodfettle could sense my discomfort from the recent embarrassed affair, even pausing on several occasions to comment before overriding curiosity by going about her chores. By late afternoon I was seated by the window with a bottle of brandy watching and listening to the fall of rain until the gate creaked open to confirm that Dorothea was home. I roused myself to move upstairs and not have to face the wife I despised. I had barely stepped on the first stair when the sound of Dorothea's voice caused me to stop.

"Ralph Chatterfortth, please be so noble as to put my mind at rest with assurance that it was not you but rather someone who just looked very much like you that was seen clamped in the stocks this very day at the Market Place." cried Dorothea.

Looking round I saw Dorothea standing still and with a look of unutterable wrath from beneath her black bonnet as Mrs Goodfettle chortled from a position by the front door.

"You have not spoken to me for some weeks now and I do not care to have a conversation with you now," I replied.

"I am disgraced in having you as a husband and so wish you were a better man. Are you afflicted sir? Would you taint this good house any further and ruin my reputation and the future of your son?" asked Dorothea as she shook the rain from her bonnet.

"I am not afflicted save being married to you and I will indeed be a man of honour," I replied before turning my back to Dorothea and climbing the stairs.

In due time Thomas's simple but effective plan was ready to be told and it was quite clear that preparations had already been made. I complied to assist without hesitation and felt good for it, with any prior apprehensions nowhere to be found. With earnest abandon the scheme was put into action the following evening.

Thomas and I agreed to convene at just after midnight. It was a simple task for me to leave the bed in which I slept alone and depart from the house without being noticed. Thomas was obliged to take much more care in slipping away from Lilly, but my brother-in-law was very devious. As I met him by the church of St George, Thomas was carrying a bag, in which were two large black cloaks for each of us to wear. There were also two black scarves to cover our faces likes the Highwaymen of old. Finally I knew there to be some rope and the two pistols left in the bag, although Thomas did not reveal them at this point. By-and-by we made our way to the Dragon Club in Exeter Street but did not venture inside. Instead Thomas led me over to St Anne's gate before surreptitiously crouching down low to avoid being spotted by a coachman waiting by his carriage. Thomas had found out that this was Punting's personal coachmen as he had been observed by many residents in taking the same position every evening to take his inebriated master home to their residence on the edge of Trafalgar Park.

We both moved the short distance to the back of the carriage, stooping low at all times. Thomas pushed the scarf over his mouth and pulled a pistol from the bag and moved to the brink of where the coachman stood as he tended the horse.

"Stay calm and quiet and no harm shall come to you," Thomas demanded as he thrust the pistol close to the coachman's face

"I have no money sir," cried the disbelieving coachman

"I do not want your money," sneered Thomas before calling over to me, "bind and gag him."

I also raised my scarf and hastily moved forward with the rope to secure the poor fellow around his arms and legs, and to gag him with a length of cloth. Once the knots were secured tightly, Thomas concealed the pistol beneath his cloak and passed the other pistol to me. I reluctantly took the weapon and concealed it under my own cloak, with a trembling hand, vowing never to use it whatever the circumstance. The coachman was briskly dragged over to the edge of a nearby garden and secreted behind a high hedge and under an apple tree.

Thomas instructed me to sit in the coachman's seat on the carriage and slouch low, still concealing my face beneath the scarf. He then moved out of sight as we were both made to wait for some time. I began to have doubt on reflection as I looked up at the dark outline of the spire. Heaven help me, I thought, if this plot was to fail. I might be killed or face a lawsuit or jail. My desire for revenge could perpetuate discord beyond anything I had known before. Then I heard footsteps but it was just an old gentleman out for a stroll. He paused by the carriage for a moment and lifted his hat, winking at the same time from beneath the street lamp. I simply nodded and made no leave to speak. The man moved on and very soon I heard more footsteps approaching. I sat placidly in my seat, expecting another midnight stroller to walk by.

"If you please Hudson, take me home," cried Punting as he clumsily climbed into the seat behind me. I stalled for a moment and pulled the scarf higher over my face.

"Well Hudson can we go now sir as it would be preferable to be home before morning dawns," yelled Punting in anger.

Thomas was slinking nearby and in an instant was sat next to Punting with his pistol drawn and the barrel pressed to Punting's forehead. "Lead on to the stocks coachman," cried Thomas in triumph.

"I – I do not wish to come to any harm," Punting stammered as I drew the horse forward to go down past the cathedral and on to the high street. "Will you be content with my wallet and jewellery?" asked Punting.

"No sir, just remove all of your clothes and consider this, it ain't long since I shot down the last man with this here pistol as he dared to cross me," said Thomas in his mimicked accent.

Punting did as he was told until he was naked, with only the pile of clothes upon his lap retaining his modesty, although the streets were empty to save him any embarrassment. We made the stocks in good time and Thomas threw me a set of keys that had somehow been taken from a Peeler. The broken, miserable and very naked figure of Punting was ushered out of the carriage and was quickly secured in the stocks. Thomas and I then stood by to gain full enjoyment of the joke, deriving so much entertainment from the situation. For a while we stood with our backs to the stocks smoking and laughing outright before taking our leave in the carriage as Punting fought and struggled in vain to break free. His cries for help echoed around the square and could still be heard as I stopped the carriage on Ivy Street, from where we both fled on foot back to Harnham and home.

Chapter XX - *The unfortunate reappearance of a miserable wretch seeking revenge.*

Despite the disguise it was very obvious to Punting that the only person with the motive to take such action against him was I. However there was no reproachful attempt by Punting to take revenge, save for ensuring my membership to the Dragon Club was forthwith cancelled. In truth I had not even the slightest of curious intentions of returning to the club anyway. The Magistrate, Sidney Stroker, avoided and ignored me as a disgraced member in exile but it was of no real inconvenience. However there was one man who was roused to take notice of the indignant retribution dealt to Punting. There was a rough Hand that worked on the Punting estate called Dick Trottle, although Thomas and I knew him better as The Stork.

Upon hearing about the circumstances that led to the arrogant landowner spending a cold night shivering in the stocks, there was no concealing the involvement of a chancer called Ralph

Chatterforth assisted by a mysterious masked accomplice with a pistol in hand. Trottle knew that I was Ralph and that I had sworn to not know the identity of the violent stranger who had threatened his friends.

One evening I was enjoying the goodness of some tobacco and mollified from the harshness of life by way of several jars of ale in a small inconspicuous Inn near Fisherton. All the rooms were gloomy and filled with strangers and I was able to withdraw into the confines of my own company. Having perhaps been too bold with a sense of unbounded liberty I did not sense that others were corroborating my true identity as a stranger amongst thieves. I recall a raw, dank, blustery fateful night as I left the Inn for home, buttoning my coat tightly. Another man paused on the corner nearby as I slunk down the road. In a moment his footsteps were audible behind me and I could not help but look back with suspicion. I moved off in the direction of the new train station and hoped the stranger would go in another direction. Home was across the meadows and I suddenly feared the solitude of the open fields in the dark gloom. I kept my course but so did he. I turned the corner quickly to the station and hurried up to the main building, At length I could hear the man getting closer and I moved faster still. I reached Brunel's building and rushed inside to mill with a small crowd present. The whole place was shrouded in unbroken darkness with every gas light extinguished and despite my fear I wondered why so many were present at the station at such a late hour.

"Ah Ralph Chatterforth, how is the child I brought from London?" muttered a voice I recognised instantly. I turned to look through the murk into the piercing eyes of Dick Trottle, The Stork.

"Good Evening, this is quite surprise?" I replied politely whilst trying to stay calm. "The boy is well and part of a loving family."

"I have sought you out Chatterforth for I recollect that you told me that you had no knowledge of the whereabouts of the masked stranger who killed the Slymetoe brothers. And yet you conspired with the very same scoundrel to set upon Noah Punting. Would say that makes you a liar sir." Trottle said smiling.

When I heard these words I began to tremble. The conversation was a short one and I did not hesitate to push my way through the assembled crowd. Consequently Trottle followed, but with more force than I and causing a number of indignant gentlemen to raise their voices in protest. I moved on with determination as I knew the matter was very serious indeed. In no time I had reached the track when my fear was momentarily lost by the scene of phrenzy and carnage afore me. Under the light of the moon I could see a train engine apart from the track with two carriages buckled and resting uneasily behind. A number of sheep and cows lay dead across the track as local butchers sought to take any edible flesh away. Several other animals were injured and showing their pain whilst others lay feebly waiting to die. They were tended to with kindness but ultimately slaughtered. Trottle had also stopped in his tracks behind me and took in the sight of such a horrible accident.

"Lead me to the masked man or join the cattle in their fate," said Trottle softly in my ear.

With these words I walked forward on to the track, anxious to somehow get away as Trottle's boots creaked loudly as he rushed along the rail in pursuit. He drew close as my way was blocked by several dead animals before Trottle stumbled forward, knocking me to the ground. He grabbed hold of my head and pushed my nose hard into the earth, causing it to break and bleed. Trottle laughed realising that nobody could see him clearly in the darkness as he attacked, and even better was the fact that the still dead body of an engineer lay nearby. My own dead body would not seem too conspicuous now.

"I hope you are comfortable Chatterforth and able to tell me now the name of the masked stranger," said Trottle. "Tell me now or cry your last and join the poor fellow yonder."

Despite trying I could not alter my position and wriggle free with any amount of contortion, and I knew that I would be killed if I equally divulged or withheld Thomas's name. I stayed silent in suspense as my chance of life remained twitching in the balance. A church bell sounded loudly and then tolled several times more, distracting Trottle for a moment and he relaxed his grip. I somehow eased free and with all the speed I could muster tried to escape. Trottle grabbed my collar and pulled me back, crashing my bruised body hard against a stricken carriage and on to the floor once more.

"Just like these dying beasts it is time to put you out of your misery," cried Trottle as he raised a boot to crash upon my head. He struck hard but I moved just in time and was only dealt a glancing but painful blow. I lay wearied and exhausted as Trottle watched with masochistic pleasure and saw an opportunity to end my life. He picked up a large rock and rocked it to and fro as he kicked a boot hard against my swollen red cheek. I shrank back in pain and awaited certain death as the formality was prolonged by several sneering taunts. And then a loud rumble, pain and darkness.

I was unable to move and somehow found myself crushed under Trottle's large frame. I pushed hard but could not move my attacker's limp and lifeless body because of the force on top of him. I heard the agonised bleat of a bull that was quickly cut short. The huge weight upon Trottle relented as two fat gentlemen moved the dead beast to one side. I heard Trottle pronounced dead too as I crawled away to safety. The poor rough creature had fallen from the coach on to Trottle as he was about to take me with a fatal blow. In turn Trottle had fallen on me and ironically saved my life as the perfect buffer from the weight of the stricken bull.

Unnoticed by the crowd I slipped away in badly torn clothes and a body covered in cuts and bruises, but I was alive.

The next day I tried to comprehend my constant misfortune and of course confided in Thomas of the event of the previous night. I feared that Lilly could sense my troubles as I called at the Endstreet house for she was very tearful in my presence and on several occasion leant down to kiss me on the cheek as I sat on a sofa, just as my late mother had done when I was a child. I recall several uneasy glances from Thomas too as I babbled my tale with rather a fretful disposition, almost affected to tears. Thomas opened some wine and we both smoked. I began to stop shuddering, enjoying the company and conversation as Thomas gave reassurance that any danger had now passed. I was simply a victim of unfortunate circumstance and that my life could only get better. Lilly asserted that I would stay and dine that evening as she feared that Dorothea was not feeding me well. I returned home on a very foggy night resolving once more to positively adapt to the events of the life before me.

Chapter XXI - *Unexpectedly I am set forth to proceed with adventure in Europe and become something of a Gigolo*

For several months my life was simply a monotony, a boring monotony. I looked so glum and withdrawn that even Dorothea noticed and took a kind of pity. One evening in the spring of 1857 I was summoned for a meeting in the drawing-room. Dorothea remarked that I was like a restless bird stuck in a cage and that my mood was affecting the entire household. I declared that I had no care for how anybody else felt and that I would not seek to change.

"You are ruined Ralph Chatterforth," cried Dorothea, "such a ridiculous weak man. Yet you still cling to this life as my husband in name. I could show courage and have you taken back to the asylum to be rid of you but no doubt your dainty little sister would cause trouble."

"You are so practical my dear," I returned with a slightly drunken slur having enjoyed several glasses of ale in town. "Am I to be alarmed as to what other plan you may have brewing?"

"No, you shall not be alarmed but on the contrary probably quite cheerful," replied Dorothea.

"How can that be?" said I, turning my back to go and pour a large glass of brandy.

Dorothea looked at me with a disdainful expression of face, quite angered by my uncouth firmness. "Now," she said imperiously, "here is my proposition. I am willing to do anything to take you from this house for the sake of the general happiness of all concerned. It unfortunately cannot be permanent as we cannot become the scandalous talk of Salisbury society." She made a short pause to look at me again with a wrathful air. "After reflection I should be happy to make available a large sum of money in order that you may travel and enjoy the delights of Europe for several months at a time. I shall make it known in public that your absence is due to business opportunities. Consequently we shall lead separate lives and no doubt both be happy."

"Can this really be you Dorothea?" I asked rapturously. "I am spared from this awful life as your husband and you are willing to pay for me to be gone."

"For Heaven's sake spare me your pitiful gloating," cried Dorothea, "I only do this so I do not have to suffer your presence for as long as possible."

"I thank you for your compassion," I returned with a contemptuous laugh. "This will truly be no great penance, and I fear without this opportunity I would die of madness. But what of my sister and my job at the Assizes?"

"I will leave it you to explain to Lilly and ensure the parting is not too painful," Dorothea replied. "According to Judge Brownwig, a position shall be kept open for your pitiful job whenever you shall return. Do we have an agreement or do you wish to confound me?"

"We have an agreement," replied I, smiling and then laughing. This was a triumph to behold.

Dorothea left the room without another word and I hurried away to the nearest Inn and enjoyed several more glasses of ale in celebration.

Next morning, feeling a little uncomfortable, I went to see Lilly to inform her that I would be travelling for much of that year. I began by being positive and cheerful, explaining that I had several exciting engagements overseas, and not mentioning the prospect that the following years could follow in a similar vein. My apprehension was not to be realised as to my surprise Lilly embraced me and did not cry.

"I am not afraid or worried that you choose to travel Ralph as I believe you are so unhappy as things stand and it can only be for the better," said little Lilly. "I should like so much that you will return as the blithe and confident brother I know so well."

I replied that I had no doubt that it would be the case and hugged Lilly to reassure her. We then took a stroll through Harnham on a lovely spring day, stopping by the river and reminiscing about the happy days of our childhood. I felt so calm and happy, yet felt strangely hollow inside as I watched my kind sister teasing and laughing.

In the summer I departed for Rome and enjoyed a fabulous voyage on a calm sea and under a constant blue sky. Away from the turmoil of my life in Salisbury, I found peace and solitude at a grand hotel in the ancient Italian city. I read a great deal and started to write this book as the tale of my own inconsequential life. There were many good companions amongst my fellow travellers, with whom I would share wine and conversation by the hearth. I wrote many long letters to Lilly and confirmed my happiness, finding further joy in every reply.

I led this life for several years as time slipped away without much great incident, moving from city to city and becoming an accustomed traveller. I took life easily as I saw so many wonderful sights in Rome, Naples, Geneva and Paris. I drank endless bottles of fine wine and made love to countless beautiful women. Indeed in Naples I met the most gorgeous twins from Oxford, and under escort. I complimented them both on their beauty as the grey haired wiry gentleman who sat with them was eyeing me drily with suspicion, pulling at his moustache in concerned contemplation. Unperturbed, I made advances to engage in conversation with the ladies, enchanting them both and ensuring the escort's continued discomfort. I addressed the gentleman directly as we waited for dinner to be served and I asked if I may dine with them. He was hesitant but I swore to be good company and the pleading from the twins ensured he would oblige.

We took our place at the table and dinner was quickly served, whilst I demonstrated only polite manners. A good red wine was served with veal, which the escort known as Mr Trimble enjoyed in abundance despite appearing weary and exhausted from the recent journey. When the dinner was over we all moved back to a place by the fire and in no time Mr Trimble had fallen into a slumber. The two young ladies became even more attentive and giddy as we drank some brandy. Finally they both stood and beckoned for me to follow, which I did only after a little hesitation. I walked up the grand staircase and straight to the ladies' room, where I was encouraged to close my eyes. On opening them again, the twins were there before me lying naked on the outside of the bed. In short, with much tenderness I made love to them both.

I awoke the next morning to find the ladies both hurried and flustered as Mr Trimble pounded heavily on the door. Naked and bewildered, I was ushered into a wardrobe to hide, holding my clothes, as the twins quickly dressed.

"I have very strong reason to believe that you entertained a gentleman last night," said Mr Trimble as he looked around the room. I watched through a crack in the door, unable to dress for fear of making a noise and alerting the angry escort.

"Why good Lord Mr Trimble, you may say what you like but it is not true of course," replied one of the twins.

Some moments passed in silence before dust caused me to sneeze loudly. Before Mr Trimble could move I rushed from my hiding place and raced towards the door, leaving my clothes in a heap behind. Mr Trimble shouted in anger and set off in pursuit as I ran naked through the hotel, causing several female guests and one male guest to faint as they made their way to breakfast. Thankfully I made it to my room and pleaded with a maid to let me in, which she did after dropping some sheets and covering her eyes. I locked the door behind and in the ensuing minutes that followed was forced to dress quickly and gather my meagre belongings as Mr Trimble knocked heavily on the door, demanding that I face him.

I was forced to escape out of the window, surviving a drop from considerable height, and then leave Naples with haste for fear of being challenged to a duel of honour. Now, I am quite happy to tell this tale although it was not such a comfortable situation at the time. Of course I relayed the whole story, and particularly the lovemaking, to Thomas, Edwin and Daniel on my return to Salisbury. I gave such an account with some fervour and was often asked to repeat it. That was true also of the time that I entertained a Duchess in Paris as the Duke slept in the next room. Unlike Mr Trimble, he remained oblivious to the whole situation.

During those travelling years, I only returned to Salisbury on two occasions each year, when I spent most of the time with Lilly and my friends. I saw little of Dorothea or the boy we called our son, Arthur Chatterforth, save for the funeral of Dorothea and Thomas's father, who died from consumption in 1859. It was then I saw my wife as a lonely empty soul, staring ahead without expression as the other mourners passed her by. Confounding the differences in our relationship I did at least try and offer condolence but failed as Dorothea instantly rebuffed me, and very publicly too with a wave of her arm and a sharp turn of her head. I approached Thomas as well to convey my sorrow but quite frankly he was smiling and at perfect ease as if unconcerned by his father's passing. He did of course have the good fortune of being comforted by my loving sister.

Chapter XXII - *The Endstreet business is in decline and as a consequence Dorothea's health deteriorates. An article in The Times bears tidings of great concern.*

The time soon came for the renewal of my former life in Salisbury as alas the days of carefree travelling ended once I returned home in the summer of 1860. First and foremost, there was no longer the money available to fund my wild exploits as the Endstreet family business, with Dorothea at the helm, began to decrease in capital value. Competition from the north and from abroad was sufficient to drive down prices and therefore profit. And then to top it all, the trusted Accountant Mr Tamper had proven to be an embezzler. By the time his crime was realised, when the Endstreet books showed such insufficient return that it was not possible to trim the numbers to steal without detection, the crook Tamper had fled. He knew his time had run out and left Dorothea in a state of total humiliation upon the crime being discovered. Many tried to mollify her but not on any account was she to be calmed, making sure that Tamper's despicable deed was reported in The Times no less.

As Dorothea perused The Times on a fine sunny July morning, she was so preoccupied in finding the piece on Tamper that she took no notice of any other news that day. I clearly recall the church clock striking the hour just as Dorothea threw the newspaper to the floor in disgust at the small column attributed to the crime that was well hidden several pages in. She was certain that Tamper had fled to London and that a distinct and visible report would secure his capture and the return of the stolen wealth. Dorothea wished me a good morning with an ill-humoured face and retired to her bedroom, where she remained all day.

Left alone I picked up the newspaper and was immediately drawn to the startling story on the front page. A young boy barely much younger than my own son Arthur had been brutally murdered in a place called Road Hill House that was not far from Frome, which was indeed in turn not far from Salisbury. The case was quickly to become infamous and I remember reading the story with such horror, yet Dorothea had not even glanced at the headline. However

I was to be struck with even greater incredulity as I opened the paper to read on.

As a consequence of continuing to read the Road Hill House article, I was drawn to another scandal that had shocked London. At first I simply glanced at the headline, 'Unscrupulous Baby-Farmers Tried And Sentenced To Hang'. Then I read on with unease about how a man and woman had taken a good commission to provide rich child-less couples with babies born into, and taken from, desperate slum families. It was thought at first that the mothers were party to the deal, keen to accept a fee and lose the burden of raising a child. I cast my eyes with anger as it was conveyed that the babies were nearly always stolen, with the evil couple having an accomplice in a villainous Doctor who was able to use his position to deliver and steal the babies at birth. The mother was told that the child had died as it was whisked away down the dark back street and alleys of London. Another, a crooked Pawnbroker, would arrange for customers to purchase the babies by placing coded adverts in society papers, promising discreet adoption of a healthy child. Unfortunately the babies would not always survive and die before they could be sold, to be buried without dignity in a dusty yard. When the couple were arrested they were holding two wan babies, too weak from hunger to cry. The Doctor and the Pawnbroker had fled but the couple had been brought to justice. They were related as Auntie and Nephew and went by the names of Evelina and Reginald Grittle.

A sickness in my stomach followed as I read and digested these words. My conscience was in anguish and indubitably I would not act to conceal what had been found out. Surely this terrible secret would be uncovered was my initial concern as I sat in remorseful apprehension. I was roused from my worry as Gertrude Stimple, the Nanny, brought Arthur in to see me. He ran forward to greet me, his supposed father, with a large smile and raised his wide eyes to meet my concerned stare. Stimple encouraged me to pick the boy up and I did so with shaking hands. Arthur and I came together as I hugged him with tears in my eyes. May God forgive me for a mother was missing such a beautiful child.

After that I stood a little and watched Arthur play before Stimple took him to the nursery. It is a painful narrative that I must write and I feel now as I did then with such a disagreeable sensation taking control of my whole body. I resisted the temptation to awaken the resting Dorothea and tell her what had been discovered. Instead, and after bundling up the newspaper that revealed the truth about the Grittles, I made my way at full speed to confront Thomas Endstreet.

As the newspaper was placed in front of him, Thomas looked embarrassed before he made a pretence of being as shocked as I. The tone in which he spoke showed great concern but betrayed an obvious guilt.

"This is very inconvenient indeed," said Thomas timidly. "But you must not show the slightest alarm or anxiety and the secret about Arthur will remain just that. Panic and the treasured reputation of the Chatterforths will be in jeopardy."

"How can you be so cold sir without time to reflect?" I asked. "It is as if you knew the truth before I came to you with this newspaper."

"Let it pass Ralph and ask me no more questions," returned Thomas in obvious agitation. "This revelation is done with and the newspaper should be disposed of. In truth nothing has changed."

"The devil has taken you Thomas." I cried loudly. "I should never have joined you on this wicked escapade."

"But you did and you are therefore not innocent. Spare no more time in pity but just go home and forget what you have found out. If you do not, be afraid of the consequences, and above all be afraid of me," rejoined Thomas as he clasped a hand on my collar.

I pulled Thomas's hand away after a moment's reflection, "maybe my friend you should fear me."

Meanwhile, Lilly entered the room and forced both Thomas and I to resume some degree of composure, although we stood in silence for some time as my sister spoke softly on an array of different subjects. I left soon after with a supposed apologetic bow of the head as Thomas sternly reminded me to "understand that the situation was no more than business." He then turned to go and subtly dispose of the newspaper.

This was not the end of the matter and it was only a short time later that further correspondence on the scandal of the Grittles in The Times was to signify a much greater degree of concern within such despicable circumstances.

This time, only two days later, it was Thomas who was rapid of foot in making his way to my house with that day's Times under his arm. As I opened the door, Thomas charged in completely flustered and giddy with worry. Dorothea had once again secluded herself in her bedroom, with the curtain drawn and unable to face neither the light of day nor the crumbling Endstreet business empire that was now close to ruin.

Thomas laid out the newspaper on a table, too stunned to speak at first before simply urging me to read another article on the Grittle scandal. Feeling perturbed I stood stroking my chin, with the scraping sound of my hand against the bristles making the only sound in an otherwise silent room. As I read the article I became more and more affected by what was written, and I found my chest tightening and was overcome by a shortness of breath. By the last word, I needed to sit down and was completely struck dumb.

Notwithstanding it was apparent that two rich bothers, and both highly successful businessmen in London, had benevolently pledged to help some of the Grittle's victims find their stolen children. Frederick and Allan Tinkerton had only recently returned from America and felt so saddened and humbled by the plight of so many mothers losing their babies, that they had publicly offered a large reward to track down the infants whereabouts to the four corner's of England if necessary. Perchance Evelina Grittle had kept a record of every transaction made, giving up the book when she was arrested on hoping to find clemency. A hope that had now been ended by the noose.

The majority of infants that had survived had already been rescued to the dismay of the untrue parents and the delight of the pining mothers. A large number of the transactions had been completed in London itself or in the counties that surrounded the capital. Indeed Twickenham had been the new home for most. The rich couples who had bought their children unscrupulously from such disparate characters were now named and shamed in The Times. Many now faced certain social and financial ruin, and the majority had even been charged with conspiracy. The final paragraph claimed that two children had been taken further afield to Brighton and Salisbury. With great uneasiness I re-read the line to confirm that it did indeed state Salisbury, finding only a small crumb of comfort in that it was quoted that very little further information was available. However the Tinkerton brothers had arranged for private detectives to be brought over from America 'to search every inch of both towns to bring the infants home'. Harassed by these thoughts I slumped back in my chair, devoid of all hope.

"I am sorry for this," said Thomas, "as we now face a very significant difficulty. These Tinkerton brothers are only being charitable I suppose but we must be both bold and shrewd to outwit their Agents. We must work as a team along with Daniel Drumdale and Edwin Gurden and protect Lilly and Dorothea at all costs."

"Are we not obliged to declare our position through innocence and end this cruel situation for Arthur's true mother?" I proclaimed in desperation.

"Never Ralph, never," Thomas shouted, "for then we shall be in disgrace and face a cruel life beyond any tears of an unfortunate and unworthy woman in rags."

"Have you no heart sir?" I asked, standing to confront Thomas.

"I do indeed and it is full of the affection and devotion for my family and not for strangers who threaten their livelihood. The Endstreet business is all but finished and Dorothea's health is diminishing by the day. Would you put the final nail in the coffin and see your sister on the streets?" cried Thomas.

I knew he was right and that my desire to do the right thing came from a weak position. There was no point in protesting further.

"It is just so, we must prepare to evade our would-be captors and protect the family," I confirmed as I sat back down with my head in my hands.

"If we are cautious, cunning and alert then there is no doubt that we shall succeed," said Thomas whilst laying a comforting hand on my shoulder.

Summer passed before a drawn out and gloomy autumn took its place. I returned to work at the court with no conception of if or when Tinkerton's Agent may show his face in Salisbury. Every stranger's face began to haunt me as little by little a constant nervousness took hold. For months I held firm with this black cloud hanging over me as Dorothea became bed-ridden, weary and bitter as the Endstreet business empire finally collapsed. This once proud and domineering lady was reduced to spending her days in a darkened room, waited on by the Housekeeper Mrs Goodfettle as our only remaining Domestic. The rest of the staff had been dismissed, including the Nanny, Gertrude Stimple, and a great deal of elegant furniture sold as a means to survival. As I sat before a pitiful fire each night, there was now only a few pathetic chattels adorning each room. Above Dorothea would bang on the floor with a stick, demanding that I tend to her like a servant as Mrs Goodfettle cared for Arthur. I was often obliged to take this frail ghost of a woman a bowl of hot soup before she faced a night of miserable nightmares. The mood in that room was always sombre and every time I was pushed to remember the fierce strong woman that I had married, who was now so frail and colourless and on the edge of madness. I did try and offer companionship but was greeted with nothing but scowling and hard sullen stares. Time would not soften her mood but rather darken it further.

With great constraint I remained loyal to Dorothea and did not run away, if only to stay close to my sister. I am glad to say that Lilly and Thomas did not labour under any great difficulty as they both found work and were also able to retain a Housekeeper at the time to take care of the children. Thomas took a position of Bookkeeper with the Railway and Lilly worked hard and long hours as a Seamstress on Milford Street.

 When it came round to Christmas time I had begun to dismiss the idea that Tinkerton's Agent would indeed make any kind of appearance. It was on Christmas Day that Thomas entreated me with a plan to restore our lives to a brighter and more comfortable standing. I had taken Arthur to Thomas's house for the festivities, leaving Mrs Goodfettle with Dorothea. As the children played, Thomas stoked as good a fire as I had been accustomed to for some time and opened a bottle of brandy.

"Ralph, I have been thinking very rationally of late and would like to make a proposal of a superb opportunity for a brighter future," said Thomas with a cheery tone and rosy cheeks.

"Say what it is," I returned.

"With an adequate sum saved and with strength of purpose, I resolve that the Endstreets and the Chatterforths leave Salisbury and England for a better life on a foreign shore," Thomas replied.

"I can tell that you have quite made up your mind, and do you have a destination in mind?" I asked,

"Yes, I submit that we take a ship from Southampton to begin a new life in America when the time is right. We shall all emigrate together," cried Thomas.

"Does my good sister approve as she is so happy and accustomed to living in the shadow of the spire? And what of Dorothea?" said I.

"Lilly informed me that she would only consider such a move if her brother was also by her side," replied Thomas.

"And Dorothea?" I repeated.

"We will need to make necessary arrangement for Dorothea but I fancy she will remain here," said Thomas rather coldly.

I thought of the opportunity to escape Dorothea and all my troubles and felt exalted inside. "When will our ship set sail?" I asked.

"As soon as we can gather enough money we will make provision for Dorothea and then be at sea with our goods and chattels. Our children will grow old together in a new country," replied Thomas.

I smiled and raised my glass for more brandy and then gave a toast to the voyage, remembering that of course my son would have to be by my side.

"I have calculated that we should be ready to leave before next Christmas arrives," confirmed Thomas.

I would have to wait in anticipation for another year and pray that no great changes would come to contrive and alter our newly drawn plan.

Chapter XXIII - *The humiliation of Edwin Gurden as Daniel Drumdale has cause to leave Salisbury. Danger thickens with the arrival of an American known as Clouds.*

By the spring of 1861, I could still not help speculating that bad times were still to come. The first sign was rather an odd occurrence. Edwin and Hetty Gurden were invited to a dinner-party in Alderbury courtesy of Hetty's cousin. As a man of little social experience, Edwin struggled to converse with the other guests and was very quickly unable to disguise a terrible stammer. An association with Mick Mickle was revealed by default after two rather cruel gentlemen were drawn to humiliate my poor friend at every opportunity, leaving him completely agitated and out of words through shortness of breath. The other guests laughed at the fun, whilst Hetty wept quietly behind a handkerchief in total embarrassment. This unpleasant scene was to continue for some time as the two men continued in their sharp ripostes until another guest finally called an end.

Edwin was encouraged by Hetty to collect his hat and coat so they could leave, and they soon hurried to the door. For a moment Edwin stopped before making a second entrance into the dining room to confront his tormentors.

"Why the ridiculous man has returned," said the first man, laughing.

"Yes," shouted Edwin, "to bring you bad news. I have a friend who is feared by every criminal frequenting every Inn from here to Lands End. When he hears how I have been so badly provoked he will want to teach you gentlemen a lesson. B-b-b-b-e, warned," Edwin stammered finally in the excitement.

"And what is your friend's name? In case I should wish to make enquiries about this crook to be feared," cried the first man, still laughing.

"Mick Mickle," returned Edwin, "and dare you present me with your names gentlemen?"

"Why of course as I cannot be so rude, I am Noah Punting and this is Arthur Daffrey," replied Punting.

Further misfortune soon followed amongst my circle of friends when Daniel Drumdale's father was exposed as an embezzler and through the shame, Daniel was forced to flee Salisbury with his family to start a new life in Bristol. It was on the Sunday evening after Daniel had left that Edwin revived the role of Mick Mickle and put on his pitiful disguise once more. He chose to follow Punting and Daffrey down the High Street as they made their way to the Dragon Club after enjoying several jars of ale at the Old George. The cathedral rang a doleful chime as the two drunken fellows reached the corner of New Street and Mick Mickle sprung forward, holding a large sword before him

"Pray tell me Daffrey," said Punting, "whoever can this gentleman be?"

"Maybe he will do us the honour of presenting himself," returned Daffrey.

"I-I-I-I a-a-a-m Mick Mickle, friend of Edwin Gurden," stammered Mick Mickle.

"But you are not sir," laughed Punting, "you are Edwin Gurden in a frightfully poor wig and hat."

"You cur, I-I-I shall make you pay for that," returned Mick Mickle as he thrust his sword towards Punting.

Daffrey had taken a step back into the dark and now moved forward quickly to knock the sword to the floor within one quick swipe. Punting then leapt forward and removed Mick Mickle's wig to reveal Edwin Gurden.

Punting snapped his finger and thumb together, "go home you ridiculous man. Go away and never come back."

Edwin turned and ran down Crane Street as tears ran down his face. Daffrey put on the discarded wig and hat before picking up the sword and holding it in the air. "I-I-I a-a-a-m Mick Mickle," he cried before laughing loudly. Punting of course joined in with the merriment.

The next event in the chain was the arrival in town of a foreigner, by name John Howard Raincord but everyone called him Clouds. He was a very tall American, immaculately dressed in fine cloth and shiny brown leather boots, always maintaining a good humour with a bright smile that showed the whitest teeth I have ever seen. Clouds took a room at The White Hart but chose to drink most evenings in the King's Head. He quickly became acquainted with the locals who frequented the Inn and made it clear that a substantial reward was on offer for the man who could lead him to the scoundrels who had "rustled a child and taken him far from home to this fair town." Tinkerton's Agent had arrived.

Despite plying many men with rum and ale, Clouds made no progress at first with his enquiries and feared a conspiracy of silence. Instead many just took advantage of his generosity and chose to mock the foreigner's strange accent. Events would have been different if Clouds' mind had been turned to the extent that he had given up the search and returned to London, but he vowed that the child would be found, dead or alive. One boorish rogue took offence when Clouds refused him a drink and made a foolish challenge, only to be promptly thrown across the room. Clouds then just shrugged his shoulders before bowing to the other drinkers, still smiling ever-so-politely. The lout made another move with a knife in hand, thinking that it was an opportune moment with the foreigner's back turned towards him. Instead, Clouds dipped his shoulder gabbed the man again and threw him forward against the wall, and without ever looking back. His attacker lay unconscious on the floor.

Word soon spread within the district of Clouds' intentions and that a fee was on offer. Many a crook was roused to venture to the King's Head but had no information to offer in the imposing presence of the reputed Agent. Now, it so happened that one evening a report was given to Bilge who immediately put on his hat, turned on his heel and slunk down the King's Head with an assured countenance. Bilge made his way over to the foreigner and looked him in the eye without uttering a single word. The room fell silent as Clouds glanced at the repulsive stranger with an immediate feeling of distrust, before breaking the silence in a deep voice.

"Were you looking for me?" He said.

"Yes, I came to seek you out as I have knowledge that will be in your interest," replied Bilge.

"Speak out and I will let you know if it is of any value," rejoined Clouds

"Give me five hundred pounds and I'll tell you all I know, but not before," replied Bilge

"Such a large sum for something that may be trivial when it is told," cried Clouds.

"Then make me a bid for enough to assure you that I can be of assistance," returned Bilge.

"Very well, twenty pounds is the initial sum for such a disclosure," said Clouds. "And I'll make it up to fifty if I like the information"

Bilge agreed and the two men moved back into the shadows, where twenty pounds was exchanged for whispered conversation. Clouds was happy with what he heard and made up the bounty to fifty pounds and then returned to the centre of the floor to address the Inn with his newly purchased intelligence. Bilge skulked behind with a wry knowing smile on his face, conscious that he would have to slip away with some haste and cunning. Danger lurked in every corner with so many petty thieves and pick-pockets present, ready to steal his bounty. The crowd gathered round to hear Clouds speak.

"Regarding this information for which I have paid a handsome reward," cried Clouds. "I have the name of an accomplice who helped bring the child to Salisbury. If anyone can take me to this man, they shall be richly rewarded."

A low murmur greeted the announcement as Bilge prepared to leave with the Inn so pre-occupied, but curiosity held him back. Surely the brash American Agent would not get a response.

"And who is the man?" asked a rough looking fellow with a ginger beard, stood at the back

"He is a rogue and a cheat and goes by the name of Mick Mickle," replied Clouds.

The crowd conversed in whispers and shrugged shoulders that carried an air of considerable irritation. Some had heard the name but none knew where Mick Mickle could be found.

"Curse him, is there no-one that can tell me where this crook resides?" asked Clouds again.

"If we knew his whereabouts it would not be information that would be kept," shouted a snivelling pick-pocket.

Clouds looked suspiciously at Bilge who cried, "It is no fault of mine that he cannot be found. If you wish to clap eyes upon this boy again then you must find Mick Mickle."

"Very good then I shall find the scoundrel," retorted Clouds.

At this point a portly man stepped forward and asked to speak with Clouds in private. Clouds motioned for the man to step outside and the pair were followed by a curious Bilge.

"With regard to this here Mick Mickle," said the man, "I can't say for certain but I believe my master had an altercation with this man just the other day."

"You do not believe this man surely?" interrupted Bilge.

"I believe him just as I believed you and maybe I am a fool for doing so," rejoined Clouds. "How can you prove this to be so and what reward do you seek?" asked Clouds, turning back to the rosy cheeked fellow.

"Well I can take you to my master this very evening as I am due to take him home from the Dragon Club," the man replied. "All I ask is for fifty pounds for my trouble."

"Ah! You shall not be so lucky to gain such a reward," cried Bilge.

"Oh to be sure, you shall have it immediately," replied Clouds. He then proceeded to hand the man a large note, drawing the interest of a nearby crook. He stepped forward with menace only to be instantly punched in the face by Clouds and then dragged over to be thrown into the Avon. "He should know better than to cross me," said Clouds.

The portly man could not fail to take notice of the threat and resolved to take Clouds to wait by his cart, where the man's master would be present shortly. Bilge set forth to join them and the three men made their way to The Close. They lingered about for at least an hour before the man's master turned off Exeter Street and through St Ann's Gate.

"Hallo Prumple, show a leg man and take me home this instant," cried a loud hoarse voice.

"Sir, I have a gentleman here who has a business proposition that carries a hefty reward," Prumple replied nervously.

"What's the meaning of this?" cried the master, looking angrily round," what sort of business could be arranged at such an ungodly hour?"

"I beg your pardon sir for the time of our meeting," replied Clouds, "but I understand that you have information that can assist me. If this is the case then I shall reward you with a very large sum of money."

The master moved forward with great precipitation, "I'm your man so don't lag sir but tell me what you wish to hear."

"Can you tell me your name sir before we strike a deal?" Clouds inquired.

"Why of course, Noah Punting at your service," replied Punting with a theatrical bow.

"John Howard Raincord at your service sir, although people just call me Clouds," the tall American stated. "The information I seek is the whereabouts of the crook known as Mick Mickle."

"And the reward?" Punting entreated with a knowing grin.

"Five Hundred pounds, half now and half when I have stood in front of Mickle," returned Clouds.

"So-so," said the exceedingly rich Punting, "but you have found a friend in me who has the means to lead you straight to the scoundrel. I will of course oblige and tell you where the man lives, but he will not appear to be in the same guise as the Mick Mickle you have heard of. In fact he goes by the name of Edwin Gurden and was prone to wear this very disguise I have here."

Clouds merely nodded in acceptance as Punting retrieved Edwin's pilfered hat and wig from the back of his cart, before shortly exchanging half of the reward for Edwin's address. Nearby, Bilge mused on this information for a moment with a meditative expression and then retired back into the shadows before leaving the scene with some haste.

Clouds bowed respectfully towards Punting and vowed to visit Edwin Gurden first thing the next day.

Chapter XIV - Confirming *the terrible murder of a friend and an encounter with Clouds that precipitates the need for escape. My spirits are raised by a chance encounter and congress with a former female companion.*

It was on that fateful day that I was rudely awoken from my sleep by a heavy pounding on the front door. As if I could not already hear this din, the decrepit Dorothea began banging the wall of her bedroom with a stick to draw my attention further.

I threw open the window and shouted down, "Hush down there and explain why you are making all that noise."

In an instant Thomas stood back from the door and looked up at me with a white haunted face and cried, "Ralph, you must get up and come quickly. It is Edwin, he has been murdered, strangled no less in his own Drawing Room."

"Hell's Fire!" I shouted and immediately felt sick in my stomach.

Without a single pause, I dressed with haste and fled to join Thomas in his cart. We moved through the streets at the swiftest pace and soon reached the gate to Edwin's garden. On entering the house, the first thing I heard was the constant sobbing of Hetty Gurden. She greeted Thomas and I with tears streaming down her cheeks and an absolute look of horror. Her daughter, Josephine stood by in silence with a rueful face, but did not cry. The two were led away by the Housekeeper, and we were now greeted by the imposing figure of a policeman, who introduced himself as Inspector Longborne. We introduced ourselves in turn, and Thomas said that we were friends of the Gurden family.

"Ah," said Longborne, "the poor Mrs Gurden was the one who discovered her husband's body. Now we must do everything we can to bring the scoundrels responsible to justice."

"They must hang," said Thomas impetuously.

"Quite, but first we must catch them," pursued Longborne. "Do you know of any reason why anybody would wish to kill your friend?"

"Perhaps it was a burglar, who Edwin chanced upon in his own home," I offered.

"But nothing was stolen," replied Longborne.

The Inspector stepped forward and motioned for Thomas and I to follow him to the Drawing Room. In the middle of the floor lay the stricken body of Edwin Gurden. The room was in an immaculate condition and nothing indeed had been disturbed. We all looked on for a moment or so in silence, until interrupted by the voice of a stranger who had entered the house unannounced.

"Well am I to assume this unfortunate fellow is now the late Mr Edwin Gurden?" the stranger said whilst wiping his chin.

"You are correct in your assumption," replied Longborne, "and who are you sir? What is the purpose of your visit?"

"John Howard Raincord at your service sir," returned Clouds, "and I was hoping that Mr Gurden would be of great assistance to me in a very grave matter indeed."

"Perhaps you would like to share the purpose of your intended meeting with Mr Gurden?" Longborne rejoined.

"Sure, I was hoping to take the liberty of questioning Mr Gurden about his role in abducting a child from London some five years ago. I understand he was known to use an alias under disguise. A crook known locally as Mick Mickle." Clouds replied and then produced the hat and wig used by Edwin when he became Mickle.

"May I ask what evidence you have to support this supposition?" Longborne resumed his questioning. "Am I right in thinking you are the American agent hired by the Tinkerton brothers and reputedly displaying large amount of money in every Salisbury tavern?"

"Unquestionably that could only be me," cried Clouds. "As for Mr Gurden, my intelligence was very reliable and I am sure that the stolen child now resides with a friend of Mr Gurden. Now I have been happy to answer your questions and I have formally introduced myself but I do not have the pleasure of knowing who else is present here. I note that one is a policeman but these other two gentlemen, please confirm if you were friends with this unfortunate wretch?"

"How dare you call him a wretch," cried Thomas, "I demand an apology this very instant or shall take the matter further."

Clouds moved forward and looked down on us both before placing a hand on Thomas's shoulder and said in a softened voice, "I do feel obliged to apologise but I guess you have indeed confirmed yourself as a close friend."

"Sure enough," I assented, "and proud to be called a friend. I do not believe your story about Edwin stealing a child. I admit to reading the story in The Times but I am sure you are totally wrong in your deduction."

"I can apprehend why you would say that, being a close friend and all. Can I ask your name sir?" Clouds asked in a loud voice.

At first I stood in silence, before replying with some apprehension, "I am Ralph Chatterforth."

"And I Thomas Endstreet," added Thomas immediately.

"I take it you are both fine upstanding gentlemen with wives and children that befit your social standing?" returned Clouds.

"Of course," assented Thomas in a confident tone.

"I would say that it would not be a strenuous endeavour to allow me to see your children if you should have a son, and to then of course be sure that the stolen boy is not with you," said Clouds with a condescending air.

"Although I would be very confident that we could both be detached from such an accusation, I do not see how giving any consent to see our sons would prove anything," cried an affronted Thomas. "If I recall the child was taken as a baby some five years ago and would now not be recognisable."

"I note the reasons for your objection, but believe me I will know if it is the child," rejoined Clouds with confidence. "Due to the gravity of the situation will you yield to my request and I will be more than happy to meet your children under the scrutiny of this fine officer here."

"I will not allow you to see my son at present," I said petulantly whilst being concerned as to how this overpowering foreigner may prove that Arthur is the abducted child, which of course he was.

"Why would that be Mr Chatterforth?" Clouds asked whilst looking down on me.

"Because he is very ill and has taken to his bed," I replied with a cunning lie.

"I am sorry to hear that," rejoined Clouds, "but will be more than happy to wait until he is better."

"In the meantime I will relent and allow you to see my son this very morning," confirmed Thomas.

Thereupon arrangements were made for Clouds to briefly see Thomas's son, Toby, away from the suspicious gaze of Lilly. Inspector Longborne was indeed in attendance and watched with a puzzled frown as Clouds quickly confirmed that Toby was not the boy. Clouds resolved to return when my son was feeling better and left our company. Once Longborne had gone it was time for Thomas and I to devise a plan to ensure that Clouds never got to meet Arthur.

The encounter with Clouds was so highly disagreeable that Thomas and I knew we would have to be quick witted to foil him. Our scrupulous plan was quickly put in to motion. Arthur was smuggled under darkness to be taken into the care of Thomas's eminent Great Aunt Matilda, who lived in The Close no less. It was explained that I had cause to dismiss the Housekeeper, Mrs Goodfettle and now needed to personally tend to the bed-ridden Dorothea until a new Housekeeper could be hired. There was truth in this as I did indeed dismiss Mrs Goodfettle and Dorothea was now so delirious with madness that her mind was sufficiently softened that she did not notice, and nor did she comprehend that Arthur had gone too. This enabled the same tale to be told to Lilly, although the motive was embellished with the notion that it was in preparation for our families to depart for a new life in America. The whole plan or story began as a small acorn and grew into a tree with branches representing every conceivable explanation for our actions.

It was declared to Lilly that the Endstreets would sail for America within a month and take Arthur along as their own. I would follow when Dorothea was fit to travel and sufficient funds had been raised. For the most part there was a great deal of truth in the principal intention of this proposal, although my fate was never to follow a straight path.

I reluctantly put a bell in Dorothea's room so that she could attract my attention when required. At first her impatience was deplorable and the bell rang loud and often throughout the day and night. I was attentive at first being present more than not in the house having taken an absence from my work due to the situation. But

Dorothea's madness had turned her into a violent wretch who would do nothing but shout loudly and throw whatever was to hand. I had to now keep her door locked for the safety of all concerned. On one occasion she grabbed me by the throat after appearing from behind the door, squeezing so tight that I passed out and fell to the floor. Dorothea left me where I lay and went back to bed. She was asleep when I came to and I took the opportunity to remove any small objects from her room to save my skin from any more bruises. With thanks to Thomas, I was able to secure some strong sedative drugs and once administered by mixing with her food, my deranged wife was left to sleep for most of the hours of each day in her sombre room. I had peace.

News came through that the treacherous Bilge's life had not been spared for the undoubted murder of Edwin Gurden. He was however not brought to justice by way of the gallows but found staggering along Scots Lane with a shirt soaked in blood. He fell at the feet of a priest and supposedly died after confessing many sins, including killing Edwin. The identity of his killer was not revealed nor ever discovered and the list of suspects would have been many. I had no doubt that Clouds had struck him down for slowing his progress in finding the stolen child. Recent events had strengthened my resolve to escape at the soonest opportunity.

Edwin was buried with humility and dignity at St George's Church despite the heavy rain that never ceased for a moment on the day of the funeral. As the coffin was lowered into the ground and Hetty Gurden began to wail I looked up to see the lanky figure of Clouds watching from a under a tree at the end of the graveyard. His eyes were piercing despite the gloom and entirely focussed on me. I glanced away and then back again and the figure had gone.

Daniel Drumdale had returned to pay his respects and joined Thomas and I at the Rose and Crown after the funeral as we reminisced about our days at the Twizzle Academy in the Close. I felt nervous and could not help but look anxiously about in case Clouds was present. Thomas caught my eye on several occasions and encouraged me to drink more heartily, especially as he had some good news to announce.

"Just yesterday I was faced with a highly encouraging circumstance when a very upright gentleman showed a distinct interest in purchasing my house," said Thomas. "By this morning we had agreed a price and the deal is done."

"Well, well!" I returned, "so you are to be successful in raising the money to leave for America."

"Indeed, I plan to arrange passage from Southampton by early next week," cried Thomas.

"Upon my life, one feels desperately jealous in comparison to the exciting new life that lies ahead for you both," said Daniel. "When will you set sail Ralph?"

"To be candid with you, it may take some time as Dorothea is clearly too insane to travel," I replied

"Not a trifling situation indeed," confirmed Daniel.

"Unquestionably though it is a difficulty that Ralph will overcome," said a triumphant Thomas. "I expect him to finish my mad sister off for good and bury her in the garden, then put the house up for sale and set sail to join us."

"Do not imagine for a moment that is true," I replied after noticing that several other drinkers had heard Thomas's assertion. "I will simply have to bide my time and travel at the soonest convenience."

"If you please but if you simply wait for Dorothea to die it will be a long time coming," retorted Thomas loudly. "She was put on this earth to torment and if that means simply surviving to an old age to spite you then so be it."

"How about you Daniel, can you be encouraged to come to America as well?" I asked in order to change the subject.

"We are so comfortable and happy in Bristol that I would not wish to change anything," Daniel replied.

"Stuff and nonsense, you should come," a drunken Thomas cried out, acquiring the attention of all those present.

"We will not be going," returned Daniel.

Thankfully Thomas did not press the matter further but ordered more ale. I looked around the crowded Inn and was immediately drawn to the tall figure of Clouds at the back of the room, slinking by the hearth. He caught my observant glance and smiled broadly by way of reply, raising a glass of ale in the process. Had there been sufficient information in Thomas's loud uttering for Clouds to suspect our plan? It was a consequence that Clouds was sure to watch my every move, following me like a shadow until he had mastered the case. I tried to stay calm and simply raised my glass by way of acknowledgement. As I drank on with my friends I could not resist stealing a look over to see if Clouds was still present and whenever I did so he returned a bright knowing smile. We encountered each other's glance several times in this way and I began to feel more and more awkward until after a short time my tormentor was gone. Disposed of this concern for now I began to relax and enjoy the company of my friends. I gave no indication at all to Thomas that Clouds had been present as I feared he may have confronted him in his state of inebriation. Instead we truly raised a glass to the memory of our dear friend, the sorely missed Edwin Gurden.

There was nobody visibly in waiting as we left the Rose and Crown but I still feared that Clouds was nearby. I twitched with nerves as a gate slammed loudly and then jumped backwards having been so distracted that I was nearly trampled underfoot by the arrival of a carriage from London. Thomas cried out a warning but long after the carriage had come to halt.

I made slow progress in pursuit of Thomas and Daniel as they clambered up the small hill behind the Inn. It was a clear evening and I stopped for a moment to admire the cathedral spire in the twilight before curiously and fatefully looking back to see who had arrived in the carriage. Two rather portly gentlemen and a fashionably dressed lady made their way to the Inn door under the light of a bright gas lamp. In an instant the lady looked obliquely towards me and I caught sight of her fair face. It was Janet from Plymouth with whom I made love surreptitiously in the very same Inn several years before. I looked back up the hill and could no longer see my friends but instead of trying to catch them up I resolved to return to the Rose and Crown and renew my acquaintance with Janet.

After the briefest of consideration I simply called after Janet before she was shown to her room. The Innkeeper eyed me narrowly with suspicion as Janet looked round cautiously before her face filled with great surprise.

"I will only say that to be honourable you will need to entertain the lady in the lounge and not in her room," cried the Innkeeper.

"But he is my husband," said Janet

"I do not believe it as earlier he was here and drinking a great deal of ale," rejoined the Innkeeper.

"Waiting for my dear wife to arrive," I replied hastily in keeping with the pretence.

"Well if you are to stay the night it will be another ten shillings," said the Innkeeper.

Janet immediately opened her purse and handed the Innkeeper ten shillings, "happy to oblige."

I took the trunk from the Innkeeper and carried it up to the cold and damp room. Janet shivered with cold and drew her coat close round her. Without speaking I lit a lamp and then stirred a fire before drawing up two chairs.

"Oh my gracious!" said Janet as she finally began to warm, "I've found you." She then began to cry.

"You must compose yourself, please be calm," I said and reached out to hold Janet's hand. In an instant she stood up and fell in to my arms before we kissed passionately.

"I have suffered so much since we were last together," whispered Janet. "Through it all I believed that there would be no hope in life of ever seeing you again."

"Are you still being mistreated by your ignorant brute of a husband?" I asked with some ire.

"He died a number of years ago from shock," cried Janet.

"What was the cause of his shock?" I returned.

"That I was pregnant and he was not the father. He knew it was impossible and flew into such a rage that he took off his belt and went to beat me. As I cowered in the corner, he turned blue in the face and clutched his chest. He lay dead on the floor within a few minutes and I was spared." Janet explained with her head bowed.

"Surely that is to be applauded," I interposed without any sensitivity.

"In some ways yes, but his haughty relatives looked down on me as if I had killed him with a knife and tried hard to dispute the small fortune my husband had bequeathed me in his will," returned Janet. "Eventually I secretly bought a small cottage near Brixham and moved there with my son, away from the hatred of my husband's family. Until this trip to London on a matter of business I have remained in Brixham as a lonely widow."

"For what business did you go to London?" I inquired.

"A Great Aunt had died and had left one hundred pounds in her will," replied Janet.

A thought suddenly struck me and I felt both scared and excited at the very notion of what it entailed. I stood up before the now cheerful fire as Janet sat down again to be closer to the warmth, holding a shawl tight around her shoulders. I looked down at Janet's round pretty face showing tear soaked large brown eyes that were almost hidden from beneath her long brown hair. Janet looked so beautiful and also so vulnerable as she glanced from the roaring fireplace to meet my gaze.

"The matter of the child, do you know who the father is?" I asked coaxingly.

"Yes," Janet sighed as she dropped her head down.

"My dear girl, surely it is not me?" I returned.

"Yes," she repeated and sighed again.

I went to move the lantern to give more light but my hand was shaking so much I almost dropped it. Part of me wanted to remonstrate and deny Janet's assertion whilst another wanted to weep tears of joy.

"He is now six years old and born nine months on from our night of passion," Janet confirmed. "I thought of trying to contact you but decided against it through fear of ruining your marriage."

"You are so honourable but my marriage is in but name only and my wife now taken by lunacy to top it all," I rejoined whilst sitting back down and gently taking Janet's hand to hold. "What is the boy's name? Does he look like me?"

"I named him Ralph after you and yes if you saw him there would be no doubt in your mind that he was your son." Janet spoke with a heartier refrain.

"I need to see him somehow," I said.

"I cannot bring him to Salisbury so you will need to come to Brixham," Janet returned

I paused for a moment to recall my current precarious situation, "I will need to take care of a serious business matter first."

"After it is taken care of do you suppose that you can come to Brixham?" Janet asked whilst staring hard into my eyes.

"I suppose it is possible," I suggested whilst contemplating that it was highly unlikely with a new life beckoning in America. "Please don't distress yourself when you are back home by worrying about my arrival."

"No I will not as I am sure you will come to see us," Janet cried and fell into my arms again. As we kissed and held each other tight, I could not truly contemplate how my life had been turned upside down yet again and within a matter of hours due to a chance meeting.

In the softened light I carried Janet over to the bed and once again we made love, just as we had done in the same Inn some seven years before. When morning arrived we made love again as the birds sang loudly outside. I joined Janet for breakfast and she could not disguise her expectations for me to somehow become a loving father and husband. I played along in accordance with her wishes but felt terrible inside for such deceit. As we finally said goodbye by the side of the carriage, Janet's head drooped so low that I could not see her face. Through breakfast she had been nothing but a picture of love and now she was so dejected and quiet before beginning to whimper. I held up her tear soaked face and kissed her wet cheeks. Janet smiled and her tears soon dried before she climbed aboard the carriage. As the carriage pulled away I was left alone and felt condemned in my wretched life. Now it was I who shed a tear drawing several disapproving and expressive looks from passers by.

Troubled by such fraught emotions, I quickly proceeded on foot to my home. The morning was foggy and every house on the route home was partially cloaked in an eerie mist. It made my situation seem even more dismal and I felt more alone than I had ever done before. How I longed for the carefree days when I travelled in Europe or strolled nonchalantly by the Avon with Emma Toopey. Upon arriving home I waited by the gate for quite some time before feeling the effects of the cold. From the outside the house looked abandoned with all the shutters ajar and the curtains drawn open, and I could not even see a light in Dorothea's bedroom. Mournfully I considered that perhaps my wife had failed to rise and died in her sleep. If it was so then I was to blame for abandoning her, even if such an event would have shortened my troubles by some degree.

I hurried into the house and all seemed very quiet and still until I heard shuffling sounds coming from the kitchen. Curiously I made my way over and opened the kitchen door. The room was lit and sitting at the table were Dorothea and Arthur, both enjoying a bowl of porridge.

"Why is the boy here?" I asked, "he is meant to be tended to by Thomas's Great Aunt."

"He's a good boy and run home to see his mother. He's alright now, not in any danger now he's home. My lovely boy, so much more of a man than his father." Dorothea rambled on incoherently and squeezed the child so tightly he squealed.

"Did he come here by himself?" I rejoined, praying inside that Clouds had not seen him arrive.

"Not a bit of it, the kind American man brought him here," replied Dorothea as she rocked nervously in the chair.

I twitched at the news and bestowed a furious look upon Arthur for running away. However there was something amiss. There sat the boy I had called my son for five long years and yet he had somehow acquired a small scar at the bottom of his left cheek.

"Why did you run away?" I asked the boy but he would not reply as if told not to speak. This was not like Arthur at all.

I moved forward and lifted the boy up by his lapels and shook him with some force. "Why did you run away?" I repeated.

"Get off me mister," the boy cried with an accent from the streets of London and without any recognition of his father.

"Put the boy down Chatterforth," Clouds voice boomed out from behind me and I released my grip, leaving the lad to fall to the floor.

"What is going on?" I said through gritted teeth.

"I have simply done you a favour and returned your son home. I take it this is your boy?" Clouds asked.

"Yes he's my boy," replied Dorothea in a flood of tears.

"No he is not," I added quickly sensing a trick.

"So who is to be believed?" rejoined Clouds.

"Please let me explain," I whispered and took Clouds by the arm and led him to the corner of the kitchen. "My wife is suffering from lunacy and the truth is that she would declare any child placed in front of her to be her son. On the other hand I am of sane mind and of course know this not to be my son. He is still being nursed through his illness by kind relatives."

"My time here is drawing to a close and I will soon return to London with the stolen child and collect a handsome commission," returned Clouds whilst frowning in frustration. "You can rest assured of that Ralph Chatterforth."

"I am afraid you have wasted your time here Mr Raincord, but out of curiosity who is this child and why have you brought him here?" I asked.

"He is the stolen child's twin brother. They even have identical and unusual birthmarks in the shape of a four leaf clover. That is how I can be so sure about the boy's current appearance. I had the lad brought down to Salisbury last night so he could be ready to meet his brother for the first time in five years." returned Clouds, as he ushered the lad away despite Dorothea's sobbing and wailing.

"How did he get the scar on his cheek?" I inquired.

"You are very observant," faltered Clouds. "It was the result of a fight with another urchin. Good day to you Chatterforth and I wish your son a speedy recovery so we can bring this matter to a close."

Almost as soon as the words had escaped his lips, Clouds had gone and taken the boy with him. I managed to sedate Dorothea by drugging a glass of water and once she had ceased from taking hysterical convulsions, I led her up to the bedroom and left her sitting on the bed with a prolonged vacant stare, lost to reality.

Chapter XV - *The last instalment and the last night alive for a persistent foe. A time for farewell to loved ones and a heinous thing is done to bring this sorry tale to a close.*

Troubled by such a range of emotions I eagerly proceeded by foot to see Thomas and find out how quickly our plans could be put into practice. If the situation was to be prolonged then I feared being unmasked as the child snatcher and sent to jail, with Thomas accompanying me and poor Lilly left as a destitute mother. At length when I reached the Endstreet residence, Thomas beckoned me in with an eager hand and an ashen face. Lilly immediately sank into my arms and began to sob as the children sat quietly in the hall. It was evident that several trunks were being packed in readiness for a journey.

"Please don't cry Lilly," I whispered softly and affectionately pressed my hand on her back.

"I am sorry dear Ralph but we have such distressing news," replied Lilly in a faint voice as Thomas raised his eyes to the ceiling in exasperation.

"Please compose yourself for the children," said Thomas, "they seem very alarmed. Tend to them and I will explain the turn of events to Ralph."

"Very good," returned Lilly as she continued to sob. With a drooped head she took the children into the kitchen.

"Is it all up? Does she know the truth about Arthur?" I cried drawing closer to Thomas.

Thomas clenched his teeth and took one look around to ensure Lilly had gone. "You can depend on it that she is not aware of how Arthur was taken from London. I fear that Lilly is more concerned about our current financial predicament."

"I believed it to be apparent that you still had some wealth and now enough to sail for America. Is that not now the case?" I asked with great concern.

"I have the money but I also have a long line of creditors ready to beat down the door and take it all. I owe much more than I have to give and will be in a debtor's prison by the weekend if we do not make our escape." Thomas continued with an expression of unmitigated defeat. I had never seen such a look in all the time I had known him.

"In other words we are all doomed," I cried.

"Not quite," Thomas replied as he turned to address me with bloodshot red eyes. "I am taking my family to a smallholding near Romsey, where a close friend will give me board for the evening. Tomorrow evening we will sail from Southampton and leave all our troubles behind."

"Can you truly trust this friend?" I asked, knowing that Thomas kept company with many desperate and villainous rogues.

"I have no choice but to trust him or by tomorrow I will be penniless if I stay in Salisbury," Thomas confessed.

"How did you come to such debt?" I inquired.

"Through gambling and much dishonesty," replied Thomas, waving his hand in despair.

"But what of Arthur? Will you take him with you?" I asked

"Of course," Thomas answered after a pause. "You will need to collect Arthur from the Close this evening and bring him under cover of darkness to the top of St Ann's street. My carriage will be waiting there at nine o'clock and we will take the boy from you and off to America."

"I will need to avoid Clouds at all costs as I now know that he will certainly recognise Arthur as the stolen child that he seeks," I said before describing the earlier events involving the trick played by Clouds using Arthur's twin brother.

"I cannot believe such a thing!" exclaimed Thomas, shaking with concern. "You must be extremely diligent Ralph or else all will fail. If you are not at St Ann's Street I will assume you have failed and leave without the boy."

"Ah, then I will take that as fair for the sake of Lilly. I will need to be cunning and shrewd as I fear that Clouds is watching my every move." I said as Lilly came back into the hallway.

Lilly looked at me in silence with great affection whilst trying not to shed any more tears. Finally she ran over and locked herself in my arms as if it was the last time we would ever meet.

"I understand the sacrifice that must be made but cannot bear that we will be apart for so long. I fear I may never see you again," cried Lilly.

"My poor sister you must be strong and we will all know good fortune again. I promise," I replied whilst trying not to sound anxious.

"I have said to Thomas that we should remain here and pass our lives together in Salisbury, come what may. I would rather that than be rich or know any fortune at all," returned Lilly, full of spirit.

"The purpose of our adjournment from Salisbury is to avoid more than living a life as a debtor or pauper. I fear that both Ralph and I will end up in jail," rejoined Thomas.

"What crime have you committed?" asked Lilly, clearly shocked.

"There is a misunderstanding over a business transaction to which both Ralph and I were party," replied Thomas. "It was simply an inadvertent oversight but we could both end up before the magistrate by the end of the week. We have no choice but to flee."

"What will become of you my dear brother? Will you not still be brought to task when we have gone?" Lilly returned, panting for breath.

"I have been endeavouring to prepare my own escape to another town and will soon be able to raise the money for Dorothea and I to join you in America," I lied and was sure that Lilly was not fooled,

Lilly merely nodded and did not question any further on the true extent of our deceit. I looked on in shame, struck dumb through disdain for my own desperate character. Thomas moved over and gently lay his hand on Lilly's soft white cheek but she flinched as if the touch was very cold. Lilly then resumed the task of loading the trunk for the journey without another word, dismissive in her action of both her husband and brother.

I did not linger in the Endstreet house for long but made my way home to rest in preparation for the deed I would undertake that very evening. To attempt any other plan or venture at this hour was doomed to fail, and yet was our only course of action also in vain? I did expend a great deal of thought about simply running away but in short would have not been able to live with the thought of such cowardice hanging over me for the rest of my days. It was Dorothea that roused me from my sombre reflection at around midday with a loud ring of her bell. Knowing she would be hungry I took up some tea and toast but Dorothea ate but a little as she stared at me full in the face the whole time with a pale haunted complexion. Perhaps I should have tried to explain our predicament but I am sure it would have been rejected through ignorance. Dorothea began to reminisce about our very first meeting and yet I had not heard her talk or refer to the past for such a long time. She spoke in a quiet benevolent voice and began to smile as we ended up having a long chat by the fire before she retired to bed once more. I took her hand between mine and Dorothea fell asleep, blissfully free of pain and anguish. My wife had once been so proud and strong of will, and I so reliant upon her. Perhaps I might have been a better husband but then perhaps she might have been a better wife.

Instinctively I packed some belongings into a bag, principally clothes, food and keepsakes. In a separate case I secured this hefty parchment that described the course of my wretched life. The bag and case were left by the kitchen door should I need to leave Salisbury in a hurry. At last the time came and I put on my coat before walking down to The Close at speed. In due time I had crossed Harnham Bridge, looking around at every opportunity and wondering if Clouds was waiting nearby. I came to the house where Arthur was being looked after and quickly passed through the garden gate. Thomas's Great Aunt Matilda received me in an affectionate manner but her mood changed to sadness when I explained that I needed to take Arthur away. The boy's bag was duly packed as I looked on shamefaced at the innocent boy, identical in appearance to his urchin of a brother. It would need to be assured that they would never meet if I was to succeed and yet I was still perturbed with guilt. A good soul would have been obliged to hand the boy over and confess. As it was I gave only a little consideration to such a notion and hurried Arthur to put on his coat, despite protestations from the boy and Great Aunt Matilda alike. It was evident that he had greatly enjoyed his time in this house.

It was now dusk as I took Arthur by one hand and carried his small case in the other. We walked along The Close and around the Cathedral, which was masked on one side by a flimsy birdcage scaffold courtesy of Gilbert Scott's restoration. I recall there was quite an eerie wind that held a sharp chill within and had ensured that there were only a few hardy souls idling around. Pushing on at a pace I looked up to see a figure coming down the path from St Ann's Gate. I had begun to feel a little uncomfortable and to wish myself well away from Salisbury. A stout fellow walked by tapping an expensive walking stick as he went. The man smiled and wished us both a good evening but I could barely look him in the eye, and could do no more than nod in acknowledgement. It was with excessive anxiety that I quickened my step, and ensured Arthur did the same, in such haste to reach the gate and make my way up St Ann's street to safety. I checked my pocket watch and it showed ten minutes to nine as the rain began to fall.

St Ann's gate was in sight through the murk of the evening but I felt rather uneasy as another figure made its way along the path that ran from the Bishop's Palace, stooping low against the wind and rain. In a moment I would be at the gate but then so would be the stranger walking ahead. I gripped Arthur's glove with some force and caused him to cry out. Looking down at the boy I apologised before slowing the pace in the hope that the stranger would walk on ahead. Instead the man stopped and turned to walk towards us, straightening up to his full height in the process. As if faced by a horrible apparition, I stopped instantly, recognising the tall smiling figure of Clouds standing in the gloom.

"Chatterforth, is it possible that your son is well again and you felt a brisk walk would do him good?" Clouds said with a condescending intent in his voice.

"I cannot say, please let me pass as I must get the boy to a physician," I replied without any thought and encouraged Arthur to hold his collar above his chin.

"You are very good, but the game is over," returned Clouds, advancing as he spoke.

I looked about and could do no less in the circumstances but drop Arthur's case before picking up the boy and turning to run. Clouds was taken by surprise by my action and I had carried Arthur some yards towards the cathedral before our pursuer gave chase. It did not take Clouds long to get near to us but with some fortune his heavy American boots slid badly on the wet grass and he fell with quite a tumble. I dashed on and came to the foot of the flimsy birdcage scaffold just as Clouds had roused himself to give chase once more. There was a chance to be stolen and so unbeknown to

Clouds I hurried Arthur up the first ladder and followed him at pace. No sooner had we reached the top of the ladder and climbed upon a rickety plank, than I heard Clouds run past below. Arthur looked frightened and bewildered as I pressed him to stay silent and still. My pocket watch showed it was nearly nine o'clock, and Thomas and Lilly would now be waiting with a carriage less than a mile away. I was conscious that the boy and I would have to go very soon but we had only been seated for a matter of a minute when Clouds returned to the foot of the scaffold. The American looked anxiously about before seemingly making a shrewd deduction. I knew in a moment that we were about to be discovered and did not look down for confirmation. Instead I ushered Arthur to the back of the scaffold and on to the next ladder that rested precariously on two more ramshackle planks of wood. The ladder moved to and fro as we climbed and I feared it would topple, sending the boy and I crashing to the floor. In due time the heavy tread of Cloud's boots as he climbed the first ladder echoed down below. As we drew a little nearer to the top of the scaffold I could hear Clouds making his was along the creaking plank underneath. Feeling tired and defeated I pushed the boy up onto the next plank and urged him to crawl to the end and out of sight. Forlorn, I climbed from the ladder too and sat down with helpless abandon. The ladder began to rattle and shake as Clouds began to climb. Soon he was in sight and stopped to smile up at me.

"Ralph I do believe something is amiss," said Clouds.

"Mr Raincord," I said quite calmly, "there is something which I have earnestly concealed until this very night. But I believe there is no delicacy or concern to conceal it any longer."

"I knew beforehand, of course I did," interrupted Clouds, "so do not think you can win any grace or favour by making some pitiful confession at this juncture."

"Then I shall not lay anything bare before you," I returned, "but surely it is you that should seek grace of favour?"

"Really," Clouds answered whilst laughing, "may I be permitted to ask why that would be?"

"Because I am an evil wretch who cannot be trusted," I replied without removing the sharp stare of my eyes from his face for a moment.

Clouds was angered by my remark and instantly began to climb the ladder towards me. During the discourse, Arthur was shivering in the darkness at the far end of the plank. There was but one hope of escaping within such an intensified situation. I resolved to rigidly bide my time, sitting quite still as my foe got ever nearer. My last memory of Clouds was that he was a fellow of noble appearance despite being so full of scorn. With a strong gallant hand the American tried to grab my leg but was distracted by the load chime of the bell that rang from the bases of the spire. I knew it was about to strike at nine o'clock precisely by way of diversion, and present the opportunity that I quickly took. With all the force I could summon I kicked hard upon Clouds' face before watching him teeter and then lurch in panic. It was to no avail as the American fell backwards in the darkness, his body crashing hard on the earth below. At this time I had managed to hook the ladder with my heel so that it did not follow Clouds downwards and leave Arthur and I trapped on the ledge. Steady of purpose I led Arthur, silent and bewildered back down.

Clouds lay motionless upon the floor and showed no sign of stirring. I tried to shut such a gruesome sight out from the boy's gaze, pushing him forward with haste. It was hard to resist one final glance back at body, but in that moment I heard a distinct murmur. Clouds' death was in fact to be a lingering one as he lay unable to move and muttering painful curses. I made no attempt to help him and instead fixed my hat firmly upon my head and rushed the shaken boy towards St Ann's Street,

As it was by no means certain that Thomas would still be waiting for us at some fifteen minutes past the hour, I proceeded with some concern. Upon our arrival however it was wonderful to see that

Thomas had been prepared to wait, albeit due to being badgered by Lilly.

"Where the devil have you been?" shouted Thomas with a fierce gesture. "Another five minutes and I would have been gone, I swear."

"An unexpected complication," I replied, "but it is one I have taken care of."

In the next moment several loud Peelers' whistles distinctly sounded from the direction of The Close. Thomas instantaneously looked hard at me as it was immediately evident that the commotion was the result of my complication.

"Oh my gracious, whatever is happening down by the Cathedral?" cried Lilly as she climbed from the carriage.

"I am sure it is nothing to concern us," I answered.

"I saw a man fall and think he might be dead. He had been talking to father and was very angry," said Arthur in a low voice.

"Ralph," cried Lilly, "whatever happened?"

"I don't know what comes over the boy sometimes. He has such an imagination, just like his father," I returned, recoiling with some anxiety.

"I don't believe you Ralph. I am your sister and know when you are lying," said Lilly, eying me narrowly as she spoke.

"Am I to go with you?" Arthur asked Lilly, breaking the dreadful pitiful silence.

Lilly merely nodded and bowed to kiss the boy on the head. In that instant a terrific yell sounded very loudly nearby and the muffled footsteps of a gathered throng could be heard distinctly. Several more voices took up the cry and it was evident that the crowd were heading our way. I have no idea how they set upon my trail so quickly.

"We must go," screamed Thomas, "get the boy on board."

Thomas helped Arthur up and I passed up his bag. I can say nothing of the final look that he accorded me other than it was as if he really disliked me. As for Lilly, she now bore the weight of knowing her brother was not a good man, although at our moment of parting there was only speculation in her mind as to what I had done. Surely even in the innermost recesses of her innocent thoughts there would be no capability to contemplate just how evil I had been through such a wicked life. Lilly had been truly proud of me but I had betrayed her. With such tears of sadness she kissed me delicately on the cheek before turning away without another glance in my direction.

"God bless you for what lies ahead Ralph," cried Thomas before moving the cart away at speed.

"I fear it will not be enough," I shouted hastily but I doubt anyone heard.

"He's up here I am sure," cried a voice nearby as the noise from the crowd grew louder.

I crouched behind a wall and peered over, trembling in fear and feeling so very alone. The crowd was very large and most were carrying lamps that shone brightly in the gloom of night. The gleam grew sharper as the mob got nearer, their footsteps quickening by the second. There was no point in trying to outrun my pursuers as I was so helplessly outnumbered. If I headed into the country then my chances were as slim as the fox being chased by the local Hunt. If I headed down Culver Street then I was sure that another mob was already making its way up Milford Street to cut me off. Although improbable my only option was to find a place to hide but I fretted fearfully on where I could go. Panic stricken I clambered over a nearby fence and landed in a small well-kept garden. Thankfully the blinds had been drawn at all the windows at the rear of the house. Several voices cried out with fury from the other side of the fence and I could now hear the sound of several horses cantering by.

"I will pay a handsome reward to whoever takes him alive," cried an extremely posh fellow.

Many others immediately took up the cry with an extreme eagerness to expedite my capture. I moved from my crouched position by the wall and ventured forward in the darkness, staying shrunk down and desperate to find some convenient hole in which to hide. Upon reaching the house I moved carefully along the wall, hastily feeling my way as I heard someone attempt to climb the wall, doubtless to check if I had taken refuge in the garden. It was by incredible chance that I stumbled into a small brick appendage, complete with strong wooden doors at the front. Creeping round I pulled firmly on the handle, expecting it to be locked fast. To my surprise the door came free and I quickly slipped inside, spurred on by the noise of several men landing heavily on their feet behind. I was just able to fasten the door shut before falling forward from a ledge into a large hole and total darkness. It was a long way down and I hit the floor with some force, landing uncomfortably on a stacked pile of coal. I lay still in the cellar praying for survival, wincing in pain.

Up above my pursuers could be heard in mumbled conversation as they walked by the cellar. Several excited shouts followed declaring that the wretch must be nearby and that he would be captured soon. Circumstance would surely now ensure my capture and I prepared for the worst but in desperation buried myself under the coal until I was almost on the verge of suffocation. A hand was laid upon the door above and it was opened with a shudder. Through the faintest of cracks in the mound of coal I could see two distinct silhouettes against the moonlight and instantly a dim lamp was held down into the cellar.

"Is the dog in there?" A man asked.

"Cannot be sure," came the reply, "perhaps you should go down and check."

Another voice joined the conversation, causing the two men to start, "what exactly do you think you are doing in my coal cellar?"

"Beg your pardon sir, but we are on the trail of a murderer. He killed a man this very evening by the cathedral and was seen by several witnesses. A reward is on offer for his capture." The first man replied by way of a humble explanation.

"Do you know who the wretch is?" The posh man of the house asked as his silhouette came into view.

"Not his name but we have a good description and know what he was wearing from the colour of his coat, trousers and shirt and even the distinctive make of boots upon his feet. We have witnesses who will confirm his identity in a second," said the second man. "It is also said that he had a small boy with him and we believe it to be the child stolen from London."

In the instant and tragic moment that I had sent Clouds to his death I had not taken the time to consider that the act had been observed. Thankfully it appeared that I was not known to these witnesses and at least Arthur was now gone from the scene.

The lamp was held down into the cellar again and all three silhouettes leaned forward.

"I should say that in all probability the murderer has not found refuge here," cried the posh man. "Now I wish you luck in apprehending him and to be sure he does not come here later, I shall secure the door."

The heavy door was shut loudly, throwing the cellar into total darkness once more, and I heard the sound of a key locking me in. I frantically pulled myself from the heavy pile of coal that had shielded me from capture and sighed with some relief upon the fact that I had not been discovered. Now I needed to bide my time and effect an escape.

In due time a beam of light came into the bottom of the cellar as a member of the household collected some coal in a scuttle. I observed that there was just sufficient aperture for my frame to squeeze through. In the meantime I held my position for several monotonous hours, until I was sure the household had retired to bed.

I could hardly find the door in the darkness and had to carefully move a great deal of coal aside to make the room to slip through. Thankfully the door gave way after a couple of firm shoves, but I scarcely had time to ensure a soft exit and instead tumbled through the opening on to a hard wooden floor, taking several lumps of coal with me and a great deal of soot. I hesitated for a moment as I lay on the floor, listening for any stirring upstairs in case my loud clattering had alerted the household.. Thankfully there was only silence save the ticking of a large clock which I observed after casting a hurried glance down the hallway.

I stood up slowly and carefully surveyed my surroundings with every slow footstep I took towards the staircase. Silently I made my way to the top and then crept along the landing to the master bedroom. After pushing the door ajar I peered in and could hear both the master of the house and his wife snoring loudly. I traversed into the room slowly, and with caution, continuing to tread with remarkable care. Looking nervously about I spied several sets of the master's clothes hanging in a wardrobe that sat with the doors open. It was situated close by and I was able to take the first hanger with ease before moving away as quickly as I could, startled as the master drowsily mumbled in his sleep and I feared he had awakened. With some relief I left the bedroom and made my way back downstairs.

After finding the drawing room, I briskly exchanged the man's grey suit for my ripped and stained clothes. I threw my clothes back into the coal cellar, although the soot trail through the house would ensure that my presence would have been quickly realised by the morning. I also exchanged my distinctive boots for some shiny black shoes and then encased myself in a large black coat. The shoes and coat had been conveniently left by the front door.

I got out of the house and immediately made my way back down St Ann's street. My right knee was hurting badly having been injured during the fall into the cellar and gave me something of a limp, and the appearance of a wretched cripple. I started in alarm on several occasions as members of the mob walked incessantly nearby, still searching for the murderer in his distinctive clothing. I was not approached in my new clothes but speculation came into my thoughts that my presence in the house I had just left may be realised imminently, if say a maid was to venture downstairs. I made up my mind to quicken the pace and reach my journey's end sooner rather than later. Once I had walked down Exeter Street and passed the Dragon Club, I felt sure I would not encounter any further problems. Just as I began to relax my stride, several shouts and loud whistles echoed in the night air, although at some great distance behind. Was the commotion due to the discovery of my discarded clothes? Hastily I pressed on, fearing the very worst, and made my way through to Harnham by way of small, narrow lanes and muddy fields. I arrived at length in my neighbourhood and passed many large gardens and houses before thankfully finding my own house in total darkness and with nobody loitering nearby.

Being very anxious, I did not light any lamps but simply sat down in my favourite armchair and tried to consider my plight with a weary head. I assumed Dorothea was sleeping soundly in her room and did think to check on her. My selfish and principle concern was that my identity would somehow be discovered and the Peelers would come to take me for certain fate at the Gallows. Even if this was not the case, I could not comprehend walking around town in case of being spotted by the witnesses to Cloud's death. I sat slouched in a weary state as my conscience sat heavily on my thoughts. Finally sleep won the day and I fell into a deep slumber.

It was this very morning that I awoke and readily undertook to take control of my destiny. As I write the final words of this sorry tale, Dorothea lies still in death upstairs, killed by the poison administered to her breakfast just one hour ago. Doubtless dear reader you have made up your mind that I am indeed a heartless wretch, and I cannot disagree. With my wife now dead, nay murdered, I took to calmly washing and dressing myself before taking refreshment for the journey ahead. Very soon after scribing my final full-stop on this pitiful tale, I will gather my packed bags and then seal the pages of this script in a large envelope. On this seemingly quiet and serene morning I will then abandon this house, so full of unhappy memories, and burn it to the ground by way of single flame and a great deal of lamp oil. As soon as the fire is well stoked, I shall stroll down to The Close under the rays of the morning sun. For one last time I will turn my head and look up the beautiful serene spire, and doubtless have a tear in my eye. It is then my intention to take this script to Thomas's Great Aunt and leave it with her for safekeeping, with instruction that it be held unopened until I return. Of course I shall not return. Instead I will make my way on foot and head for Devon, using my money to buy food and sleeping under hedgerows along the way. I propose to be reunited with Janet and my true born son, to at last lead the life that I had always hoped for. So I close this tale with wonder as to who may ever get to read about my sorrowful life. Farewell and bless thee, whoever you are, and I trust you are a better person than I.

Lightning Source UK Ltd.
Milton Keynes UK
UKHW021239181119
353758UK00010B/2647/P